Afterwards

Afterwards

K M Kendrick

British Library Cataloguing in Publication Data

A Record of this Publication is available from the British Library

ISBN 978-1-914199-66-0

This edition published 2024 by The Red Telephone
Manchester, England

Girl

This is the story of my death. And of what happened next.

They don't understand what is happening at first. They arrive confused, frightened, and entirely naked. They have no memory of what their life was like before. I am the only one who does, and I have no idea why.

I like to help them, if I can. It can help just to see another human. I show them where their things are. I try not to hang around once they've calmed down. I've never been much of a social person, even before.

It never gets fully light here. I used to love that time, back home, when the streetlamps were flickering on, and the sky was becoming a deep indigo. It felt like a twisted joke when I arrived here: a messed up version of Heaven where the stuff you love becomes, well, hellish.

I know I'm dead because I remember dying. I took an overdose when I found out I was pregnant. An overreaction, in hindsight. It was a proper overdose, designed to kill: I did my research. I became sick, and sleepy, and at the very last moment repentant and cowardly: ohgodnowhatdidido? Too late, here I am.

The first few days in this place were predictably nightmarish. I woke up stark naked, in the middle of the night. I remember screaming with cold, and fear. I had never felt cold like this when I'd been alive; it felt as though my blood was freezing on the inside. I curled into a ball and wished to die all over again. Except this time I didn't. I remained miserably alive, in Hell.

It wasn't until I'd calmed down that I found the bundle which had been left for me. Clothes, shoes, a knife and some food. I didn't stop to wonder who my benefactor was. I dressed, I ate and then I curled up again and cried myself to sleep, hoping to wake up somewhere else.

There isn't much to look at in this world. I remember the old world being so full; of people and things, lights and noise. This world is quiet, and dark. I spend my days trying to find shelter for the night. You can't stay in the same place because you might get found. So you look for somewhere new each night. A tree with leaves is OK if you can climb it; if you can get high enough up they probably won't see you. Most of the trees are bare but you can still camp behind them.

Some days I want them to find me.

The tree I slept behind last night is a huge old skeleton. I've been here a couple of days now, which is unusual for me, but I like this old fella. One of its limbs is pointing out towards the edge of the trees as though it's trying to direct me. It has character. I'll probably move on today though.

I've started leaving markers around the woods to help me to navigate. I carve a heart shape into the bark. *Sorry old man.*

It's the middle of the morning before I start to pack away my few possessions. I'll travel in the direction I've decided to call North. There is no reason for this decision and it isn't really North. It's as meaningless as everything else in this place.

I've just picked up my bundle and am about to walk when a tiny noise immediately puts me on my guard. I stop and look around, trying to seem as though I'm not looking. I spot him almost straightaway. I remove the knife from the pack.

'Come out.'

Nothing.

'Come out. Now!'

Still nothing. I move towards the trees, holding the knife in front of me.

'Who are you?'

I can see him a little more clearly now. I relax a little.

'Oh. You're new.'

He's a boy of around twelve or thirteen. He's staring at me with terror in his eyes.

'It's alright. I'll help you. There must be some things around here for you. Let's see.'

I find his pack behind one of the trees.

'Look. You have some clothes here. And food. Oh, and—' I hold up a bow.

I half turn my back as he dresses. You can never be totally sure about them, but he looks alright. When he's dressed I hand him the rest and he eats, hungrily.

'You'll be fine, now,' I lie. 'Just stay hidden at night.'

He is staring at me with wide eyes. He looks like he is going to cry. For a moment something stirs in me; something I've locked away. Then I turn away from him and begin to walk.

After a few minutes I look back. The boy is behind me. I stop walking.

When he reaches me I say, 'Look. You can't come with me. I can't even look after myself. I'll get you killed.'

He just stares at me. Sometimes they can't remember how to talk. He must be a mute.

'Just stay here, okay?'

He stops walking. For a moment I feel something – disappointment maybe, or guilt. Then I carry on.

I walk until the late afternoon. I finally stop when the light is disappearing. I'm still in the woods. The clearing in front of me looks disturbingly similar to one I spent the night in a few days ago. That should have been way back, in the opposite direction.

It's more open than I'd like but I'll just have to take my chances. Soon it'll be too dark to continue.

I sit on a rock and eat the remains of my breakfast. The fading light is casting eerie shadows across the landscape from the skeletal trees and jagged hills. I daren't risk a fire, not here.

He appears in the distance. He's followed me all day. He looks exhausted; he's walking in zig-zags. Pity finally overpowers self-preservation. When he reaches me I offer him my blanket. He accepts and falls asleep immediately, while I watch him and shiver.

I lived in a city. Cars passed our house day and night. There was always light. I had a telescope but you couldn't see many stars because of light pollution. So every now and again we'd go off somewhere into the countryside with a blanket and the telescope and just look at the stars.

I miss stars.

I finally fall asleep. I'm awoken by a noise I don't recognise. It sounds like an animal. My hand goes to my knife. I stand over the boy and wait. He stirs. *Don't wake up.* The last thing I need is him panicking and crying right now.

There is a snuffling sound to my left. I close my eyes even though it's completely dark. It doesn't sound too big. It's getting closer. I wait until I actually feel its breath on my skin and I thrust forward with the knife. It makes a thin squeal and I hear it drop, heavily. I stand motionless for a few minutes in case there are any more but everything is silent.

Sleep has left me now. I'm alone with my thoughts.

Another memory appears, unasked for. Me and Mum. We're in the kitchen, making a cake. I can smell it as it cooks; it smells really nice. I'm happy. I hug Mum, and then out of nowhere she starts to cry. Big crying, as she used to say, not just a sniffle. She won't tell me why. I wonder whether I did something wrong. It isn't till later that I understand.

The boy wakes with the meagre morning light.

'Hi,' I say.

He stares at me for a moment. Then he says, 'Hi.'

I smile. I think that's my first smile in this place. I've almost forgotten how.

'You can talk!'

He nods. 'Yes.'

'Are you hungry?'

'Yes.'

I use the first light of the day to help me skin the animal I killed last night.

'What is that?'

'An animal. It was him or us. And now we can eat him.'

'OK.'

I make a fire. That's one thing that's easy enough here; everything is tinderbox dry. Keeping it small and hidden isn't quite as easy.

We tear off strips of meat and cook them in small chunks, eating as we go. Then I wrap up the rest to eat later.

'Can I stay with you?'

He looks at me with pleading eyes. I don't know how to refuse.

'Alright. But you have to take care of yourself. I can barely take care of me.'

'Alright.' He seems to relax a little. 'Where are we?' he asks.

'I don't know. I woke up here like you did. Do you remember anything from before?'

'Before? What do you mean?'

That would be a no then. 'Never mind. Do you have a name?'

He stares at me blankly. I consider him: short black hair, brown skin, big brown eyes. He reminds me of my cousin. 'I'm going to call you Ali.'

He nods. 'What should I call you?'

I think about this. I had a name, back then. But the person attached to it was so different from me. 'I don't know.'

'What about Girl? I could call you Girl.'

I shrug. 'Alright.'

It doesn't take long for me to discover that not only is Ali not mute, he's very talkative. Annoyingly talkative. He's a question-asker.

'Where do the things come from? The packs? When we arrive?'

'I don't know. Where do you think they come from?'

'I think someone is looking after us.'

I look around at the dead landscape. The earth here has been scorched in a wide arc. It grins at me unpleasantly. I can see no goodness here.

When I look back at the boy I see the hope in his eyes.

'Yes, maybe,' I say.

There's something I should probably share with you at this point. It seems like you've earned it. You've stayed with me this far.

I have a secret, and it goes like this: the truly ironic part of all of this is that the thing the overdose was designed to cure is still here with me; I am still pregnant, the only lost soul in the whole of the underworld who is with child.

My life had been pretty normal until my fifteenth year. It was just me and Mum, living in a council flat. My dad didn't exist to me in any real sense; he was a story Mum told every now and then. Sometimes the details changed as though she had made him up entirely.

We were happy. Take a look at fifteen year old me: I was confident, doing well at school (take *that* statistical probability). I had a boyfriend, sort of. He wasn't my baby's father. He was a sweet, nerdy kid from my school year. George. We had fun together that was never going to amount to a lifetime commitment. We'd bunk off school together every now and again and do something more enjoyable. We lived a couple of miles from the seaside so we'd walk up there sometimes and play in the arcade or mess about on the beach.

I barely recognise that happy, carefree girl: taking selfies on the pier, getting detentions. Thinking too much about her hair. A normal teenager.

It changed. Why did it change?

How did I get to *here*?

I know I am pregnant because a) I feel crappy all of the time and b) I still have all of the symptoms: sore boobs, nausea, pain. No period, if periods are still a thing here. Who knows?

And also, I just feel it. It's as though the whole death thing never happened to me. It's like I'm exactly the same person I was before, except I'm in this shitty place and I remember dying. So there it is. In about seven months Hell is going to hear the pitter patter. If I can survive that long.

'Do you remember before?'

'Yes.'

'Well, what was it like?'

'Big. And complicated.'

'What do you mean?'

'Well – there were lots of things. We had so much stuff. Phones, iPad, TVs.'

'What are they?'

'Just things. They helped us talk to each other.'

'Oh.' A momentary pause. 'How?'

I sigh. 'Enough, Ali. Enough questions.'

'Please? Just tell me.'

'Alright. Last one. We could see each other and hear one another's voices. And we could send messages.'

I could see him trying to decide if he could risk another question. 'No. I need a bit of alone time. I've been on my own for weeks, and now you. It's too much, all in one go.'

He looks a little crestfallen, then smiles broadly. 'I'll get some firewood,' he says.

'Be careful,' I warn him. 'Keep looking around you.'

'You *do* care about me!'

'No. I just don't want to have to rescue you.'

He disappears into the leafless wood.

I sit still, enjoying the quiet left behind in the boy's wake. It *is* nice to have some company. Even if he talks too much. I'm starting to realise that I've probably spent too much time alone. I've adjusted to it, and now it's hard to change back.

There is a faint breeze, which is unusual. It blows the dust around in swirls around my feet. I wiggle my feet and it causes the dirt to make new patterns in the air. You make your own amusement here.

I've been daydreaming for a while when I realise that Ali should have returned by now. I pick up my knife and follow his footprints.

A few metres away I find him in a clearing. He's in a tree. Below the tree are two – what are they? I can't focus on them properly. They are looking up at him. Something about them is repulsive; they're beasts. I feel sick just looking at them. I want to kill them, to completely destroy them. I know I'm outnumbered. I go back to the camp and find Ali's bow. I've never used one of these before, but it seems like my best option. I try to keep myself hidden and aim the arrow towards the nearest one. It makes a hissing noise in the air and lands nowhere near them. I try again and miss again and this time they see me.

The nearest creature comes charging at me making angry noises. It's still out of focus. I discard the bow and charge towards it with my knife. At the last moment the creature seems to panic and the two of them run away.

I'm shaking. I walk over to the tree and hold out my hand to Ali. He takes it and climbs down clumsily.

'Let's go. They could come back.'

'Alright.'

We go back to the camp and gather our things quickly. Ali looks scared.

'What were they?'

'I don't know.'

'They were horrible.'

'Let's just go.'

We walk in the opposite direction to the creatures, to minimise the risk of meeting them again. The day isn't too hot so far; the wind is keeping us cool. If it continues we should be able to walk most of the day if we have to. Maybe we won't have to. Maybe we'll get lucky today.

Half a day's walking takes us out of the forest. This is progress, but it also leaves us vulnerable to attack. We can't walk for long in open ground.

'Let's stop here a while and figure out what to do,' I say. Ali looks pleased at this suggestion and immediately starts rummaging for the food in my pack.

Lunch is difficult. The wind is blowing the dust around so much it's impossible to eat and the meat is becoming ruined. Ali looks like he wants to cry again so I stand over him while he eats, annoyed with myself for being soft.

'Thank you,' he says, quietly.

The dust storm solves our visibility problem anyway. It'll be impossible for someone to see us through this. We can walk on. We just have to hope it lasts till we get to shelter. We walk, coughing and blinking and trying to swim through the dust and hoping against hope that there isn't anything in the middle of the storm that we don't want to meet.

The dust storm is followed by a regular storm. Rain is infrequent here, but it does occur, and it's drinkable. This rainfall is pretty heavy; fat, globular drops which we catch with our tongues. Once I've put out our empties to refill Ali and I set about splashing one another.

When the rain stops the landscape becomes visible again and I see something not entirely unexpected: the edge of the forest. Of course, I can't be sure it's the same one. There might be lots of forests here. But at the same time I *am* certain. Somehow, while walking in a straight line, Ali and I have come full circle.
    'Is that…' begins Ali.
    'Try not to think about it,' I say.
    Our only other option is to try to go around the forest. We choose a direction and walk.

We've been walking for a while when we see what seems to be a camp with tents and a few wooden huts. It doesn't look inviting. Around it are poles stuck in the ground, with what look worryingly like human skulls on top of them. But it's directly in our path.
    'We're going to have to turn around,' I sigh.
    'But we've walked all day!'
    'What choice do we have?'
    As we turn to go back we see four, five, six figures in the distance. And there are more behind us.
    'What should we do?' whispers Ali, unhappily. 'Are they going to hurt us?'
    'Ssh. It'll be OK. I'll talk to them.' I'm panicking inside. Having to pretend for Ali's sake is good; it makes me feel more in control.
    As they get closer I see that they're human. That doesn't make

13

me feel much better. We're completely outnumbered so if they decide to rob us or worse we don't stand much chance.

'We're not alone,' I shout, as they approach. 'There are more of us. We're the scouting party.'

There's a man at the front of the mob. 'We've been following you for half a day. There's no one else.'

My hand finds my knife. Ali's sobbing, quietly. The man holds up his hands.

'We're not going to hurt you. Put the knife away.'

'Why should I trust you?'

'Because even with the knife you don't stand a chance. Your best option is to trust us.'

'Convenient for you.'

'Look, just make a decision. We have other things to do.'

I look at Ali. He looks miserable but he gives a tiny nod.

'Alright,' I say. I place the knife in my pack, without taking my eyes off the group approaching us. The man seems to relax a little.

'Okay. Fine. Follow us.'

They pass us and we fall into step behind them.

'This is good, isn't it?' asks Ali. 'They might help us.'

'We'll see,' I say.

They lead us into the village where we are shown to a place with seats made from bundled hay. Ali's looking happier by the second.

'They're going to look after us, Girl. We'll be OK.'

The man who seems to be their leader approaches us. 'Welcome to our town.'

I look around at the ragged collection of tents.

'Thanks.'

'Where are you from and how long have you been here?'

Good question. 'I don't know how long I've been here.' My hand drifts to my stomach. 'A month, maybe two? It's hard to tell.' I nod towards Ali. 'The boy's new. We came from over there.' I point. 'What about you? How long have you been here?'

'I've seen twelve season changes. It's easier to survive once you know the rules.'

'The rules?'

'Yeah. You'll see. Meantime get some food. Someone will find you a place to sleep. You look exhausted.'

That's true. Every bone in my body seems to ache.

'See?' whispers Ali, when the man leaves. 'See? I told you.'

'I still don't trust them. Why are they helping us?'

'Because they're nice.'

'I don't think nice exists in this world.'

'You're nice.'

'No, I'm not.'

'Yes, you are.'

A little while later a girl with pale skin and freckles shows us to an empty tent. 'You can stay here if you want.'

'Whose is it?' I ask.

'Someone who doesn't need it,' she says, walking away.

'Why? Why don't they need it?' I ask, already knowing the answer. The girl has gone.

The tent is empty apart from a blanket in the corner. Ali puts his pack down and sits on the blanket. 'It's nice.' He wrinkles his nose. 'Smells funny, though.'

It does smell strange.

'Hey, move off the blanket a minute.'

He does, and I move it tentatively.

'Eurgh! What are they?'

The blanket was concealing a pile of what look worryingly like finger bones. Some of them still have stuff attached. I think I can see a fingernail. I'm struggling to keep myself from vomiting. I leave the tent in a hurry and find the girl. She's sitting with another girl, eating.

'Hey,' I say. She looks at me briefly, then turns back to her meal. 'Hey! Why have you put us in a tent that has… that has…' I can't bring myself to say it. 'There are bones there.'

She shrugs. 'So get rid of them.'

'What kind of a messed up place is this? Who has human bones in their bed?'

She turns back to me. Her surprised look only lasts a second. 'Not my problem. Sort it out yourself. I'm not your servant.'

My frustration is building. 'So helpful!'

'Stop being a baby.'

I want to hit this girl. All of the fear and the horror is being replaced by anger. Fury is starting to consume me. I grab the girl and pull her to her feet.

'Hey! What are you doing? You psycho!'

'Why are you being like this? I'm asking you for help.'

'Let go of me!'

'What's going on?'

It's the man who we met on the road. I let go of the girl. She glares at me.

'Your latest acquisition has just gone crazy. Sort it out or get rid of her.'

He turns to me. 'What's going on?'

'She took us to a tent with human bones in it. And when I told her, she was...' I'm struggling to justify my anger. '...Unhelpful,' I finish, lamely.

The man gestures for the girl to go. She leaves with her friend, giving me a final nasty look.

'Human bones?' he repeats. I nod. 'Hmm. Well, the guy who slept there before was a bit strange. He lost it, towards the end. It happens, sometimes.'

'But where did he get them from?'

'Let me see.' I take him to the tent. Ali's sitting outside, looking miserable.

The man goes inside for a moment. When he comes back he has the blanket, with the bones inside.

'They're not human,' he says. 'I can understand how you made the mistake. They're demon bones.'

'Demons? What do you mean?'

'You must have seen them. They live here too, unfortunately. Pure evil. They disguise themselves, make it so we can't see them properly.'

I nod. 'I *have* seen them. So these bones are from those... things? How do you know?'

'Must be. Nothing else they can be. We had a few attacks

before you came and some of them died. I guess he kept a memento.' He lifts the blanket. 'I'll get rid of these.'

'Thank you.'

He walks away, leaving Ali and me alone with the smelly tent. We sit outside for a while.

'Well, this is home now, at least for a while,' I say. 'We'd better get used to it.'

'Can we get another blanket?'

'I'll ask. Later.'

'OK.'

Another time, another world. I should have been in maths but the sky was too bright; the morning had knocked on my door and asked me to play out, so I did. I went to the meadow near the motorway and found a tree with low branches. I climbed up and sat and listened to the buzzing and the traffic noise.

I'd been sitting there for three quarters of an hour when I heard a loud noise from the direction of the road. A motorbike came flying over the embankment and down towards the meadow. Over the gorse, nosediving into the long grass. The rider was catapulted into some bushes.

I froze. I didn't know any first aid; what could I do? I sat there and hoped for someone else to come but no one did. Eventually I forced myself to get up and have a look.

He was in a bad way, but alive. His leg was twisted under him and there was blood seeping from a large cut on his head.

Don't die I remember whispering. *Don't die in front of me.*

We get another blanket and fashion a sort of bed.

'It'll have to do,' I say.

'It still smells,' complains Ali.

'It's all we have.'

The next day the man comes back to the tent early in the morning. 'Get up,' he says.

'Why? What do you want us to do?'

'We need to talk to you. You need to know some things.'

I shake Ali who isn't pleased at being woken before he's ready. He rubs his eyes.

'What is it?'

'They want us to go to some sort of meeting. They have things to tell us.'

'Why can't they do it later?'

'I don't know. Come on, we have to go.'

He stands up, awkward with sleep, and stretches.

'Alright. Do we get to eat?'

'Hopefully.'

They're sitting around a fire which is cooking something. This cheers Ali up. The man gestures for us to sit, which we do.

I'm getting a little tired of being ordered about but I decide to bite my tongue. Temporarily.

'We need to discuss some things,' the man said. 'First – names. I'm called Conrad. Have you two got names?'

I nod. 'This is Ali. I called him that. And I'm Girl,' I say, smiling at Ali.

'Ali. Nice name. What made you think of it?'

'He looks a bit like my cousin.'

'What do you mean?'

'My relative.'

'I don't understand. You mean someone you knew? Someone you arrived with?'

Oh. Of course.

'No. I mean from before. Ali was in my family.'

The meaning of my words takes a moment to settle on his face.

'You mean – you can remember?'

I nod. 'Everything.'

The man looks incredulous. 'It isn't possible.'

I shrug. 'Okay.'

'I mean – none of us can remember. Some of us think there isn't a before. I've always thought it was just a story.'

I'm not sure what to say, so I say: 'How did you get your name?'

18

'It was given to me, when I arrived. I just knew what I was called. I assumed you were the same.'

I shook my head.

There is a woman sitting next to him and she says something quietly.

'We'll talk about this later. We're running out of time. For now you need to know a few things.'

'What things?'

'The rules of the game.'

Ali and I glance at each other. 'What game?' I ask.

'This. The game. The reason we're all here.'

'But…'

'No!' His voice has a slight edge now. 'You need to listen. Really listen, okay? For all of our safety.' I nod. 'Right. Good.' He takes a breath. 'In less than two hours a group of demons is going to attack us. Now unless I explain a few things to you you'll get yourself killed and worse, you might break the rules.'

'Why is that worse?' asks Ali.

'I'll explain.'

Later that morning Ali and I are sitting behind barricades waiting for the arrival of – what? Demons, monsters. We've been given weapons. Ali is crying, but quietly so that no one will hear.

'It's alright,' I whisper. 'We're going to hide. We don't need to fight.'

'But you heard him. We have to fight. Otherwise we're breaking the rules and they'll kill all of us.'

'You don't really believe him do you?'

Ali nodded. 'Yes.'

'Well, we'll stay together. I won't let anything bad happen to you.'

'You can't stop it.'

'I can try.'

Conrad had explained to us what he referred to as 'The rules'.

'We're here for a purpose. We're here to kill demons. They attack us, we attack them. If you kill one of them, you get supplies. Food, clothes, whatever you need. But they're clever, and quick.'

19

I'd asked him what would happen if we refuse to fight. If we decided to take our chances finding food, as we had up till now. The question visibly angered him.

'You can't!' he said. 'That's not an option. If one of us breaks the rules we all pay.' It had happened once. The next day a disease had taken hold in the village. Twenty people died. As he told us about that he became unfocused for a moment. Then he shook it off.

'It's a clear system,' he said. 'We follow the rules. We get food. And we're good at it. We've won the last twenty fights.'

'But why?' I asked. 'What's the point?'

He shrugged. 'If you want to stay alive it's what you have to do.'

I hear it before I see it. A cry, a screech, like an enormous bird. It makes my veins freeze.

Ali and I had hid, earlier.

'I can't fight them,' Ali had told me with certainty. 'I just can't.'

I wasn't sure what I was capable of but I didn't particularly want to find out.

'We'll just hide, wait it out,' I said.

'But what if he's right? What if we cause something bad to happen?'

'We'll leave tomorrow anyway.'

'OK.'

But it's here, a metre or two from our hiding place. I can hear it and I can smell it. It's making me want to vomit. I grip my knife so hard it's making my hands hurt. We can hear it moving clumsily around, somewhere in front of us. Death, our death, stomping and thrashing and stinking. I have to stop it. I have no choice.

I wait until it sounds really close and I jump over the barricade wall and land on the creature. It's easier than I expected to fight this thing; in fact it feels good, right. I swing the knife at it. It's swiping back at me with a weapon of its own. I feel enraged. I want to kill it. Human and demon lock into a frenzied dance, tearing at each other wildly.

I believe I would have killed it except suddenly it's over;

they're retreating. I feel unsatisfied and angry. I run after the beast but Conrad stands in my way.

'Stop. Let it go.'

'Why? Get out of the way!' I snarl.

He laughs. I want to hit him. 'I can't fault your enthusiasm,' he says. 'But they've gone. The game's over. Better luck next time.'

The adrenaline is still coursing through my body. Then suddenly it stops, and I feel nauseous. I vomit on the ground. Conrad pats my back. I shove his hand away.

'You're going to do alright,' he says. 'You've just got to get used to it. It can be overwhelming at first.'

I sit on the ground for a few minutes, normality coming back to me in shifts. After a while I remember Ali and go back to our hiding place.

He's curled up behind the barricade. He looks like he's been crying.

'You OK?'

He looks at me like he's scared.

'Hey. What's wrong?'

He just shakes his head.

'I just got a bit crazy. It's OK. You know I won't hurt you.'

'I don't like it here,' he says.

I sit down next to him. 'Well, we don't have to stay very long. We'll just get our strength back and then we'll go, OK?'

He nods, miserably.

Neither of us sleeps well that night. When I finally drift off I'm awoken shortly after by Ali, crying in his sleep. I put my arms around him until it stops.

The next day we get up groggy and go to find food. Conrad and a couple of the others have cooked some fresh meat; it smells good. He hands us a couple of plates and we help ourselves. I start to eat and then I notice that Ali hasn't touched his.

'Come on. You need to eat or we'll never get to leave.'

'But look.'

He points at his plate. The meat is covered with tiny wriggling white grubs.

'Ugh!' I immediately look down at my own plate. It looks fine. I hand it to Ali.

'You need to eat too!' he says.

'I've lost my appetite.'

But the moment Ali touches the plate the food starts to crawl with maggots. We both stare at it, then at Conrad, who shrugs.

'Boy didn't fight,' he says. *I warned you.*

Ali starts to cry.

'What kind of messed up system is this?' I yell, throwing the plate. 'He's just a kid. He's not a fighter.'

'Normally kids like him don't survive more than a few days. You're not doing him a favour by protecting him.'

Anger is coursing through me again but it's directionless. I want someone to shout at.

'Save it for the next battle,' suggests Conrad. 'And if I were you, I'd get the kid to fight this time. It'll only get worse if he doesn't.'

I used to have a recurring dream, back when I was alive. I was walking up the steps of a lighthouse. It was tall and seemed never-ending, but eventually I reached the top. I looked around at the sea and for a moment everything was perfect; calm and beautiful. Then I tried to switch the lamp on but instead everything went completely dark.

That's a little bit like being here. Like someone switched a light off somewhere and no one knows how to put it back on. Everybody's given up being nice; there's no point. It's all about survival.

The next battle isn't until a few days from now. That gives Ali and me a little bit of breathing room to work out what we're going to do.

'I want to leave,' says Ali, about twenty times an hour.

'We will,' I keep repeating. But my mind is turning over our options and none of them look good. Eventually I come to a decision.

'I'm going to train you to fight.'

Ali looks at me dubiously but doesn't immediately object.

'I'm not saying you'll be assassin material,' I continue, 'but all you have to do is inflict some kind of injury. I'll help you. You get fed, we get to stay alive.'

He puts his head in his hands. Then after a while he looks up and nods.

We start immediately. 'They gave you this,' I say, handing him the bow. 'So maybe we'll start with that.' I point at the dark spot on the wooden wall. 'Try to hit that spot.'

He lines up the arrow and releases it. It flies in the right direction but bounces harmlessly off the wood.

'OK, no natural aptitude. Never mind. Try again.'

He practises for a while. After an hour or so his aim is beginning to improve. I decide to try a little hand to hand combat. I haven't told Ali I'm pregnant and I decide now isn't the time.

'Come on, hurt me,' I say.

He approaches me nervously. He raises his hand; I deflect it. He starts to giggle.

'Oh *come on*, Ali.'

He straightens his face then tries again with the same result. This happens several times until finally I give up.

'I think the bow and arrow will be your thing,' I decide. 'Keep practising. You won't even need to be near the demons. You can fire your arrows from your hiding place.'

He nods. He actually looks quite happy, and his next meal is maggot-free.

By the time the next battle comes around Ali can aim reasonably well. But he's shaking all morning; he can barely hold the bow.

'You just need one shot on target,' I tell him. 'I'll do the rest.'

The other residents of the village get increasingly tense as the fight approaches. Conrad is jittery and brittle; I start to avoid him. He's making me more nervous, if that's possible.

The battle begins in the same way as the previous one. A loud, screeching cry and suddenly the creatures are all over the village. It hurts my eyes to try to look at them; they're always out of focus. They fill me with horror and revulsion; I want to hurt them, to stop them from making me feel like this.

This fight goes better for me; I still don't get the kill, although every cell of my body wants to destroy the thing. But it retreats, limping and bleeding when the fight ends.

I go to find Ali, feeling good. As I approach he is looking at something in his hands. He jumps when he hears me and closes his hand around whatever he was looking at.

'How did it go?' I ask.

He shakes his head.

'Nothing?' I sigh.

'I couldn't stop shaking.'

He looks so sad I decide not to say anything else, and just hug him.

The next meal is another grub-feast. Ali starts to cry again when he sees it. I sigh and grab a handful of grubs.

'It's still food,' I say, shoving the wriggling handful into my mouth. It tastes really horrible but Ali follows my lead and begins to eat the wormy meal.

Later that day Ali and I are sitting together in one of the trees, keeping watch. It's sunset, if it can really be called that in a place without daylight. The sky is a sort of purple-red. Almost beautiful.

'What will I do?' asks Ali. 'I can't fight. I've tried.'

I hold my hands wide. 'You just have to keep trying. I'm not sure we have a choice.'

He's looking at something in his hand again.

'What is that?'

He looks at me strangely, then holds open his hand. He's holding a severed finger. I want to vomit.

'What is that? And why are you holding it?'

I think of the previous occupant of our tent. Maybe Ali is losing his mind like that guy. Maybe that's what eating grubs does to you.

'It came from – the thing. That you were fighting. You cut it off with your knife.'

I stare at him for a moment. 'No, that's not possible. It didn't look like…' I pause. I don't know what it looked like.

Ali looks up at me. 'It's human,' he says. I look at the finger. It does look human. It *is* human.

'But it can't be,' I say.

'Why? We don't know what they really look like behind that weird mask. What if they're humans, like us?'

'They're not. I just know they're not.'

But I'm no longer certain. I decide that the best tactic is just to be direct. I approach Conrad later that day.

'What are the things we're fighting?' I ask.

'Demons. I told you.' He sounds irritated.

'Then why do they look like us? How do we know they're not human?'

He stares at me like I just insulted his Grandma.

'I told you. They disguise themselves as humans. You know what they are. You can feel it.'

I *can* feel it. And I want to believe what he says. I decide to ignore the tiny nagging voice in my brain. I know they're demons. I *know* it.

When I return to Ali I can't meet his eyes.

'What did he say?'

'I was right. They're demons who take human shape sometimes.'

'But that makes no sense. You know that.'

I sigh. 'Ali, I know you're scared. We'll work something out. I promise.'

'You're not listening to me. It's not right. It's all wrong! The man who had our hut *knew*.'

'He was deranged.'

'According to Conrad.'

'Yes, according to Conrad. He's our leader. We're supposed to listen to him.'

'He isn't *my* leader.' He turns away from me, curling his body up into a defensive ball.

'Ali…'

'Go away.'

'Fine.'

I walk away from him.

I take a risk and leave the village. I want to walk and think. The woods begin a few metres from the village wall. I wander around the jagged trees for a while, till I find one with low enough branches for me to climb. I sit among the dead limbs and remember.

After I saw the motorcycle accident I stopped caring, for a while. Or more accurately, I pretended to stop caring. I was the teen cliché; alcohol, drugs, boys. Well, one boy. I can't even remember what was so fascinating about him. I think I just needed a distraction.

He rode a motorcycle too. I'm sure a psychologist would have an opinion about that. I was always asking to go out on the bike; and I wanted him to take risks. It's like I wanted the accident to happen to me. It never did; instead I had a different kind of accident. The kind which makes your boyfriend run away if he's an arsehole.

I sit in the tree with my hand on my belly. It's still flat. Perhaps I'm wrong. I can't be certain of anything.

'Hey!'

Conrad is standing below my tree.

'You shouldn't leave the village. It isn't safe.'

'I needed some time to myself.'

'Well, you can't be here. You could be attacked. Or you could draw attention from something and bring it back to the village.'

'*Something?*'

'There's all sorts of crazy stuff out there. You haven't seen anything yet.'

'I won't be long. I don't want to go back yet.'

To my immense irritation he sits.

'Well, I'm not leaving you.'

'Why not? I'm fine.'

'You never know.' He leans back against the tree trunk. 'So. Tell me about what you remember. From before.'

26

Such a big question. An impossible question.

'It was busy, with people, and things. Nobody had any time. My mum…' I paused as my thoughts clouded. 'She was a nurse. She cared for people. She worked at the hospital and was always tired.' I'm not sure why I'm telling him this.

'I wish I could remember,' he says. 'Sometimes I think I can but it's probably just my imagination.'

Suddenly I see a clear image in my head; a different Conrad, in another place. He's scruffy, dishevelled and kind of fat; the sort of guy who would be labelled a slacker. He's in an untidy room eating food from a plastic packet. Am I imagining it? Should I tell him about it?

Hmm. I don't know what Conrad imagines his life was like but I'm betting it isn't this.

'What's wrong?' he asks.

'Nothing. I just want to be alone.'

'Too bad.' He stretches out, hands behind his head. 'You know, your little friend is going to get us in trouble.'

'What do you suggest we do? He's not a fighter.'

'He needs to learn. If he doesn't he can't stay. We've learned that the hard way.'

'Then I'm not staying either.'

'If you're going to survive here you'll have to get smarter. You need to choose your friends better. He's a liability.'

Conrad's starting to seriously irritate me.

'If I go back will you leave me alone?'

'If that's what you want.'

'It is.'

The tiny ration of daylight is beginning to fade now anyway. I climb down and begin to walk back, trying to ignore Conrad.

I'm almost back when I see her, crouching in some bushes. She's folded up on herself, as if she's trying to shut the world out. A newbie.

'Hey,' I say, trying not to make the sigh in my voice too obvious. 'Are you okay? Have you found your things?'

She won't speak to me. I help her find her pack and bring her back to the camp. There's a chorus of groans as I bring her in, but a couple of the girls rally round and I leave her with them.

That night I have an odd dream. It doesn't feel like a dream; it feels like I'm seeing somebody else's life. I'm back on earth, in an alley somewhere. There's a boy on the ground. He's surrounded by other boys who are kicking the living crap out of him. He must be in pain but he's laughing hysterically. Then suddenly he seems to notice me. He's staring right at me as though I don't belong.

The next attack is in two days. Ali doesn't want to train; it's like he's given up.

'Come on. You have to be able to defend yourself.'

'I don't want to.'

'Conrad will kick you out of the village.'

He just shrugs. I don't know what to do.

When the attack begins I tell Ali to stay behind me. Conrad wants me near the front with him this time; that's where the main fight takes place. In spite of everything I can't help being a tiny bit proud that he thinks I'm a good fighter. Unfortunately it puts Ali in more danger; we're in the thick of the battle here.

The fight doesn't go well this time. There are too many; I'm quickly surrounded. I'm knocked over within a minute. Conrad and another guy have to wade in and help me. Two of the creatures are trying to drag me away. Conrad kills one of them, I think, and the other one finally lets go and carries away the body of its comrade. My pride has suffered a bit but otherwise I'm OK.

'Sorry,' I say.

Conrad frowns. 'I don't know why they all attacked you. That doesn't usually happen. I wouldn't have suggested you fight here if I thought that could happen.'

I look around for Ali. 'Hey. Where are you?' I call. I look behind the bush where he had been hiding. Nothing.

'Have you seen Ali?'

Conrad shrugs.

'They got him.' This was Dan, the girl I had fought with on the first day here.

'What? What do you mean?'

'They took him. Sorry.' She doesn't sound sorry. She sounds indifferent.

'No. No! I have to help him!' I turn to follow them out of the village but Conrad grabs my arm.

'You can't. Your friend will be dead by now.'

'You're *wrong*. I need to help him.' I push past him.

'Wait. Wait! I'll go with you!'

'No. Why? I don't need you.' I'm furious and frightened and I just want to *do* something. I have to help Ali. Why is he trying to stop me?

'You know nothing about them, or about the other things that are out there. You've been here a couple of months, right? There are things out there you can't imagine. I've seen stuff I can't even describe to you. You need my help.'

'I've been here long enough. I know these woods.'

'You *think* you do but you've only seen the things they wanted you to see.'

'Who?'

He shakes his head. 'Which way are you planning to go?'

I look at the woods and gesture vaguely towards them.

He rolls his eyes. 'Look.' He points in the direction I had indicated. 'That path is completely blocked. The trees have grown across the path.' He points a little to the left. 'That side is full of poisonous fungi. Breathe that shit in and you'll be dead in seconds.' He points somewhere else. 'That way…'

'Right. OK. I get it. So which way *should* I go?'

'You shouldn't. You should stay here…'

I make an exasperated sound and stand up. 'I'll figure it out.'

'…I *was* about to say, but I know you won't do that. So in that case, your best option is to try and get through the briars.'

'The briars? What's that?'

'You'll see. But it won't be easy.'

'I don't care. I'm leaving now. If you want to come with me you'd better get on with it.'

'At least let's get some food. You're not being rational.'

I want to punch him in his rational face. Instead I succumb to a different urge and vomit. Conrad is staring at me.

'Are you alright?'

I nod. 'I'm fine. Let's go.'

'Just give me a few minutes. That won't make a difference if he's still alive, will it?'

I sigh. 'Just be quick or I'm going without you.'

Conrad says that the creatures live in the middle of the woods.

'Have you been there?'

He shakes his head. 'The only person I've ever known who's been there and came back was the man who lived in your hut. The one who went crazy. He spent a few days there before he managed to escape. It got inside his head.'

The forest is gloomy and difficult to walk through. The roots have grown out of the ground and created a thorny carpet which covers the forest floor entirely. Every step we take is an effort.

'How do they pass it to get to us?' I wonder.

'I told you. They're not human. They probably don't feel it.'

By the end of the morning we're exhausted and I can still see the edge of the woods where we came in.

'This is impossible!' I shout.

'Still think they're human?' asks Conrad.

I shrug. 'It doesn't matter anymore. I just need to find Ali.'

'Why does he matter to you? You've only known him a few weeks.'

'He does matter. He's all I have.'

Conrad's face is wearing a *you'd-better-get-use-to-it* expression that I choose to ignore.

I keep telling myself that the roots will thin out soon but they just don't. I'm starting to think getting to Ali will be impossible. On top of everything else I'm dizzy and nauseous. Conrad has noticed I'm finding it tough; I think he's waiting for me to give up and turn back but I won't, even if it kills me. I'm on the point of fainting when he suggests we stop to eat.

'How far do you think it is?' I ask.

He shrugs. 'I told you, I've never been there. This wasn't my idea, remember.'

We eat our food in bad tempered silence. We can't even sit; the ground's too thorny. So we eat quickly and start walking again.

We haven't been going for long when we hear a noise: like twigs snapping. We stop walking and crouch behind a large trunk.

After a few moments we hear something in the clearing. Two somethings. They're searching. For us? But they can't know we're coming. They're speaking in a language I don't recognise.

I glance at Conrad. He's looking up into the tree; I think he's assessing it as a hiding place. It won't conceal us as it has no leaves but they might not notice us if we're above them. We don't need to find out, however. After a minute or so the voices fade away.

'This is good,' whispers Conrad. 'It means we must be getting close. If we assume that they're scouts from their camp then all we need to do is follow their trail. That'll get us to them. No idea what we're going to do at that point though.'

'We have to find a way to help Ali,' I say.

It's easy enough to follow the scouts. This seems to be a well-worn path; all the brambles have been trodden down. We're both jittery though; we're listening for the smallest noise ahead. Every now and then we stop and just wait. Nothing happens, so we continue.

After a while Conrad stops again.

'This doesn't seem right,' he says. 'We should have seen something by now. They'll have patrols, like we do. I think they know we're here.'

We both look around but it seems we're too late. Blurred figures appear all around us. A blanket is thrown over me and I can feel something being tied around me. I can't breathe. I vomit in the bag. I'm going to suffocate. I'm dying all over again.

Boy

The pavement is hard underneath my cheek and stones pierce my skin like tiny teeth. I lie still, pained, queasy, hoping that my lack of movement will convince them that I'm unconscious or dead. Then pain explodes in my stomach once again as one of them directs a booted kick my way.

I'm laughing. It all seems so… pointless. And suddenly it's so funny. My laughter is irritating the guys kicking the shit out of me which is even funnier.

And that's when I see her.

She looks like a ghost. Maybe she is one. She's tall, strong, cropped black hair. She's got this angry look about her, like I said something to annoy her.

A siren sounds somewhere nearby and the boys run away, shouting abuse at me as they go. I lie still.

'Hey. Are you alright?'

A random passer-by. Where were you five minutes ago? And do I look alright? Idiot.

'Listen, I'm going to ring for an ambulance. You stay there.'

Like I'm going to be moving any time soon. I lie still and looked at the sky. It's a beautiful night, even when you've taken a beating. My eyes lose their focus a little and there she is again: graceful, furious, terrifyingly beautiful. She's staring at me.

'Hey. Who are you?' I croak. The idiot assumes I'm speaking to him.

'I'm Jake. Just stay still. They're on their way.'

The girl frowns at me as though she's confused, and then she disappears. Another spectre conjured up by my malfunctioning brain. I groan with pain and frustration.

'Can you hear me? Can you tell me your name?'

A light is being shone into my eyes. I must have zoned out for a bit; now I'm on a stretcher. I manage to say something that even to me sounds like 'Muhmuh.'

The paramedics keep talking to me as I get bundled into the back of an ambulance. Judging by their faces I must look pretty bad. I want them to leave me alone; I feel tired and cold. The pain in my head is growing and my eyes lose their focus. I need to sleep.

I'm not there anymore. I'm in an empty field. The sky's no longer completely dark. And I'm naked.

Oh, right. Reality hits me like a claw hammer. I'm dead. That was a pretty bad beating they gave me.

I'm oddly unafraid. I get to my feet, and stretch. All of the pain is gone. The voices have gone too. I feel good. My shit life is over. Let's see what the afterlife has to offer. I'm not even cold, despite my lack of clothing.

I find a bundle nearby which solves that particular problem. It's like it's been made for me. There are the clothes, all in my size. There's also food, and a couple of nifty looking hunting knives. I dress and try some of the meat; not too bad. Then I pick up the pack and start to walk. It doesn't seem to matter much which direction I go.

I've walked for a while when I see something in the distance. It's too dark to see clearly but it looks like a person, walking towards me. I take one of the knives out of my pack and hide in in my sleeve. Living on the streets for a while makes you kind of paranoid.

Yeah, it's definitely a person, and they're heading for me.

It takes a few minutes for us to reach each other. Whatever this place is, it's spacious. Empty, really.

He's an old man. He seems unsurprised to see me.

'Hello,' he says.

'Hi,' I reply. What do you say in this situation? Small talk has never been my thing and this scenario is quite frankly, weird. 'Where am I?'

'This is Afterwards,' says the man.

'As in Heaven? Or Hell, maybe?'

'Perhaps,' says the man. 'I've been asked to find you. I need to take you to the shrine.'

'Shrine? Like a religious thing?'

'You'll see.'

'And what if I don't want to go with you?'

The man looks surprised. 'You can do whatever you want, obviously. But you might find it difficult to survive without the help of my mistress.'

I look around at the empty landscape.

'Did your mistress leave me these things?' I ask. The man nods.

'She'll help you. But you will have to earn her help.'

I shrug. 'Makes no difference to me. Let's go.'

Girl

I'm not dead. Well, I'm not more dead. But I passed out for a while.

The blanket has been taken off my head. The vomit smell has gone, too. I'm still in the forest, except this bit looks like someone lives here. There are things lying around: clothes, tools, blankets. The thorns have been cut away.

I sit up, suddenly alert. Where am I?

I can hear voices nearby. A man talking to a child, I think. The child sounds like—

'Ali?'

'Girl!'

He bounds through the trees and hugs me. 'You're alright!' he says.

'So are you! I thought you were – I thought they killed you.'

'They brought me here. I was right! They're people! They...'

'Stop! You're talking too fast. What do you mean?'

'You'll see. Come on!'

He grabs my hand.

'Come *on.*'

He pulls me towards the door. I'm still a bit dizzy.

'Just wait. Give me a minute.'

He makes an impatient tutting sound. I take a few breaths and then follow him.

'Look. Look around!'

I look about. My blood freezes. 'Oh my God, they're all around us!'

The beasts, or whatever they are, are swarming over the entire forest.

Ali looks crestfallen.

'You mean you can't see?' he says.

'See what?'

One of the things is walking towards us. 'Get behind me,' I snap at Ali. He starts laughing.

'It's fine. They're people. Look. Really look.'

I try to look at them but it hurts my eyes too much. The smell is making me feel sick all over again. The beast has reached us and is speaking to Ali but I can't understand what it's saying. He nods then looks at me.

'He says to close your eyes.'

I look at Ali warily. 'I'm not closing my eyes.'

'Just do it!' he says, impatiently. 'Trust me.'

'I trust *you*.'

He tuts and places his hands over my eyes. 'Now reach out your hand.'

I do. It connects with an arm. It's hairy, but human hairy, not monster hairy. I remove my hand quickly.

'See?' laughs Ali. 'Now open your eyes.'

A man is standing in front of me. The smell is gone. Well, mostly. Everyone smells bad all of the time.

'What's going on?' I demand.

The man, a short, skinny guy, holds up his hands. 'I know it's confusing. I'm not a demon. None of us are.'

'What did you do?' I say. 'How come I can see you now?'

He points at a place where a blanket has been tied between some trees, making a roof. 'Let's sit down.'

The ground has been cleared here too, and blankets and rugs have been spread to make it almost comfortable. The man gestures for us to sit, so we do.

'You woke up here, right? A few weeks ago.' I nod. 'Ali tells me you can remember. Before.' Another nod. 'That's a rare gift. I've only known one other like you. He started our movement.'

'Movement?'

'The resistance. That's what we are.'

'Resistance to what?'

'I'm getting to that.'

I can't help staring at the man. 'How come I can see you now? Before you looked – well, I don't know what you looked like. But I wanted to kill you. You made me feel sick.'

The man smiles. 'I know. That's how it works. It's like a trick of the mind that this place plays. The good thing is, once you see through it, it doesn't work anymore. Ever.'

'But why?'

The man takes a breath. 'This place we're all in. It's a kind of game. They call it Afterwards, because its participants are drawn from, well, before. From our old world.'

'A game? Whose game?'

He spreads his hands wide. 'We don't know who they are, exactly. All we know is that they control this place. They choose their players from the dead of our world. We wake up here and they give us what we need to survive, as long as we fight for them. If we don't, they make it very tough for us.'

I nod. 'That's what Conrad said.'

'Conrad. The man you were with?'

I nod. 'He said that if we didn't fight the village would be punished.'

'That's right. We're already part of one of the teams when we wake up. We're given clothes and weapons and sooner or later the rest of the team finds us and we learn to fight. Or die in the process, which is what usually happens.'

'But why? Are we being punished? Is this Hell?'

The man shakes his head. 'The guy I told you about said that back on earth people used to make animals fight each other. He said that we're like those animals. We don't matter to them, whoever or whatever they are. We're entertainment.'

I process this slowly. 'That's why we're here? To kill each other as sport?'

He nods and then draws himself up. 'Anyway, a few of us are trying to find a way to fight back. We're the resistance. We live here, in the forest. They haven't found us so far.'

'How many of you are there?' I ask.

He looks a little defensive. 'Not enough. But our numbers are growing. Instead of fighting the others we're rescuing them, showing them the truth. We're more or less between the two villages so it's easy enough to join one of the raiding parties and pull a couple of people out.'

'How does the disguise thing work?' I ask.

'*They* do that. It's supposed to make us hate each other.

Anyone who isn't part of your group takes on the appearance of something evil. It works to our advantage though because it means everyone looks the same. Less chance of anyone noticing that we're here.'

'Can I speak to the other guy? The one who remembers?'

He shakes his head. 'As soon as they found out that he was different he was killed. They sent someone after him, an assassin. My guess is that they saw him as dangerous.'

'So does that mean I'm dangerous?'

He nods. 'Could be. Which is why we're not going to shout about your ability. We'll keep it quiet and use it.'

There's so much to think about. Then something else occurs to me.

'Where's Conrad?' I ask. 'Is he here somewhere?'

'We can't help him,' says the man. 'Some of them are like that. I'm guessing he's been here a while?'

I nod. 'Twelve seasons.'

'They become fixed after a while. They can't see things differently. We try to get new people before they get to that point.' He pauses. 'I know it's a lot to think about. Sometimes I think it's better not to know. But that would be letting them win.'

My mind is cartwheeling.

Can it be true? *How* can it be true? I've never been religious. As far as I was concerned you lived your life and that was that. Game over. My views have changed on that.

But this? Who are these beings, who feed us and clothe us and then watch while we kill each other? This is Hell, but it's a Hell which doesn't care if you're a bad person. It's indifferent.

And what can these people, this resistance movement, really hope to achieve against beings who control the world we live in? Our situation is hopeless.

I sit with Ali for a while. Part of me can hardly believe he's here. I want to grab his cheeks like a grandma just to make sure he's real.

'What is it?' he asks.

38

'I'm glad I found you,' I say.

'Me too,' he says. 'You'd never survive here without me.'

The day gets older and hotter and I find myself struggling to breathe.

'What's wrong?' asks Ali.

I'm taking in little gulps, snatching at the air. I hold my hand up to tell him I'm OK. I know what this is. I've had panic attacks before. I try to slow my breathing and focus on something, anything. I feel like I'm being suffocated.

'I'm getting someone,' says Ali, scrabbling to his feet.

'No,' I say, breathlessly. 'I'm OK. I just need… open space.'

He watches me dubiously as I stand and begin to move away.

'I'll come too.'

I shake my head. 'Not this time. I won't go far, I promise.'

He pouts but doesn't follow me.

I walk around the camp. It isn't much to look at: three or four makeshift tents made out of blankets knotted together and a couple of wooden dens. I see a few people; they look normal. It seems the man was right about that, at least.

Is it all true? For all I know it could be part of an even more elaborate deception. It *feels* true but that seems to be no guarantee.

I wander into the woods and I find to my surprise that this part isn't covered in briar. It's pretty open and empty and I can feel my breath returning.

I sit by a tree, checking for insects before I do. There aren't that many here but the ones we have are pretty nasty; biting, stinging, venomous things. If what he says is true then are they part of it? Or were they already here? Too many questions and no answers.

Why am I different? Have I been brought here for a reason? Does *that* have anything to do with it?

I place my hand on my belly and close my eyes.

'Are you alright?'

A dark-skinned woman with untidy grey hair is looking at me.

'Yes,' I say.

'Only – you're sitting in a corner by yourself. Makes me wonder.'

'I'm fine. Thank you.'

There's something odd about her. What is it?

'You need to take care of yourself you know. In your condition.'

I stare at her.

'What did you say?'

'You heard me. Girl in your condition. Shouldn't be sitting in the dirt, in my opinion.' She smiles. 'Oh, don't worry. I see plenty of things I shouldn't see. It's a talent of mine.'

'How did you know?' I ask.

She shrugs. 'Does it matter? I'm just an interfering old busybody, I suppose. Got a lot on your mind, haven't you?'

I nod. 'You could say that.'

'Well, can't help you much with that. Doubt you'd need my help anyway. You've always been stronger than you think you are.'

I frown. 'Who are you?'

'An interested nobody. My name's Jane.'

'How long have you been here?'

'Oh, a while now. Want some water?'

I shake my head.

'Well, don't sit down there too long.' She seems about to leave when she turns back towards me. 'Hey – scorpion. Look out.'

I jump up. There's a small green scorpion inches from me.

'Thanks!' I say.

'Keep your eye out, Rosie. There's worse things than that in this place.'

The blood drains from my face.

'How do you know my name? My old name?'

'I told you. I see things. Like I see that young man who's going to try and kill you.' She fixes a serious eye on me. 'You've got some challenges ahead. But you're up to it, I think. Just be careful, alright?'

I stare at her as she picks up the hem of her long dress and starts to walk away. 'Which young man?' I call.

'You'll see.'

She disappears into the lengthening shadows within the forest.

Boy

I'm being forced to kneel in front of this weird looking woman in a robe. Long white hair and a face like vinegar.

She looks like someone from one of those stop-motion animation films they used to put on the TV at Christmas and Easter. My dad would put those films on and make his way through a six pack of strong cheap lager. He was an uncomplicated man.

She's been talking for a while about how the world has been created by her and some other people. She seems to want to impress me with her power so I'm trying to look impressed. I'm kind of uncomfortable in this kneeling position though.

'We made it as a test. A sort of purgatory, if you like. To find the strongest and bravest.'

She has this soft voice, soothing. It all feels a little phony though. Like someone described to her what a goddess ought to look like and this is what she came up with. And I don't buy what she's saying about this being a test. She seems to be implying that if I do well I get to go to Heaven. I know that's not true. I wouldn't want to be part of any Heaven which would allow me as a member. I'm paraphrasing someone there, aren't I? Huh. Clever me.

'There are some of our own who don't understand what we're doing,' she's saying. 'Some of them have started to work against us.'

My knees are really starting to feel sore. Fuck it – what's the worst that could happen? I stand up. There's a loud intake of breath around me. The goddess lady makes a soothing sound.

'Let him stand if he wants to.'

'My knees are hurting,' I say, conversationally.

'The enemies of this world have sent someone – a champion, of sorts. She is quite dangerous to us, in her own way. That is why we've chosen you to stop her.'

I nod. 'Alright. Stop a girl. I can do that. But why should I? I mean, what do I get?'

'Apart from your life?'

I shrug. 'I'm already dead. Doesn't matter that much if I get deader.'

'There are worse things than death,' she says. She's intending to be menacing. I just don't care enough about my life or any of it to be intimidated. She seems to realise this after a moment.

'We'll make it worth your while,' she says. 'We have it in our power to make this world very comfortable for you.'

'And the next?'

'That isn't within my power.'

I think about it for a moment. 'Well, it's not like I have anything else to do, anyway. I'll take your job on.'

'I know you will,' she says, with a slight smile. 'You'll be provided with some men to help you reach her. They'll be under your command.'

This is sounding considerably better than I'd hoped.

'So who is this girl? Do I get a picture or something?'

'You'll know. You'll recognise her.'

Girl

My mum got ill a few weeks after my sixteenth birthday. Well, I suppose she'd been ill longer than that. She just didn't tell me. I'm not sure she'd have told me at all if she'd had the choice. As it was, she needed to prepare me.

'I need to know that you're not going to let this ruin your life. You have to make yourself get through this. Get your A Levels. Go to a good university. I wish I could help you but I don't know if... if I'll be there. You might have to do it by yourself.'

The news changed me. I cried for a few days, and then I became angry: at myself, at the illness, the world. At her. How dare she tell me to get on with my life? How dare she ask me not to miss her?

I wanted to go off the rails. I wanted to stop being the well behaved kid I'd always been. I wanted to fuck my life up.

I don't sleep well that night. There's just too much to think about. I finally doze off in the early hours of the morning and wake up a short while later, bruised and sickly. When Ali bounces over I'm still groggy.

'Girl. Wake up! It's time to eat.'

'Ugh. No thanks. I'm OK.'

'Come *on*. Don't be lazy. It's time to get up.'

'Go away, Ali. I'm tired.'

He makes an exasperated noise. 'Fine. I'll have to bring it here.'

'No! Ali, I...'

He runs off. I groan and turn over. He comes back minutes later with a plate full of meat and leaves.

'I'm not eating that,' I say, clutching my stomach.

'What's wrong?' he asks, helping himself to the food.

I don't feel ready to tell him the truth yet. 'I didn't sleep well and I have a headache. And you're not helping.'

This doesn't deter him. He sits beside me.

'Want to go hunting later?' he says.

I stare at him. He laughs.

'I learned how to use my bow. I'm helping us to catch food for everyone. Are you proud of me?'

I smile, despite the nausea. 'I am. Well done.'

'So we can go out together if you want, later.'

I lie around for a while. My bed is a couple of blankets folded together on the ground. I stretch out on the dusty ground, drawing pictures in the dirt. I used to enjoy drawing geometric designs, interlocking circles and triangles in complicated structures. My mum thought maybe one day I could sell them. I begin to draw a circle and spiral it outwards. I start to add details but it doesn't look right. I obliterate it with more dirt.

'Hey. What's that man called we spoke to yesterday?' I ask Ali.

'John. Why?'

'Can we go and see him? I have some questions.'

He shrugs. 'I suppose.'

Ali leads me further into the forest. The trees thicken and everything becomes darker. I begin to hear voices ahead.

'Sounds like a meeting,' says Ali. We step out into a large clearing. There's a group of people there, including John.

Conrad is in front of them, tied up. He's covered in blood and bruises.

'Hey! They can't do that!'

I push my way through the group towards Conrad. 'Let him go!' I snap at John.

John shakes his head. 'He knows where we are now and he'll bring others and attack us. That's what this place does.'

Conrad is staring straight ahead. I can tell he isn't seeing me.

'So what are you going to do? Kill him?'

John shakes his head. 'That's playing their game. We won't do it.'

'So, what? Why are you keeping him here?'

'We're trying to get through to him. But he keeps fighting us.'

'Of course he does. You're a demon, as far as he knows. Please, just let him go.'

'We can't.'

'Then let me try to speak to him.'

John thinks about this for a moment. Then he stands aside.

'Go ahead.'

I walk up to Conrad slowly. After a moment his eyes begin to focus on me.

'You,' he says. 'You're alright. I thought you were dead.'

'I'm fine. You have to listen to me. The bone-man was right. The demons aren't demons. They're people.' He's looking at me with a glazed-over expression. 'Are you listening? Conrad?' He seems to have zoned out again.

'What did you do to him?' I shout at John.

'He was trying to kill us,' replies John, calmly. 'We had to defend ourselves, that's all.'

'Please let him go.'

'No. We can't. And even if we did he wouldn't be able to get through the forest. He stays, as our prisoner.'

Conrad makes an animal-like noise and starts trying to pull his arms free.

'Put him near my tent,' says John. Conrad is led away, struggling and shouting. 'We'll look after him, as well as we can. But he can't go.'

I don't know what to think about any of it.

I leave the village, alone. I walk back to the edge of the forest and find a tree to climb. I sit by myself, listening. There's no sound. The leaves should rustle but there's no breeze. Everything is completely still. I realise that I'm holding my breath.

I'm a trapped animal. I have to fight, or die. If I die, who knows if I'll wake up to something worse?

And now I have Ali to consider. He won't survive for long without me looking out for him. And Conrad. I have to help him, somehow.

So many things to think about. I didn't ask for any of this.

John tells me that they've been working together for a while. They try to find the new arrivals to the world; they use the raids on the other village to rescue them.

Life has been difficult, he says. They've had to endure sickness after sickness. They've had to learn to find food.

'But I think we've had help,' he says. 'We'd never have survived otherwise.'

'What do you mean, help?'

'One of *them*,' he says. 'One of their own has been reversing the plagues they sent to us. The sickness doesn't last more than a couple of days. And we find unexpected food parcels when we really need it.'

This makes me think of something. 'Do you know an old woman named Jane?'

He stares at me. 'There are no old people here. You must have realised that by now. We don't survive long enough.'

'Oh.' So *that* was what had felt so odd about her.

'Why did you ask that question?'

I tell him about her, leaving out the conversation about the pregnancy. His eyes are nearly popping out of his head.

'She must have been the one. It's the only explanation.'

'She said someone's coming for me. To kill me.'

He nods. 'We'll put extra guards out from now on. We'll be prepared. Don't worry.' He has a feverish look about him, like a religious zealot who's just been told tomorrow's judgement day. I decide that there's never going to be a better time to come clean about my situation.

'I haven't been totally honest,' I say. 'There's something you don't know about me.'

Ali chooses that exact moment to come crashing over, waving something small, furry and dead. 'Look what I caught! I'm getting better. You need…' It seems to register that we were talking about something. He sits, looking a little crestfallen.

John looks at me questioningly but the moment has gone.

'It doesn't matter,' I say.

'Are you sure? It sounded important.'

'Some other time.' I turn to Ali. 'Hey, that's great. You're getting really good at this.'

He grins. 'Want to eat it?'

By the time we've skinned it there's about a thimble-sized piece of meat left but it doesn't dampen his enthusiasm at all. He splits the tiny portion 50-50 and we cook it at the communal fire. I make lots of *mmm* noises as I eat it. He's grinning widely.

'I can hunt for us now!' He's so excited I can't bear to point out to him that this is the first time he's caught something edible in all the time he's been here.

Later that day I decide to find Conrad. It doesn't take long; the camp isn't very big. He's tied up but he doesn't look in worse shape than the last time I saw him.

'Can I speak to him?' I ask the man guarding him.

He shakes his head. 'Violent,' he says.

'Please? He won't hurt me. I know him.'

But he won't change his mind. 'No.' He's not a chatter.

'Let her speak to him.' John has appeared from nowhere. Is he following me?

The guard makes a strange grunt but he stands aside.

'Thanks,' I say, to John.

'Be careful,' he says. 'We'll be outside if you need us.'

What does he think a tied up, beaten up man can do to me?

'Conrad?'

His face is covered in spongy purple bruises. When he looks up however his gaze is clear.

'Girl. You're alive.'

He's forgotten about seeing me earlier.

'Hi, Conrad. Are you OK?'

He laughs, quietly. 'Not really. Have they hurt you?'

I shake my head. 'They're good people. Mainly.'

'They're not people. I wish you could see.'

'I wish *you* could see. You're being tricked.'

He stares at me. 'Well, one of us is wrong.' To my surprise he holds out his hand. 'Closer,' he says. I glance to the side, aware of John and the guard. 'You have to help me. Help me to get free.'

I glance around again. 'I can't,' I whisper. 'There are guards. What can I do?'

'Please.' He looks at me with pleading eyes.

John chooses that moment to decide we've talked for long enough. 'Come away,' he says.

'I haven't finished!' I snap.

'Yes, you have. Time to leave.'

I turn back to Conrad. 'I'll try,' I whisper.

I glare at John on my way past. He ignores me and instead walks up to Conrad. I can't hear what he says.

Later that day I talk to Ali about Conrad. His eyes grow wide as I tell him what Conrad asked me to do.

'You can't,' he says. 'What if he attacks us all again? Remember how you felt, before you saw through the demon-mask? *You* would have killed them. Conrad's even worse. He's already killed loads of them.'

He has a good point.

'I can't just leave him though,' I say.

I rest my head on my knees, as I always do when I have something to think through. If I can somehow return him to the other village I doubt he'll be back here in a hurry. But how? He'll never survive the journey in his current condition.

Then something occurs to me. I find John.

'Can I ask a question?'

He looks at me warily. 'You can ask. What is it?'

'How do you get to the other village? When you rescue the new people? It took us half a day to get past the first part of the forest. It's covered in roots and thorns.'

He stands there for a moment, thinking. 'Why do you want to know?'

'Just curious.'

'Well, I can't tell you, I'm afraid.'

'Why not?'

'I wouldn't want you to be tempted to try to help your friend.'

Damn.

'How could I help him? You have a guard there all the time.'

'Yes, we do. So don't think of it.'

'I'm just curious.'

He gives me a pull-the-other-one look and walks away.

That night I make a decision. If I can't rescue Conrad, I'll have to socialise him. Just because it's more difficult for people who've lived here longer to see through the demon-masks that doesn't mean it's impossible.

I go to see him early the next morning to explain what I'm going to do. This time the guard lets me in without an argument but I can tell he's listening closely to our conversation.

Conrad seems predictably unconvinced by my plan.

'I'm not going near any of those things,' he says. 'I don't know how you can stand it.'

I roll my eyes. 'You'll see. You have to do what I say though.'

'No.'

'It's this or you spend your life here, in this hut. I can't rescue you.'

'No.'

'Or death.'

'Those things will kill me anyway.'

'No, they won't.'

I walk to the entrance of the hut. Ali is standing just outside with one of the other villagers: a mute girl, a little older than Ali. She's looking at Conrad, warily.

'It's alright,' I say. 'I won't let him harm you.' Ali takes her hand and leads her towards Conrad. I stand between them. I can hear Conrad's breathing begin to speed up. He looks like a frightened animal.

I place a blindfold around his eyes. He starts to shout but he's still tied up so he can't do much about it.

'It's alright,' I say, firmly. The sound of my voice calms him a bit. I gesture to Ali to bring the girl closer. She doesn't look any keener than Conrad, but she allows Ali to guide her hand towards him.

He flinches when her hand touches his shoulder but his breathing slows a little, as though he's thinking.

Me and Ali glance at one another. Could it be that easy? I walk up to him and tug away the blindfold. As soon as it's gone he starts screaming. So does the girl. She runs out of the hut, crying.

I wait for Conrad to calm down so that I can talk to him about what had happened. This takes a while. I reason that this is the first contact he's had with one of the demons where he wasn't trying to kill it. So probably a natural response. I'm a little disappointed, all the same.

'What were you thinking? When you touched her hand?' I ask, when he's calm.

'That I was touching a person. A normal person.'

'That's because you were. That's the instinct you need to trust. Your other senses are lying to you.'

He actually seems to consider this. 'But how do I know you're not the one who's being deceived?'

I want to shake him. 'Think about it. Why would demons try to trick us into thinking they're human? It makes no sense that way around. You must see that.'

He goes quiet, which I take as a good sign.

'I'll come back tomorrow,' I say.

I do. Tomorrow, and the next day, and the following day. By the third day I feel we're making some real progress. Conrad has actually started to see through the mask, but only for a short time. For some reason his perception of them isn't changing completely. He's starting to come around to my way of thinking, though.

'They are like us, aren't they?' he says, after the fourth day of my socialisation training. I nod. 'You must think I'm an idiot.'

I make a face as though I'm thinking about this. 'No more than I ever did,' I say.

He gives me a look. 'Funny.' He looks suddenly pensive. 'All of those people I killed. I didn't know.'

'No, you didn't,' I say. 'Hold on to that. It wasn't your fault. That's what this place is designed to do.'

50

He looks at me sadly. I'm starting to see something in his eyes I never noticed before; kindness. And depth. I hadn't noticed their warm brown colour before, either.

Mmm.

I realise I'm staring and turn away abruptly.

'Hey – don't leave,' he says.

'I have to talk to John. I want to tell him about the progress you've made.'

'Will you come back?'

I nod, silently.

I find John in his hut. He looks bad tempered as usual. He doesn't have too much to smile about, I suppose.

His mood doesn't seem to be improved by my arrival.

'Yes?'

'I want to talk to you. About Conrad.'

He puts his hand to his head. Suddenly, I know that he was a businessman back home. I visualise him in a neatly tailored suit, sitting in the exact same position when somebody gave him bad news about stocks or something.

'I don't want to hear it,' he says. 'I know you've been trying to help him to see us. But he isn't like us. He never will be, no matter what he might say.'

Something occurs to me. 'Did he kill somebody you knew?' I ask.

He nods, slowly. 'He did. Someone I cared about, in fact. But that's not why I'm saying this. He can't be trusted.'

Anger is building inside me. 'So – you're just intending to leave him tied up, forever? Can't you at least speak to him?'

'There's no point. Besides – I don't like to look at him. He might not be a demon but he's repulsive to me. He deserves to lose his freedom. He deserves worse, but I won't play their game.'

When I leave John I'm exhausted and demoralised. All of the work I've done with Conrad over the last few days is pointless – John intends to keep him there, a bound animal, for his whole life, as penance for something he did instinctively.

Fury is building into a tight little knot in my stomach. They did this. The beings – whatever they are – who created this place. They created all of this misery and death and hurt.

There's a strange fluttering sensation in my belly. The anger subsides briefly. *Is that you?* I ask, silently. I place my hand on my stomach. It's still flat and I can't feel any movement. Maybe I imagined it.

'Hey!'

I jump. It's Ali, crashing into the room as usual.

'What's wrong?'

'Nothing. Well, everything.' I explain what John said. Ali's looking thoughtful.

'You know – I know the way back to the village. The other way, I mean. I've seen it.'

I stare at him. 'Have you?' He nods. 'Well – why didn't you tell me?'

'Because I didn't want you to release him. I thought he'd hurt us.'

'And now you believe him? And me?'

Ali nods again. 'He can see us now. He's different.'

I think about it but then shake my head. 'No – it won't work. He can't go back now. He'll be treated like a madman. And he won't be able to fight.'

We both consider this. 'But what if he goes back and shows them?' says Ali. 'If he uses the same training you used? He'd be much better at helping them because they already know him. He could change the whole village!'

'But that doesn't solve the problem of how to get him out of there.'

We agree to think about the problem for a day or two and to continue with Conrad's socialisation in the meantime. I find that I'm not sorry to be spending another few days in Conrad's company. I'm enjoying our training sessions. We're also doing less training now. We're spending most of our time together talking. He often asks about what I remember about my old life. I keep my answers deliberately sketchy until finally he notices.

'Why do you never answer my questions? About before?'

I shrug. 'I was a different person then. None of it is relevant anymore.'

'Of course it is. It's where you're from.'

I prefer to talk in general terms. I describe the colours; so much warmer than in this world. The sky could be a deep blue on a sunny day, changing to pink and orange in the evening. The clothes people wore were so bright. My favourite summer dress was pineapple yellow.

I can tell he doesn't understand everything I'm saying. Some words no longer have any meaning, here. But he listens, patiently.

The next day John comes over to wake us. I was dreaming of home. Those dreams are becoming less frequent now.

I sit up sleepily. 'What's wrong?'

'I'm having a meeting. We've got a problem.'

'Oh. Now?'

'Yes. The centre of the camp. Don't be long.'

Ali is still half asleep. 'Do they really need me to go?' he whines, rubbing his eyes.

'He said everyone. Besides, why should I have to get up and you get to stay in bed? Get up.'

He sits up, and stretches. 'You're mean.'

'Sure am. Come on.'

We make our sleepy way to the middle of the camp, the same place they took Conrad when we arrived. Most of the others are already there. We sit at the back.

John is already speaking.

'There's no reason to panic. We've been in difficult situations before. It'll resolve itself in a day or two, I think.'

'What is it?' whispers Ali.

'How should I know?' I hiss back. 'Just listen.'

'Do you have a plan?' a man named Wen asks.

'Not really. That's why we're here. I'm open to suggestions.'

A woman near the front speaks next. 'The trees are alive. They must be getting water from somewhere.'

John nods. 'I'm going to send a group into the woods later to look into that. In the meantime only drink what you need. We have a small reserve but it'll be gone soon.'

'The water!' I whisper to Ali. 'Something must have happened to the spring.'

'What about a raid on one of the villages?' calls someone near to where we're sitting.

'That's playing into their hands. Don't you understand that? It's what they want.'

'Maybe it's time we admit defeat,' says the voice. I can't see who's speaking.

'No,' replies John. 'Who is that? Come forward.'

The group shifts a little but nobody steps forward. John frowns.

'Well, I don't blame you for being scared. But we'll weather this storm like we have all of the others.'

'What about the prisoner?' asks Wen.

John looks at him, then at me. 'Don't give him any more water until this is resolved,' he says.

I stand up. 'You can't do that. It's barbaric.'

'Sit down. We have a crisis and I'm dealing with it in the best way that I can.'

'You're wrong!' I snap. 'You're pretending to be doing something good but you're as bad as they are.'

Anger is bringing tears to my eyes and I don't want him to see them so I leave. Ali follows.

'Are you OK?' he asks, putting an arm around me. I shake it off and he looks a little hurt but I'm full of anger.

'They can't do that!' I rail, uselessly. Ali just watches me, forlornly. 'They're monsters. Refusing to kill him quickly just to watch him die slowly!' I'm pacing about in the clearing.

'They won't let him die,' says Ali quietly. The words sound hollow to both of us.

I make a frustrated noise and turn away.

'Where are you going?'

'Just leave me alone. Please,' I add.

He looks wounded and I feel bad but I don't go back. I've had enough of the company of humans for a while.

There isn't much to do here. My choices are pretty much restricted to places that I can sit and just think. And they're limited too; trees are my thinking places of choice, but there are other nooks if you look for them. Today I sit on a rock at the outskirts of the forest. It's far enough away from the camp to feel like I've got some space to think but it's close enough to get back if I have to.

Today is a typical day. It's a January sort of day. Everything is cold, and flat. There's no sound. I sit on my rock and listen. Nothing.

I have to get Conrad away. Whatever I might have started feeling towards him is irrelevant. He'll die if he stays here. So what do I do? What *can* I do?

Ali's plan seems to be the best one. If we can get Conrad back to his village, he can begin to show the others the truth. Not a perfect plan, but what choice is there?

I sit on my rock for what seems like hours. Time is meaningless here. When I go back I have the start of a plan.

A couple of days later I get my opportunity. The village is almost empty; everybody else is in the forest looking for potential sources of water. There's just Conrad, the guard and a couple of the non-talkers on guard in the trees. And me.

My plan is pretty simple. I'll create a diversion. I'm thinking a small fire until I remember the dry grass and the water shortage. Hmm. Maybe not.

I'm dreaming up this slightly silly scenario in which I tell the guard the village is being attacked. I don't know if it would have worked. But then the problem solves itself.

It starts to rain. Not just drizzle; big, angry raindrops mixed with icy pellets which cut into my skin. I'm so thirsty that for a moment I just stand there and catch the water in my mouth.

The guard starts to shout something and I remember my purpose. I run to him. He's saying something about collecting the water. Then he leaves; I suppose he's decided that collecting the water is more important than watching Conrad. I know I'm never going to get a better chance.

I use my knife to cut through his ropes. This takes longer than I'd like. Once his arms are free he helps to get his legs out.

'Can you run?' I ask. He doesn't look good. I've managed to smuggle some of my own water to him, but not much.

He nods. 'I have to. I'll be OK.'

We flee from the hut through the pelting rain and head in the direction of forest. We can't see; everything is covered in a grey mist. This makes it difficult to find the right path but it also means that John and the others won't see us.

The sparse trees don't offer much protection from the rain and I don't know if this is the path Ali was talking about. But it doesn't matter. Conrad's free.

Boy

The Argonauts lady didn't get around to mentioning all of the walking I was going to have to do in this place. There's no transportation. No horses or donkeys and definitely nothing mechanical. What I wouldn't give for an Uber. Or even a bike, at this point.

So we've been told to head towards a sort of habitation on the other side of a massive hill. Not too far, she said.

I've never been much of a walker. Although I'm finding that this place agrees with me, physically. I'm fitter than I ever was in real life. My diet consists almost exclusively of red meat, kind of like beef. I haven't asked what it is. It tastes good.

I'm bored though. It seems like we've been walking uphill all day. Life isn't fast paced.

I've been thinking about what I'm going to do when I find this girl, assuming the woman is right and I recognise her as my mark (*mark* sounds like something an assassin would say, right?). I've never killed. Not that I'm aware of. There are big chunks of my life I don't have any clear memory of. The last eight years, on and off. But I'd remember murder, probably.

She said she's chosen me for the job. Said I have the skills she needs. So I'm going to put my faith in that. Besides, I reckon I'll be able to do it. Life and death don't matter that much, as it turns out. This place isn't so bad; sort of like being dropped somewhere in Northern Scotland. No Wi-Fi.

We walk and walk and by the time night comes I'm bad tempered and cursing everything. The people I'm with are looking at me with worried faces. I *am* a killer, I suppose. In theory, at least.

There's about thirty of them – mostly men, a couple of women. They all look weary and bitter. Like me, in fact. I can tell they don't love being under my command but they're shit-scared of Rosaline. Doesn't matter to me, so long as they do what I say.

When the camp finally appears, it's a bit disappointing. Just a raggedy collection of tents which look like they've seen better days. Not worth walking over a mountain for. Still, any port in a dust storm, I suppose.

I stand there for a moment. I'm tired and want to sleep but it's cold out and if we make a fire they'll see us anyway. I see no point in waiting.

'Come on,' I say. 'Let's knock on the front door.'

We're not exactly an intimidating sight; a scrawny boy leading a group of moth-eaten travellers. They'll probably laugh at us.

I don't need to knock. We're spotted long before we reach the first tent. A group of armed men are waiting for us. They don't look pleased.

'Who are you?'

'We're travellers. We're looking for a place to stay.'

'Not here. We don't accept strangers.'

'Come *on*. We've been walking all day. My feet are half-dead. Again.'

'You have your answer. Go away or we'll kill you.'

I'm debating what to do when one of my companions steps forward. She pulls a silver chain out from beneath her hood. It has a woman-shaped pendant attached. The men see it and draw back a little.

'Come in,' one of them says.

'Alright!' I nod to the woman. Why didn't I get one of those pendant things? Useful little item.

We're given food and water and some blankets. I ask for wine but I get a confused look. That's a definite disadvantage to being dead.

When we've eaten one of the men sits with us.

'What are you doing here?' he asks.

'I've been given a job to do.'

'By *them*?'

I nod, pulling myself a little taller.

'That's right.'

'What is it?'

'Can't say. Sorry.'

'Well, can we help?'

I shrug. 'I'll think about it. I need some sleep for now.'

The man looks irritated. I draw the blanket around myself and lie down, smiling. It's the little things that make the afterlife worth living.

I get up early the next day and have a walk around while most of the people are still asleep. There's nothing much to see. It's a boring little camp. I'm waiting to feel something, an instinct or intuition, telling me I'm on the right track. There's nothing.

A man's tending to the fire. I decide a bit of conversation is what I need.

He looks a bit beaten up, like he's been in a fight. He's a pretty big guy; my guess is the other fella came off worse. He looks up as I approach.

'Who are you?' he says.

'Don't know my name,' I lie. 'Who are you?'

'Conrad.' He pokes around in the fire, moodily.

'You OK?' I say. 'You look like you've been mauled.'

'Something like that,' he says.

Great. Another uncommunicative soul in the afterlife.

'Want to tell me about it?' I prompt. 'I'm a good listener.' I have a sudden inspiration. 'I bet there was a girl involved.'

He gives me a sharp look. 'Has someone been talking about me?'

Interesting. 'No. It's just that there usually is. So, what? She went off with your friend?'

He raises his eyebrows. 'No. Nothing like that. I was trying to help her. She's – different. It got me in trouble.'

This makes me listen. 'Different, how?' I ask, trying to be casual.

'It's hard to explain. She's like no one else I've met here. I don't know if that's a good thing.'

'So, where is she?' Surely it isn't going to be that easy.

'She's not here,' he says. Aw, shucks. 'I left her behind.'

'Behind? Behind where?'

He looks at me suddenly. 'Why do you want to know, stranger? What's your interest?'

I hold my hand up. 'Just making small talk.'

He frowns into the fire. It's clear that he wants the conversation to be over but I'm not ready to give up yet.

'I'm pretty new to this world. I don't really know the rules of the game yet,' I say. 'I died. I remember it. Now I'm here.'

He looks at me again. Good.

'You remember?'

'Yes. Don't you?'

He shakes his head. 'The girl... she said she could remember things too. She described it to me.'

I nod. 'Yes, there are a few of us, I think.' I'm improvising now. 'We're trying to make things right.'

He's thinking. 'You – want to help? With their cause?'

I nod. 'That's why we're here.' *What's the cause?*

He stares at me. 'Have you even seen them yet? The demons?'

This is getting weird.

'There are demons?'

'Yes. Well, no. Not really, I don't think so. This place tricks you. It makes you see them as evil things, so that you try to kill them. I've tried to explain it to the others but no one will listen.'

I sit beside him and pat him on the back. 'Don't worry,' I say. 'I believe you. I knew there was something strange going on. Now tell me more about the demons.'

He starts to explain. I must admit I'm surprised. I knew the universe was a messed up place, but I knew it as a general concept, abstract. Now I've been given concrete proof. Sadistic fucks. And somehow I've found myself employed by the bad guys.

It doesn't take me long to shrug off the moral uncertainty though. No time at all, in fact. The label mercenary fits me. I like it.

Besides, what choice do I have? We're all here to die, one way or another.

'I need your help,' I say to him. 'I need to find the girl.'

He looks worried. 'Why?'

'We're the same. We've been put here for a reason. I'm going to join her.'

He stares at me, then shakes his head. 'I can't help you.'

I have to stop myself from shouting at him.

'You can trust me.'

'I can't trust anyone.'

'Well, you're going to have to trust me. It's a matter of life and death.'

'Who for?'

I have a sudden inspiration. 'Her. They're sending someone to kill her. If I don't reach her in time…'

I just leave my words out there, lingering in the air.

'How do I know you're not here to hurt her?'

I shrug. 'You're just going to have to take a leap of faith.'

Hah. If he's stupid enough to fall for a line like that he doesn't deserve pity.

'Alright. I'll take you to her.'

I have to stop myself rubbing my hands together like an evil genius. I love it when a plan comes together.

Girl

3 November 2021

I don't remember many exact dates anymore. But that one has stuck with me.

It's not my death day. It's not my mother's death day. It's relatively insignificant. It was my last really good day. I wrote the date in my diary so that I'd remember it, because I read somewhere that we don't remember the good stuff that happens to us. The ordinary good stuff.

Mum made pancakes for breakfast. She wasn't one of those mums – she wasn't a home baking, wholesome mum but she decided on a whim to make pancakes and they actually turned out pretty well. We had them with a silly amount of syrup and watched a cheesy musical on the TV. *Mamma Mia*, I think.

I had this recital thing in the afternoon. I was learning to play the violin.

My last good day.

When I was alive I often struggled to make sense of things. I wanted to find a higher purpose to it all. Now I'm here I can see there isn't any higher purpose. It's all just a machine, turning lives over and over.

I wish I had more days like that one.

John is predictably angry. He gives me a long lecture about the possible consequences of my actions. About how I acted naively.

'You don't understand what this place does to a person's mind,' he says.

I'm only half listening. I'm watching a fly and thinking *why is there a fly?* Did they include it just to be annoying?

I wait for him to finish and then say, 'I couldn't leave him there. What you were doing to him was cruel. It was as bad as what they're doing to us.'

For a moment that stops him. Good. Then he recovers himself.

'You're wrong. You'll see. There'll be consequences.'

It sounds like a threat but he doesn't mean it in that way. It's more of a prediction.

Things go quiet for a while. I mean that in a figurative sense, because it's always quiet here. There's a lack of things.

Sometimes I think Conrad was right. That *we're* the demons. What's the difference anyway? We're capable of the same level of evil. Perhaps the masks they give us distract us from what we really are.

I'm in that sort of mood today. Thinking about too many things. Allowing it to become overwhelming.

We have a routine, of sorts. Ali goes hunting every day. Sometimes I go with him, although I'm not a good hunter.

After a few unsuccessful trips he asks me to stop going.

'You get bored and distract me,' he says.

So I ask one of the others to show me how to find non-meat sources of food. There's not much here that's edible but if you know what to look for it's there. Certain leaves, berries, mushrooms. They all have similar and deadly relatives. The differences can be minute but they're there if you know what to look for. I guess learning to survive here is just another part of the game.

I'm becoming quite good at foraging out edible plants. I remember Mum scoffing at all of the chefs on the TV boasting about foraging for fresh food. *Nobody in the real world has time to do that.* If only she could see me now. God, I wish she was here.

I've had a few close calls though. I'd only been doing it for a few days when I brought back a pile of brown berries. They looked just the same as the ones I've eaten a hundred times. Taste a bit sour but they're edible.

Luckily for me Elise, my trainer, thought to check where I found them. I told her they were by the edge of the forest. '*In the sunlight or out of it?*' I had to think but then I remembered walking into the subdued light while I picked them.

She immediately threw them into the fire.

This type of berry becomes poisonous when it hasn't grown in darkness.

'Look for them further into the forest,' she advises.

There's another type of berry that has the opposite reaction.

It must be very amusing to this world's creators to see us scrambling about for food with arbitrary toxic properties.

Things are OK. We have food and water.

I'm worried about that. I don't know what it means. Why are they leaving us alone?

'You're being...' Ali is fishing for the right word. He does this a lot.

'Pessimistic?'

'Does that mean thinking all bad stuff? 'Cos that's what you're doing.'

He's right. Even if something bad is around the corner I can't change anything so there's no point in worrying. I worry anyway.

That afternoon I'm playing a game of catch with Ali using a bundled up rag. He's getting competitive as usual and throwing really badly on purpose so that I drop it first.

'What was that?' I laugh, stretching for a particularly bad shot. As I stretch I get a sharp pain in my abdomen and sit up rapidly.

'What's wrong?' asks Ali.

'Nothing. Just a twinge.'

At that moment we hear shouting voices deep in the forest. We look at one another then rush to find out what's happening.

John is nearby. Everyone is grabbing whatever weapons they can find and hiding in trees and bushes.

'We're under attack,' one of the men tells us

John looks at me. 'Conrad.'

No. That's not possible.

'Go and look,' says John. He points to the watch post in the tree. 'But be quick.'

I walk over. They've got this telescope thing rigged up. It takes me a minute to find him but he's there, with a boy of about my age. I kind of recognise his face but I don't know where from. Then I remember: the dream that wasn't a dream. Who is he?

They're leading a nasty looking group towards us.

I grab my knife and hand Ali his bow. 'Go and hide,' I say. 'Keep out of the way. If anyone finds you use your bow.'

'What about you?'

'I'm a good fighter. I'll be fine.'

'But what if it's the person who's been sent to kill you? Shouldn't you hide too?'

'I can't.'

My heart is hammering. I gesture to Ali to go. He runs away to find somewhere to hide. I'm about to go to John when I hear a voice I recognise.

'Rosie, help. Rosie, help me!'

'Mum? Mum! Is that you?'

The voice is coming from in the trees, the same way Ali has gone.

'Rosie, please. I don't know where I am. Can you help me?'

'I'm coming!'

My eyes are filling with tears. I blink them away. I haven't got time for them.

'Mum, where are you?'

'I'm here. I'm in the trees.'

'Where?'

'Keep going.'

I'm going deeper into the shadows of the forest. The sounds of the fighting behind me are growing fainter.

'Mum?'

'I'm here. You're nearly there.'

Suddenly I stop and look around. 'Mum?'

There's no answer. I sink down to the forest floor and put my head in my hands and start to cry.

'Hey.' The voice is soft but it isn't Mum. It's Jane.

'Did you do that?' I spit at her. 'Did you make me think my mum was here?'

She nods.

'I'm sorry. I had to get you away. You'd never have left otherwise.'

I cry, big, big sobs. Jane places her hand on my back but I shrug it away. 'Go away!'

'I will. I just want you to understand something first.'

'Why do you think I'm going to listen to you after what you just did?'

'Because I think you know I had no choice. And you know that I'm the good guy.'

I wipe my eyes and curl up with my head on my arms.

'I just really miss her.'

'I know. She'd be proud of you. You're doing really well.'

'What do you mean?'

Jane smiles, a small smile without much joy in it. 'Your friends back there...' she gestures. 'They have the right idea. But they can't win. Not that way. It's like a mouse taking on a lion.'

'So where do I fit into this?'

'You're kind of like a virus, which attacks the lion from the inside. You and your baby. You're wrong. You don't belong here. And that's how we're going to end the world.'

I stare at her.

'I'm not joking,' she says. 'The reason I brought you here was to destroy this world. It shouldn't exist. It's abhorrent. I put you here to be a spanner in the works. When your baby is born the world will collapse.'

I can't believe what I'm hearing.

'*You* put me here? And now you're telling me that my existence is going to destroy this place?'

She nods. 'This was never meant to be a real world. It's more like a video game. Remember those? A real, live birth will cause a break so catastrophic that this place will self-destruct. I hope, anyway.'

'And then what? What's next?'

'I can't tell you that. But you'll find out soon enough.' She stands. 'All you need to do is keep yourself safe. You and that baby. Keep yourself out of danger.'

'So that I can put everybody else *in* danger?'

'This is how it has to be.'

'Who are you? What are you?'

'I'm a little bit like you. I'm just trying to do the right thing.'

My head is throbbing. I'm trying to tell myself that what she's saying isn't true. It's just another deception. It's no good. I already believe it.

'Can I go back now?' I say. 'The others might need my help.'

I just want to get away from her, to forget about the things she's saying.

She looks at me sadly. 'There's nothing you can do to help,' she says. 'It's too late for that.'

'What do you mean?'

'You'll find out. For now, rest. It isn't safe for you to go back just yet.'

'But what about Ali? I need to find him.'

'You don't need to worry about Ali.' She moves aside a little and points to a thicket of brambles.

'Are you there?' I call. Ali climbs out of the bush. By his expression I can tell he's been listening.

'I'm going to leave you now,' says Jane. She turns to Ali. 'I know you've heard what's been said. I want you to know that you have an important role too. You've been chosen to protect Rosie, and her baby.'

Ali nods, dumbly. He looks petrified.

'One last thing,' she says. 'Sooner or later you'll have to leave this forest. When you do, there's a place you can go, where you'll be safe. But you'll have to get there first. They'll find you eventually, and when they do they'll throw everything they can at you. The boy is dangerous but he's nothing compared to the ones who sent him. I'll help you as much as I can, but you'll have to be stronger than you've ever been.'

'What place? Where?'

'You'll know how to get there when you need to. It won't be easy, but you have to try.'

It isn't until she's gone that Ali turns to me. 'Is that real? Is the world going to end?'

'If my baby is born. So she says.'

'Your baby. You're going to have a baby.'

'Yes. Do you know what that means?'

He's thinking. 'I think so. I think I remember.' He looks troubled. 'So – either you die or everybody dies.'

'That's what she says. She wants the world to be over. And I think she might be right.'

He thinks about this for a while and finally nods. 'Alright.'

'Alright?'

'I'll protect you. Even if it ends the world.'

Boy

It was almost funny to watch Conrad's face change as he realised I'm not here to help the girl begin the revolution. I think the penny dropped when the first of them fell to the ground with an arrow to the chest.

As far as the others are concerned they're killing demons, so they have no problem with it. Only Conrad and me can see them as they really are, and I don't care. He tries to stop me but he's no match for me; he's pretty weak, despite his size. I don't kill him; he helped me, after all.

There's only one of them left and she's in pretty bad shape. It's at that moment I remember my purpose. The excitement of it almost made me forget. I go to the woman.

'Where is she?' I ask, holding her head back by her hair, knife to the throat. I'm aiming to be terrifying.

It seems to work a bit too well. She can't get her words out. She's making a gurgling sound, half crying.

'Where *is* she? The girl?'

She finally speaks. 'I… I don't know who you mean.'

I sigh. I don't even know what she looks like to describe her. Then I have a sudden inspiration. 'She came here about three weeks ago. Knows that Conrad guy.'

She nods, franticly. 'I haven't seen her since before you came. She wasn't fighting with us.'

Anger courses through me. 'For fuck's sake!' I yell, kicking the woman. How had I not noticed that she wasn't there?

'Everyone search the woods,' I shout. 'Find the girl. Now!'

They look at me worriedly but they begin searching.

I already know we're not going to find her. Someone must have known about me and got her out of there.

We search for what seems like hours. Eventually it goes dark. I send the rest back to the village but I stay, watching.

Girl

We've been trying to go back to the village for hours. We seem to be walking in circles. Finally I decide to test that theory and mark one of the trees. We find it again a couple of hours later.

'I hate this place!' I shout, to nothing in particular.

Ali sits down near the tree.

'I think we're supposed to stay here. I think that's what she wants.'

'What about what *we* want?'

'She's trying to keep you safe.'

'And we all know how that ends.'

I flop down, gloomily.

Suddenly Ali jumps up. 'Hey, wait here.'

'As though I have a choice.'

He returns a few minutes later carrying what looks like a dead squirrel.

'May as well eat.'

'You're getting good at this,' I comment, as he skins the animal. We eat it raw.

We're in the woods for days. Every time we try to leave we come back to the same place. I start to wonder whether Jane's laughing at us from somewhere.

'Well, think of it this way,' says Ali. 'If we can't get out, perhaps nobody can get in. We're safe. We have food to eat, water to drink.'

'Hmph.' I'm sitting by the same tree, arms crossed.

'You're grumpy,' says Ali, poking my arm.

'Yes, I'm grumpy. I've been looking at the same trees for four days. I'm tired. And on top of it all, my baby is going to end the world. I think I have the right to be grouchy, Ali.'

'Well stop it. Let's play a game.'

He drew a target on one of the trees by scraping the bark with a stone.

'You use your knife, I use my arrows. We see who can get closest.'

We play for half an hour or so. Ali is much better than me.

'How did you get so good?' I ask.

He shrugs. 'Practice. How did you get so bad?'

'Oy!'

A tiny sound in the trees makes us stop laughing.

'Get behind me,' I whisper.

'No.' He stands in front of me. 'You heard what she said.'

'Ali, don't…'

I'm interrupted by a bloody figure stumbling out through the trees.

'Conrad!'

I don't know whether to be relieved. But I am, all the same. Conrad falls out into the clearing and drops on to his knees. He doesn't speak.

'Conrad. It's ok. You're safe here.'

He looks up at me. His face has a long cut along his cheek. 'No. I'm not. You're not. He'll follow me. I know it. We need to leave.'

'Who? The boy we saw you with?'

'He's bad. He tricked me. I didn't mean to… I didn't know…' He covers his face with his hands. I put an arm around him.

'It's alright. What happened?'

'They're all… dead. All of them. He's really dangerous. He'll come for you. We need to leave.'

All dead… John, Wen, all of them. How can that be possible?

I look around, almost expecting to see the boy stepping out of the trees.

'Do you think we can leave now?' asks Ali. 'I mean, Conrad found the place.'

'Well, I think we have to try,' I say. I look around. 'I wish I knew which way we're supposed to go.'

We decide to go in the opposite direction from the place Conrad came from. It seems to make sense. We've only taken a few steps however when a heavy branch falls into our path, blocking it.

'We can climb over it,' says Conrad.

'I don't think we should,' I say. 'I think it's telling us to go the other way. That's how it seems to work.'

After another couple of false starts we're left with the option of going back towards the camp.

'I don't like this,' says Conrad. 'He'll still be there.'

'Neither do I,' I say. 'But we haven't much choice, have we? We can't stay here, either. We're just pawns on the chess board. We move where we're told to move.'

We walk. After a while it becomes clear that we're not approaching the camp. Eventually we leave the forest at a completely different place.

There's nobody around. We decide to keep moving.

We've dropped into a grim silence. Each of us is too wrapped up in our thoughts to want to converse. I'm thinking *should I tell Conrad about what Jane said? About my purpose?*

I'm also thinking *I'm going to end the world. Does this make me bad?*

And *who is this guy? This assassin? Do I know him?*

The thoughts bounce off each other in my head. Too many. No answers.

Boy

She isn't here and she isn't coming back. Goddammit. How could I be so stupid?

I've been waiting here for three days. I thought she'd wait a bit and then come back, but she hasn't. So now what?

I walk back to the camp. I decide that a bit of food and some rest will make the world seem like a better place, and it does for a while. Any calm I manage to find is disrupted by a visit from Her Holiness later that day though. She looks displeased.

'You need to be cleverer than that,' she says. 'Now our enemies are alerted. The girl has been moved. I don't know where she is.'

I barely look up from my meal. I don't want her to think she's intimidating me.

'Are you listening?'

'Mmm. Good meat.'

The texture of it changes and suddenly it's gross and mouldy.

'What the fu…'

'Don't be under the impression that you're irreplaceable, Niall.'

The use of my name startles me. 'You sound like my mum.'

'I'll make this as clear as I can. You need to find the girl. You need to kill the girl. If you don't do those things, you have no purpose. There will be no point to you, and I will end you.'

I look up.

'Now you *really* sound like my mum.' She gets this really angry look on her face, so I hold up my hands. 'Okay! I understand. Can I have my food back please?'

The meat changes back. 'I'll tolerate you as long as you're useful, Niall. Remember that.'

'Yep, yep. Useful. Got it. Kill the girl. Will do.'

She looks irritated. I irritated a goddess. Heh.

Girl

The forest is a day's walk behind us now. The terrain we're in now is pretty bare: the odd tree here and there and some scrubby looking bushes covered in long thorns, which seem to be the only plant that can survive.

We haven't been walking long when Ali says: 'Hey! Look at that.' He's pointing at the ground.

There are paw prints in the dried mud; loads of them, crossing each other. They're large.

'We've just got to keep walking,' I say.

'But what if…'

'I don't know, Ali,' I snap. 'We just have to keep going. What else can we do?'

By the time night arrives we're all jittery. If there is anything around, this is when we'll find out. It's Conrad's turn to take the first watch but I can't sleep anyway, so we end up talking into the night as Ali sleeps.

'Do you *really* remember life before?' he asks, midway through the evening.

'Yes. Really. Don't you believe me?'

'I do… it's just, I can't imagine anything else besides this. I can't imagine being anybody else.'

I shrug. 'Well, it exists. I was there. I wish I still was.'

'Do you?'

'Yes. I'd give anything to be back there. But I'm not, I'm here. So I just have to get on with it.'

'I wonder who I was. Whether I was a good man.'

I think back to that image I had seen of him when we first met: dishevelled, forlorn. 'I'm sure you were. I mean you *are* a good man.'

'Am I? I don't know. When I saw the boy attacking the camp my only thought was *how can I escape*? How to save my own skin.'

'That's instinct,' I say, distractedly. Was that a noise? I gesture to Conrad to be quiet.

There it is again. Definite rustling from a clump of bushes to our right. I snatch up my knife and shake Ali gently.

'Get up,' I whisper.

He looks up groggily.

'What is it?'

'Ssh. Get behind me. Now.'

There's noises all around us now. This isn't good.

The first one comes out of the darkness. It looks like a dog or a wolf; grey, thin, its lips curled back in a snarl. It's followed by another, and another. There must be at least six. And judging from the ribs I can see poking out, they're starving.

We don't even have time to think. The biggest of them attack Conrad and the rest come for me and Ali. Suddenly we're in a fury of teeth and claws and I feel my skin tear. I just keep lunging out with my knife. I don't know how Ali's doing or what he's using to fight; I'm too immersed.

I stab out at the animal that's got its teeth in my leg and it falls away with a loud yelp. But then another one's on me and I drop the knife. I'm trying to push it away with my hands but it's too strong and desperate. Then suddenly it falls away and I see Ali behind it. He's holding my bloody knife, shaking all over.

The smaller ones start to back away. Conrad's fighting two of them with the same savagery with which he used to fight human-demons back at the village and soon enough one of them is dead and the other is limping away. Finally the surviving animals retreat, leaving the three of us torn and bleeding. Conrad roars into the night, a howl of anguish and frustration.

When daylight returns we strip the dead animals for meat and pack it carefully. We're exhausted and fearful. The same thought keeps bouncing about in my head: *this is just the start. What's next?*

We walk and we walk. We're on a path I've never seen before. There's a sluggish river beside us with dark, oozing water. We've decided to follow it, for no other reason than it gives us a direction.

'Can they see us? The bad ones?'

'I think they're all bad ones, Ali.'

'But can they?'

'I don't know. Maybe she's protecting us somehow.'

As I walk my mind drifts to other places. I think about my life. It wasn't so bad, really. I could have done more with it.

Art. I was pretty good at art. I liked textiles. I was going to get a sewing machine, saved up for it, then spent it on a gold chain for the boy instead. Stupid.

'Hey. You're daydreaming again.'

'Sorry, Ali.'

Our days become walking. We wake, we eat if we can, and we walk. The land is bare and open, the river cutting across it like a wound. Sometimes I wonder if we're walking in circles again but then every now and again we see something new and it gives me hope that we're actually going somewhere.

Whole weeks go by. We're blistered and exhausted but we keep going. There's nothing else to do.

My belly is softly rounded now; the only part of me that is. I'm thinner than I ever was in life. I'm beginning to see my bones beneath my skin. Sometimes I feel the baby moving, swimming. Like there's a family of fish in there. Swish, swish.

Ali catches me looking at it.

'Can you feel it?' he says.

I nod. 'Like a fish.'

'That's weird.' He looks at my tummy. 'I can't see anything. Can I touch it?'

'Go ahead.'

He places his hand on my belly.

'Nothing. Are you sure you're having a baby? Maybe she was wrong.'

'Pretty sure.'

'Pretty sure about what?'

Conrad. This is the difficult conversation I've been avoiding.

'She's having a baby,' says Ali, without any awkwardness at all.

'You're *what*?'

'A baby,' I say. 'Do you even know what that is? Can you remember?'

'I think,' he says. 'A small person. Not fully grown. I don't know how I know that though. And what does he mean, you're having one?'

I point at my belly. 'It came with me when I arrived. It's in there, growing. Jane said…' I hesitate. Do I tell him?

'Jane said what?'

'Jane said her baby's going to end the world,' says Ali. I glare at him.

'*What?*'

'She said something about…' I pause. 'I'm not meant to be here. Nor is the baby. When he or she is born it's going to end the world. And that's what she wants. She put me here for that reason.'

Conrad is staring at me open-mouthed.

'Sorry,' I mumble. 'I know it's a lot to process.'

He goes quiet. He's frowning to himself, in thought. He does this all the time, since the massacre at the camp.

'If you don't want to help us any more I understand,' I say.

'I just need time to think,' he says.

Time is something we have too much of. The days are open and seem endlessly long. I listen to the little sounds inside the big emptiness; our feet landing on the ground, thud, thud. Our breathing. The rustle of clothing.

The fullness of my life before seems unreal to me now. How did I fit so many things inside my head? How did I not go crazy? All of the noise and the light, all of the things. Clothes. Make-up. Boys. Taking selfies and getting likes. It all seemed so important. I had to prove to myself that I was popular, that I mattered. Until finally I decided that I didn't, and that nothing would change that.

A tiny lizard skitters across our path. It leaves a winding pattern in the dirt, like a ribbon twirling in the wind. Then it stops.

'Is it looking at us?' asks Ali.

We stare at it and it stares back. Then it disappears into a crack between two rocks.

'It was probably just a lizard.' But I don't trust anything. I'm crazy-paranoid.

A few hours later a huge black bird flies over our heads and lands nearby. I've never seen a bird before in this place. Something doesn't feel right. The bird sits there for a minute or two. It isn't looking for food or water. It's just there.

'Maybe they get birds in this place,' says Ali. 'I mean, we've never been here, have we?'

Neither of us believe it.

Conrad is still with us, at least physically. He seems to have retreated into himself. I want to help but I don't know what I can say to him which won't just make things worse, so I'm just leaving him to think things through.

Later that day we're sitting by a small fire when he finally speaks.

'I thought I was doing well. I've survived so long. It turns out I was just playing into their hands. Killing people like me. Kids, like him.' He gestures to Ali.

'You didn't know. You couldn't. That's the point,' I say.

'*You* worked it out. I think I did too. I just didn't want to believe it.'

'There's no point in thinking that way. We're all victims.'

He pokes the fire morosely. 'I want to help you. I want the world to end. It's wrong.'

He stares into the flames, frowning, retreating into himself. I can't be bothered to try to draw him out. I'm too tired, physically and mentally to baby somebody else. He'll just have to deal with it all in his own time.

I'm still trying to process it all. It's as though it's become my thing, my mission, to stay alive long enough to become a kind of human bomb. But it's not my plan, is it? I don't want any of it. I just want all of them to leave me and Ali alone. Maybe Conrad too. The baby as well, I suppose. He or she doesn't seem real yet; more of a theoretical possibility. A possibility which is making its presence felt more and more by the day.

The next day we set off walking early. We've been going about an hour when we feel the first rumble. We look at one other in alarm.

'What was that?' asks Ali, wide-eyed.

The fish in my belly is doing flip-flops too. We're all unnerved.

It only lasts for a few seconds. Everything seems even quieter than before, if that's possible. We begin to breathe more easily and begin walking again.

The next one occurs a few hours later.

'That's stronger,' says Conrad. It rumbles for longer this time.

'What's happening?' asks Ali. I have no answer for him. All we can do is keep walking, and hope. All the while the thoughts won't stop. *Is this how they're going to kill me? Or is this the end of the world, ahead of schedule?*

We're all thinking the same things but none of us want to say it out loud.

The quakes rumble on all that day and the next, getting more and more severe. My nerves feel like someone's plucking at them every time it happens.

'Girl?'

'What, Ali?' I know I'm being bad tempered.

'Do you think this is how it starts? The end of the world?'

'I don't know. I don't have all of the answers.'

He looks at me forlornly. 'I'm scared.'

'I know. We all are.'

Towards the end of the second day the quakes stop. For a while this is worse, the waiting. Eventually we begin to relax. And that's when the big one starts.

From the start this one feels different. We're thrown off our feet and cracks start to appear all around us. Ali is clinging to me and shouting, 'What do we do? Girl, what do we do?' While I'm just standing there dumbly, waiting for it to end.

It lasts about a minute. When it stops I drop the ground. I've had enough.

Ali puts his arm around me. I'm fighting back tears. I know they won't help. But I really want to cry right now. It's just too much.

'It's OK,' says Ali. 'It's stopped. We're OK.'

It's early in the day but we decide to stay put for now. We don't know when the next one will hit and at least there's nothing that can fall on us here.

'We're doing alright,' Ali keeps saying. 'We're still alive. We're doing OK.'

He's trying his best to be reassuring. He can see I'm at breaking point.

The quakes begin to lessen. I start to breathe again, in and out. We're still alive.

Boy

I'm almost glad when the earthquakes start. I'm so *bored*. The girl's vanished off the face of the… the whatever this place is called, and I have no immediate plan to find her. Threats of impending death can't change the fact that I haven't got the first clue where to start.

I feel the first one when I'm in the forest taking care of personal business. It was like a cheesy scene from a movie, where the funny guy asks himself, 'What exactly did I eat last night?' Except that it's really happening and I'm in fear for my life, so it really isn't that funny.

I run back to the camp and find Ojo. 'What's happening?'

He shrugs. 'It's never happened before.'

Comforting.

It doesn't last long but there are more of them all that day, and the next. Then there's a pause. Somehow I know that won't be the end of them.

She appears during the quake-break.

'What's going on?' I ask.

She looks down her nose at me. 'We're not sure. We think it has to do with the girl. She's not supposed to be here. It's causing… problems. Which is where you come in.'

'I've told you, I don't know where she is.'

'I think I can help with that.' She hands me a piece of raggedy looking paper. 'This is where you are.' She points. 'She's somewhere over here, following *this* river.'

A map. After all this time she gives me a map.

'They're not much use, in general,' she says, reading my thoughts. 'The habitat changes regularly. We've tried to freeze the landscape temporarily to help us locate the girl.'

I nod. 'Alright, fine. But she's weeks ahead of me. How am I going to catch up?'

'We'll find a way to delay them. Start following the river and we'll make sure you reach her. And don't get it wrong this time.'

The ground is starting to shake violently. The goddess looks perturbed.

By the time this one's finished the camp's been levelled. It seems like a good time to pack up and head off, now that we finally have a plan.

I call the others together and explain what we're going to do. They don't look happy but they know better than to argue. We gather together the basics and then we're on our way.

I have to kill the girl. No screw-ups, not this time.

I feel good. I start to whistle.

Girl

We've been walking for almost two weeks now. Most of the days are identical. The cold, the hard ground, the sluggish river. Looking for those small differences to confirm that we're moving forwards.

Today we've found the skeleton of a tree by the river. It looks a little ghostly; empty limbs spread out over the murky water. Its trunk is bent as though it's bowing down over the sludge.

We decide to stop by the tree for a while, to eat and rest. We rummage around our packs for food; our supplies are starting to run out. We divide a small piece of meat into three. It makes a depressingly small meal, but at least it's something.

The last earthquake has left fissures in the ground all around us. There's one underneath the tree, exposing its thick roots. On earth the root would be crawling with woodlice and earwigs, life scrambling into every dark corner. Here there's nothing. Just an old, dead tree which looks a bit like a skeleton.

Almost nothing. As we're eating Ali notices something.

'Look!' He's found some small brown mushrooms. 'Can we eat them?'

I examine them carefully. They look like the ones we've eaten dozens of times. We're all so hungry I decide to take a risk.

'They should be fine,' I say. Conrad raises an eyebrow.

'Good enough for me,' says Ali, grabbing a handful.

It isn't long after we set off again before we realise something is wrong. We're all nauseous. Ali stops walking, clutching his stomach, and then we all come to a stop. Ali starts vomiting.

As the day goes on Conrad and I start to feel better but Ali seems to be getting worse. He's shaking and sweating. I'm getting worried about him. I wrap him up in all of the blankets we have.

He's no better the next day. The day after that he seems worse. He's feverish; he can't see us anymore.

At the end of day three of Ali's fever I look up from tending to him and Jane's standing there.

'Can you help?' I say, immediately.

She nods. 'I can.' She hands me a small bottle. 'Drops, onto his lips, two or three at a time. He'll recover.' She seems troubled. 'They broke the rules of the game. The mushrooms you ate should have been fine. They cheated. Makes me wonder what else they're prepared to do.'

'Wait,' I say. 'I thought you said they *couldn't* cheat?'

'I didn't think they could. You need to be very careful from now on.'

'So,' I'm thinking. 'What stops them from just killing me outright? A lightning bolt or a heart attack or something?'

'I might be wrong but I think that would cause the same kind of problem your baby will cause. They're not supposed to interfere, directly. It'd make the system go wrong. The designers of Afterwards, *we* – made rules, to keep the game working properly. And nobody is allowed to create new dangers. Lethal ones, at least. All new threats have to be sanctioned by a committee, to keep it fair.'

'*A committee?*'

'Yes. Afterwards is responsible for a great deal of revenue. It's taken very seriously,' she said. 'The mushrooms weren't designed to kill you, just slow you down. Still, you need to watch out. I don't know what they're prepared to do, to be totally honest.'

'It all sounds so...'

'Human?'

'Business-like,' I say, bitterly.

'So... they know where we are,' says Conrad, after a moment. She nods. 'And if they're trying to slow us down, that means they're sending *him* after us, doesn't it?' He's frozen in fear.

Another nod. 'I'll think of something,' she says. 'In the meantime, get your friend well and start walking again as soon as you can. He's still a long way behind you.'

'But they'll do other things, won't they?' I say.

'Yes, I think so.'

When Jane leaves I give Ali the first few drops of medicine. As I put the bottle into my pack I notice that we have a fresh supply of food. Conrad has the same in his pack.

84

'Well, I suppose that's one good thing to come out of this,' he says, nibbling a small piece of dried meat. 'Do you think he's any better?'

I shake my head.

Conrad's getting impatient to leave. The thought of the boy pursuing us has rattled him.

Ali's condition doesn't start to improve until the next day. It's another three days before he's fit enough to walk again. We've been stationary for nearly a whole week.

The sickness has made Ali weak, and he's grown very thin. We have to walk slowly and stop often. He's quiet too, for Ali. I ought to enjoy the quiet time, but I miss his chatter. It makes everything more normal, whatever that means here.

The days become merged into one another again. One long, boring snake of twilit days, spent walking in the cold air.

'What do you think they are, the ones who are doing this?' Conrad asks one day, as we take a break. 'Gods?'

I think about this for a few moments. 'I don't know.' I bite my lip. 'I never believed in God. What do you think?'

'I think… well, they might as well be gods, even if they're not. I mean, what does it even mean? They control us. They watch us.' He's frowning, choosing his words carefully. 'I was relatively happy before this all started. I was surviving, or I thought I was. Then you came and suddenly everything's…' He gestures to the barren surroundings. 'But at the same time you're the most incredible person I've met here. I'm happy to be here, with you. And I'm sorry if it doesn't always seem that way.'

I'm not sure what to say. I laugh, which I know is the wrong thing to do when he's laying his feelings out in front of me. 'Sorry,' I say, hastily. 'It's just, there's nothing incredible about me. Really. I was a total failure at life and I'm not doing so great at death, either. I'm just trying to get through each day. That's all.'

'You don't see it at all, do you?' asks Conrad. 'What the rest of us see. He sees it.' He gestures to Ali. 'You have this aura of strength around you. The rest of us follow you.'

'I think you're wrong,' I say. What he's saying is scaring me. 'You can't think like that. I can't be responsible for you. You have to look after yourself.'

He puts his hands on my shoulders. 'It's alright. We will.'

I look up into his eyes. There's concern and there's admiration. It's misplaced. I shrug his arms away.

'Find another hero,' I say.

My mum got sicker. She never told me what the doctors said to her, even though I asked and asked.

She wouldn't let me stay off school to help her. I didn't go anyway. My head was filled with medical words and chemical smells and bad thoughts. I didn't have any room left for Shakespeare or Newton's law. Besides, I'd met a guy. *The* guy. Motorbike guy. He was a few years older and we used to go riding around all day; sometimes in the cities, where we'd get food and coffee and hang out. Sometimes in the countryside: whizzing down quiet lanes, finding places to be alone, far from hospitals and school and problems.

One day while I was waiting for him, George walked by on the way to school.

'Are you alright?' he asked.

I nodded. 'I'm waiting for someone.'

He frowned. 'I know who you're waiting for. You should be careful.'

I remember rolling my eyes. My nerdy ex giving me unwanted advice.

'I'm fine.'

'He's not a good person.'

'Well, maybe that's OK. Maybe I don't want a good person.'

'I don't understand.'

'Just go to school, George.' *With the rest of the kids.*

George looked at me sadly. 'I'm still your friend Rosie. That hasn't changed.'

'Fine,' I snapped. 'Bye then.'

George left. My boyfriend didn't even turn up that day. I waited half an hour. Eventually I got a text saying he'd been called into work.

It's been around a week since Ali was well enough to continue walking. He's starting to sound a bit more like himself. The annoying questions have begun again. Thank God. If there is one.

'Do you think… Girl, do you think that there's anyone else like you here?'

'How should I know? I hope not, for their sake.'

'What's it like, being, you know…?' He points at my stomach. '*Pregnant*?'

'Yes. What does it feel like?'

'I feel more crappy than if I wasn't pregnant. But I don't know if it's just because of…' I point to the landscape. 'Hey, you know what?' I say. 'I think it likes you.'

Ali grins. 'Of course it does! But what do you mean?'

'Well, when you talk to me it stops wiggling. Like it's listening. You're a calming influence.'

He stands in front of me to stop me walking. He puts his hand on my belly.

'Hi there.'

The baby does a massive flip and Ali jumps backwards.

'I felt it!' he grins.

'Congratulations,' I smile, tiredly. 'You'll make a good big brother.'

Ali looks at me as though I've slapped him.

'What's wrong?' I say.

'I don't know,' he says. 'It's just – what you said. I think I was one.'

'One what?'

'A big brother. I can't remember but… I think I had a sister. A little sister.'

'You can remember?'

He nods. 'Only a little bit.' He looks upset. I put my arm around him. 'I don't know if I want to remember,' he says.

'You will,' I reply. 'It's hard. But you should remember her. She's your sister.'

'Girl...' Ali is thinking. 'Do you think it's because I'm with you? Are you changing me?'

'I don't know,' I reply. 'Does it matter?'

He shakes his head. 'I don't know what I would have done if you hadn't found me,' he says, after a moment. 'I probably would have died, straight away.'

'No. You'd have found someone else to annoy.' This makes him smile. 'Anyway, Jane said you're my protector. That means it didn't happen by chance. We were supposed to meet.'

He thinks about this. 'I haven't been doing much protecting so far, have I?' he says.

I look at his softly featured face with its anxious brown eyes and realise at that moment that I love Ali as much as I've ever loved anybody. Even my mum. 'We might not like being controlled by them, but they know what they're doing,' I tell him. 'If Jane says you're going to protect me then you will. I believe it.'

He seems satisfied with this.

'I *am* going to,' he says. 'You'll see.'

Later that day we find the next obstacle. The earthquake has made a huge ravine, right in our path. It's too steep for us to cross and there doesn't seem any way around it. It's an impassable barrier. All we can do is wait for them to catch us up.

'There must be a way to get past it,' says Conrad. 'Climb down, make a bridge, something.'

I know he's thinking about the boy. He's tense and irritable.

'The side is sheer. There's no way to climb it. And we have nothing to make a bridge.'

'So, what? We just wait for him to come and finish what he started at the camp?' He's pacing, nervously.

'No. Well, I don't know. Maybe if we follow it for a while we'll find a way to cross.'

He nods. 'Alright. Better than nothing.'

We choose a direction and walk alongside the ravine. It doesn't end; in fact it gets bigger. After a while the ground becomes rough and unstable. It slopes down into the crevasse and as we walk bits keep breaking off under our feet, making us slip constantly.

'Should we turn back?' asks Ali, after he's fallen for the third time on the difficult ground.

'That's what they want,' I reply.

'But if we can't walk on it we'll end up turning back anyway,' Conrad points out. 'And the longer we leave it the more likely we are to run into them.'

'This is so difficult,' I sigh. I feel like giving up. Sitting down and just waiting for them. What's the point in trying to fight a god? It's like using sand to build a shield against the sea.

'Come on then. Let's go back.'

It takes us another half a day to reach the point where we started to walk along the ravine, by which point it's completely dark. We set up camp, demoralised.

'Can we make a fire?' asks Ali. He asks this most nights.

'We can't risk it.'

'But it's so *cold*.'

'I know. But no.'

We're eating the last bit of some biscuit stuff Jane gave us.

'Do you think she'll bring us some more soon?' asks Ali.

'I hope so. In the meantime we have to look out for other food.'

'Are you talking about me?'

It's odd, how Jane appears. She's never ostentatious; there's no puff of smoke. It's just, suddenly she's there, as though she's been with us all along.

'We were wondering if you'd bring us some more food. We've nearly run out,' I say.

She places a bundle on the ground. 'There you are. That'll keep you going for a while.'

She sits down next to me.

'You're not here just to bring us food, are you?' I ask, suddenly aware of an unspoken *something* in her eyes.

She shakes her head. 'No.'

Conrad looks up. 'What is it?'

She looks at him, then me. 'They've caught up with you. They'll be here in less than a day.'

'*What*?' Conrad is on his feet. 'We need to get going.'

'No.' Jane seems suddenly forceful. 'Listen to me carefully. We're not going to outrun them. They've cheated, and they will continue to cheat. We'll have to face them. *You* will.'

'How?' I ask. 'There's loads of them. There's only three of us. We've got no chance.'

Jane nods. 'I know it seems that way. But that's what they'll think too. Use the weapons I've given you. I'll help as much as I can. Protect each other. Remember, those men don't care about that boy. They fear him. You have that advantage.'

'Some advantage,' says Conrad. His eyes are filled with terror. 'I've seen what *that boy* is capable of. You're leaving us to our deaths.'

'I'm sorry. Just do your best. They've... I suppose they've beaten me. Again.'

There's something in the way she says this. Suddenly I'm very angry. 'This isn't a game!' I shout.

She regards me with sad eyes. 'I'm sorry Rosie, but that's exactly what this is,' she says. Then she leaves, just like that.

Conrad is shaking. Ali is sobbing, quietly. I'm just sitting, hand on tiny bump, waiting. Resigned, I suppose. So long as it's quick, I think.

A little later Conrad stands up. 'I'm really sorry,' he says. 'I didn't think I was a coward, until... I just can't do it anymore. I'm sorry.' He walks away, without glancing back. He hasn't even taken his pack. He's just gone.

Disappointing.

'Where's he going?' asks Ali.

'Leave him,' I say. 'It won't matter. It's just us, now. We don't need him.'

He looks at me wide-eyed, as though he wants to say, '*Are you crazy*?' but has thought better of it.

We sit, side by side, and wait.

Boy

Holy cow, we've actually found them. For about a day we've been right on their tail and now I have it on good authority they're actually waiting for us. *They've given up*, were the exact words used.

Maybe a better calibre of psycho might miss the thrill of the chase. Bit too easy. But I'm sick of fucking goddamn walking all of the fucking time. Quite frankly, I want a rest. And to do that I have to get rid of the pain in the arse girl.

Today is a good day to die.

I need breakfast. One of the men killed something last night and it's roasting on a fire in front of me. It smells good. The smoke will be visible for miles but it doesn't seem to matter now. I'm pretty jubilant. I can—

'Hey. Look! It's them!'

Goddammit. Not before breakfast.

Hey. I recognise her. This is unexpected.

For a moment I'm rattled. Whatever I had in my head, this was not it. Can I do this? Sure, I decide. I don't know her. She's nothing to me. Certainly not worth dying for.

She's walking towards us, her and a young kid, like she's dropping by for a visit. May as well get this over with.

'Hey! Look alive,' I yell. The men gather around me. There's around thirty of us. The whole situation is a bit of a farce.

She's just like I remember her. Tall, pale skin, dark eyes. Arrogant-looking. Beautiful. Really fucking beautiful.

She's staring me down like she's got her own personal army at her command. It's kind of unnerving, actually.

'So I'm here,' she says, angrily.

'Yep.' God, I've turned into a monosyllabic moron. 'You are.'

She's looking at me like I'm a lower form of life. 'Get on with it then,' she says.

'What's the rush?' I hear myself saying. 'Do you want to die?'

She shrugs. 'Looks like it's going to happen whether I want it or not.'

'Who's that?' I ask, pointing at the kid.

'My friend,' she says. 'He gets to live.' She states this like it's an indisputable fact.

'No!' This is the kid. 'I didn't agree to that. I'm going to protect you. I have to protect you!'

I decide to step in. 'You're in no position to make demands,' I say.

She looks angry. 'Just agree to it, OK?'

To my own surprise I hear my voice saying, 'Fine. We leave the kid.'

She nods. 'Right. Well, you'd better do it then.'

The boy steps in front of her but she pushes him out of the way. One of my guys grabs him.

I step towards her. Sword, nice and quick, I'm thinking. Somehow my hand doesn't want to reach for the sword. Ojo raises his bow. I gesture for him to lower it. He looks at me in surprise.

She's got this contemptuous look. Like she sees through me. Like she knows me.

'You can't do it, can you?' she says.

She's right. Fuck. She's right, I'm standing there completely immobile. I can't kill this girl. Fuck.

'Don't be stupid,' I say. Lame.

I'm cursing myself inwardly. I don't know what I'm going to do but I have to do something. Everybody's staring at me.

Wait. What's that? What *is* that?

Everyone turns towards the sound. Heavy and low, a rumbling which seems to be coming from underneath the ground.

Shit.

The ground is moving. It's another earthquake, but it feels different.

Everyone's trying to back away, but nobody knows where it's coming from so we're all moving in different directions. Then the ground starts to split, except this time this fucking awful smelling gas is fizzling out from the cracks. It's hot too; my arm grazes past it and it singes my skin.

'Get back. Get back!' I'm yelling at the men. I don't even know why; I don't care what happens to them. One or two of them seem to have breathed in the gas and are now lying comatose. It's chaos.

Then with one humungous ripping sound the land breaks in two. There's a four metre wide gap between the two edges, with noxious god-knows-what in between. And she's on the other side.

This doesn't seem like a coincidence.

The drama doesn't last long. As soon as the land is split apart it comes to a lazy halt. We all sit there for a while. No-one's saying anything.

There's still bad smelling gas squirting out here and there but on the whole it's almost like nothing's happened. I walk over to the edge. God, that's deep. There'll be no climbing down that ravine.

She's watching me.

'You were lucky,' I say. She just gives me this contemptuous look. *Yeah, right.*

Suddenly a force unlike anything I've felt pushes me to the ground. Like instant super-gravity. I'm felled. My arms and legs are unable to move. I can just about move my neck enough to see that the same thing has happened to everybody else.

A voice is speaking. It seems loud; too loud.

'Oh, really. Is that necessary?'

'They need to know their place in all of this. The pawns have started believing themselves to be Queens.'

I know the voice. It's my boss. And she sounds unhappy.

'You're being ridiculous.'

'You cheated. You can't do this.'

'Well, so did you. Poisoning competitors is clearly against the rules. All I did was create a natural obstacle. *That's* allowable.'

'You can't possibly win this fight. We will find her, and she will suffer because of what you made her do.'

'We'll see.'

The next moment I can move again. I look around but my boss is nowhere around.

The girl and her friend are walking away.

Girl

We've only been waiting a few minutes when I stand up.

'Come on.'

'Where are you going?'

'We're going to find them.'

Ali stares at me like I've lost my mind.

'But they're going to kill us!'

'Not if I can avoid it. Anyway, the waiting is killing me on its own. I want to get it over with. On my terms. You stay here if you want.'

'No!'

He stands there for a moment. He looks so distressed I go over and hug him.

'Together,' I say.

'Together.'

I wish I could leave him here. I hate leading him to danger. But abandoning him in this place would be worse.

We walk back towards the river. I know that's the direction they'll be coming from. And after a few minutes we see a narrow plume of smoke. They're not being cautious. They don't care if we know they're coming. They know we're trapped.

'Is that them?' asks Ali. I nod.

'Come on.'

'I feel sick.'

'Me too.'

It takes us an hour before we're within sight of the group. There's a lot of them. We're lost. We have no chance.

The boy's staring at me. He looks different now he's not lying on the floor, bloody and dying. He's wearing this arrogance around him like an extra skin. He reminds me of the guy, motorbike guy. Cocky and self-assured. But I'm willing to bet his arrogance doesn't run that deep.

I decide to get things rolling.

'So I'm here.'

'Yep. You are.' His voice doesn't reflect the cockiness of his attitude.

'Get on with it then.'

He makes some remark about being in no rush. This isn't going how I expected at all. He's pointing at Ali now.

'Who's that?'

'My friend. He gets to live.'

Ali starts protesting loudly. It's breaking my heart to see him so upset.

The boy is trying to wrestle back control of the conversation. Then to my astonishment he agrees to let Ali live. Ali tries to hold on to me but I push him away and one of the men grabs him. I feel like a murderer. I want to tell him I'm sorry but I can't.

I turn back to the boy. As I'm looking at him I realise something: I don't know why but I'm not afraid of this kid. I don't think he's going to kill me, despite all evidence to the contrary.

'Right,' I say. 'Well, you'd better do it then.'

I'm calling his bluff, I suppose. *Let's see what you've got.* One of the other men raises his bow and my blood runs cold for a second.

The kid waves at his man to lower the bow.

I have no idea what's going on here. But I don't think this boy wants to kill me.

'You can't do it, can you?'

He stares at me and in his eyes I see pure terror. He looks like someone who had forgotten what it's like to be scared but has suddenly gone back to being a child in the dark. I almost feel sorry for him. Almost.

Wait. What's that sound?

It takes a few seconds for my brain to understand what's going on.

Another earthquake.

Suddenly everything's going crazy. The men are running in all directions. Ali has wriggled free from the man who had him and has come back to my side. The ground is cracking all around us. There's this stench coming from the breaks in the ground.

What should I do? What do I do?

I'm staring about wildly, trying to think of a plan.

But then, it stops. And we're on this side.

Oh.

'Jane,' I breathe.

'Did she do this?' asks Ali.

'I think so.'

The boy is staring across at us. I think he's starting to realise what's happened.

'You were lucky,' he says.

Lucky. Right.

Suddenly I find myself being forced to the ground by an unseen power.

'What is it? I don't like it,' says Ali.

I don't know what it is but I don't like it either. Then I hear Jane's voice. It sounds louder than usual.

'Oh, really. Is that necessary?'

She's answered by a clipped, angry sounding female voice I don't recognise. 'They need to know their place in all of this. The pawns have started believing themselves to be Queens.'

I look at Ali. 'She's the other one,' I whisper.

'Why can't I look at them?' he whispers back.

'Ssh.'

They're having an argument. About us. About me. The other one is saying she's going to find me and make me suffer. How nice.

Then they're gone, and we can stand again.

'What now?' asks Ali.

I glance over at the boy. He looks dazed.

'Come on, let's go,' I say. We grab our packs and turn back towards the ravine.

'But where?' asks Ali.

'Forwards. That's all,' I say.

It's been almost three days since the last quake. That's practically unheard of.

Fish likes the quakes. She stops moving when one begins, then starts to bounce about like a jumping bean. Perhaps she knows she's causing them. Perhaps she's doing it on purpose.

It's been many weeks since we saw the boy. After the confrontation by the river we walked back towards the ravine, and found Jane waiting for us.

'Thank you for saving us,' I remember saying, although I didn't really mean it. She's the problem, after all. Her kind. The cause of all of this. The reason I'm here.

'You're welcome,' she replied. She told us about the place she's created for me to have the baby. It's safe and comfortable.

'It's a distance away though,' she said. 'You'll have to keep walking a bit longer. Can you do that?'

I nodded wearily, wondering why she was acting as though I had a choice.

'I'll help you to cross the ravine,' she said. 'Once you get over I'll make it impassable again. They'll find a way through, but not immediately. Then head in the direction of the evening sun. Keep going that way. It'll take weeks, maybe months, but I'll help as much as I can.'

So that's what we did. We made a bridge across the narrowest part of the ravine and we crossed it, then destroyed it.

And now we're walking again. Me and Ali.

After we had been travelling for a few weeks the landscape began to change. The trees became scarce, the grass was replaced by sand. Desert. It's baking hot even though it still never gets light. Even in the middle of the day it's dusky, and the shadows are long but the heat is overwhelming. Only in the night does the cold return.

'You're getting fat,' remarks Ali, as we walk.

My round bump looks odd on my skeleton body. Every time Fish moves I see legs and arms poking out, like a scene from a horror movie. I wonder if this is what it's normally like, being pregnant? I miss Google.

'What do you think happened, with the boy?' asks Ali. 'Has he gone?'

'I doubt it.'

'Why didn't he kill you?'

I shrug. 'I don't know. Maybe Jane did something. Maybe he's just a coward.'

'Or maybe he's good. Inside.'

'He killed people, Ali. He's not a good person.'

'Oh. Yes. I forgot.' He thinks about this for a moment. 'But Conrad killed people too. And you would have if you hadn't realised.'

'That was different. The boy knew they were people. Conrad said he seemed to enjoy killing. That's the kind of person he is.'

All the same, I've thought about our meeting more than I want to. The way he looked at me was unsettling. Like he was frightened of me.

'Should we start walking again?' asks Ali. We've been resting for a couple of hours now.

I stand, reluctantly. 'I suppose so.'

'Are you alright?'

'Mmm.' In truth, I'm in pain just about everywhere. But what choice do we have? 'Let's go, then.'

We haven't been walking long before I feel the first rumbling beneath my feet.

Until the hiatus of the last few days, the earth tremors had become pretty frequent. I don't know if Jane caused that with whatever-she-did or if it's because of me. Or something else. But they've become a fact of our lives.

'Should we stop?' asks Ali.

'Not yet,' I say.

The tremors grow in intensity, as they always do. We're constantly in fear of the ground breaking beneath us; here we would be buried instantly.

A shadow falls across us. 'Hey! Look!'

The huge bird is back. It's the size of a pterodactyl. It sweeps over us as though it's assessing our potential as a snack.

'Get your bow,' I say. I take out my knife. Our weapons look puny compared to the bird, but they're all we have.

'Do you think the other one has sent it? To stop us again?' asks Ali.

'Maybe. Or it might just be part of the game.'

It's doing wide circles around us. Every time I think it might have lost interest it reappears, swooping over our heads.

'If it attacks stay behind me,' I instruct Ali. 'You're smaller. It'll probably try to carry you off.'

He looks at me, wide-eyed. 'But what if it takes you?'

'I don't think Jane will let it.'

'But she won't mind if it gets me?'

'I don't know. But I mind. So stay behind me, OK?'

He nods.

The bird has disappeared again. Then it's back, making a graceful loop before swooping down in front of us. It's looking at us. There's intelligence in its eyes.

We stop walking. 'You got your bow?' I ask.

'Yes. I don't want to shoot it though.'

'Neither do I. But we might have to.'

The quake starts up again and the bird takes to the air. This time it doesn't come back.

A few days later something appears on the horizon. A village. This isn't good.

'We'll have to try and avoid it,' I say.

That proves to be difficult. We begin walking away from it on the diagonal, to try to go past in a wide arc. But later that day we see the first of many patrols in the distance. They've seen us, without a doubt. We just have to hope that they consider us not worth the trouble to pursue.

They watch us for a while, then turn and go back towards the village. We breathe out, but not fully.

Our caution is justified later that day. We find a beaten up old cabin out in the middle of nowhere and we take a chance on it, because the sun's too hot to stay out. It's abandoned, or kind of; the skeleton of its former occupant is curled up in the corner. Ali stares at it with wide eyes, but to his credit he doesn't back away. He's braver.

After we've passed a few hours there we decide to move on. It's a bit too close to the village and they're sure to know of its existence. Perhaps the skeleton belonged to a former resident.

But when we walk back out we find that we're surrounded. There are fifteen or so people there, including...

'Conrad!' Ali at least is happy to see him.

He smiles, shyly and glances at me. I look away.

They're not trying to kill us. A tall girl with red hair and freckles approaches me. She looks unarmed but I'm not fooled. I know any unpredictable moves on my part and she'll produce a knife from her belt or her ankle or wherever she has it stashed.

'Conrad says we can trust you,' she says. 'Can we?'

I nod, mutely. She gestures for us to follow. Conrad catches us up.

'I'm so glad you...' he begins, his voice giving up mid-sentence.

'Didn't die?' I offer. There doesn't seem much else to say.

'Yes. I'm really sorry.' He has a tortured expression. I don't care even a bit.

'I know you probably hate me,' he says. 'I deserve it. I'm a coward. I just... I couldn't handle it. It was too much.' His hands are trembling. 'At least let me help you. There are things you need to know about this place.'

I don't reply. I don't feel like dealing with him right now.

Ali doesn't share my bad mood. He's happily filling Conrad in on everything he missed when he ran out on us.

'There was another quake and the ground split and all this poison gas came out. But they were on the other side, so we got away. You should have seen Girl! She stood up to him and he was scared of her, it was really weird but cool and...'

He continues talking all the way back to the village. Conrad listens silently.

It looks like every village: a few tents and wooden huts, tall fence, communal fire. As we arrive weary faces turn to look at us, then quickly lose interest.

'Hey,' I say. Conrad and the tall woman look around. 'How come they're not trying to kill us?'

They stop walking. 'That's one of the things I need to explain to you,' Conrad says. 'Things have broken down here. They haven't been fighting for a while. The camps are in pairs and something happened to the other one. They all died.'

'But how come I don't look like a demon to them?'

This time the girl speaks. 'When they all started dying the masks were failing too. Sometimes we could see the humans underneath. Then after a while they stopped working altogether.'

'And once you know, you know,' finished Conrad.

'So they just leave you alone? No fighting?' I can't keep the scepticism out of my voice.

'None. But—'

'What?'

'We don't get any help, either. As soon as the fighting stopped, so did the food. We get nothing, now. It's like we've been forgotten.'

The *we* isn't lost on me. He's made himself at home here.

'But you're surviving,' I say.

'Barely. We hunt, but there isn't much life in the desert. Water's scarce too.'

I have more questions but the girl says: 'We'll fill you in later. For now, get comfortable. Do you have any food?'

I nod. We still have a bit of dried food from Jane and Ali caught a rat yesterday, so there's that. We soon realise that there's an expectation that we'll share what we have. We attract a crowd three people deep. No wonder they were keen to find us. I make sure we have enough before I relinquish the rest.

We're found a hut and left alone to sleep. It feels good to stop walking. That's all we do. My boots are worn out at the sole. I can feel every stone and the heat of the desert sand is unbearable. My feet are blistered and sore. Ali's are the same.

'How long are we going to stay here?' asks Ali, before sleep.

'I don't know. We'll see.'

'Do you think Conrad will come with us when we leave?'

'I don't know whether I want him to. We can't rely on him.'

'Oh. OK. Just us, then?'

'Maybe.'

The truth is, part of me *does* want him to leave with us. I like him… I *liked* him. And this place does strange things to your head. I'm not sure if it's Conrad I liked or the idea of him, in the middle of all this fear and isolation.

We go to sleep immediately. I have to admit there's some

101

comfort in having other people around. I've almost let my guard down. Not quite.

A few hours later I hear a noise and I'm suddenly alert. 'Who's there?' I reach for my knife but I can't find it in the dark. I stumble over to the door and look out. Nobody's there. Whatever it was, it's gone now.

Sleep evades me after that. When Ali wakes me in the morning I'm baggy-eyed and grouchy.

'Wake up. You need to see.'

'What is it?'

He points to the end of the hut where all of our things were piled up.

There's hardly anything left. Our packs, our weapons, our boots. All gone.

Fury consumes me. How dare they? After everything we've been through? How *dare* they? I crash out of the hut towards the fire, where I find Conrad calmly eating some more of our rations. I feel like knocking it out of his hand.

'What is it?' he says.

'Someone came into our hut and took all of our stuff. You need to help me find out who. We're getting it back and then we're leaving.'

He holds his hands up. 'Right, OK. Just—'

'What?'

'I know you're angry. But think of it from their point of view. They've been alone out here for months. They have nothing.'

'That doesn't mean they can take our stuff. We need it! How are we supposed to hunt? Defend ourselves?'

'I know. I'll ask about. I'll see what I can find out.'

He walks away and begins speaking quietly to a group of men. They all have the same hollowed out look, their eyes flat and hopeless. As the anger subsides I start to feel ashamed of my selfishness. I have to remind myself that this isn't about me. I'm keeping two other people alive.

Conrad returns a while later. He has Ali's bow and a knife. It isn't mine.

'You can have it. It's the best I can do.'

'Whose is it? I'm not taking someone else's property.'

'It's mine,' he says.

'Take it back.'

'No. You're going to need to defend yourself.'

I swallow. 'Then – you're not coming with us?'

He looks surprised. 'I didn't think I'd be invited.'

I look down, shrug. 'There's nothing here. You stand a better chance with us.'

'Why do you care?'

'I don't. Make up your own mind.'

He reaches out to me but I step backwards. His shoulders sag.

'I wish I'd stayed. I wish I was a better man.'

I sigh. 'Thanks for finding Ali's bow, anyway.'

He nods and he looks like he's about to say something else when the girl comes over. I feel a stab of jealousy, despite myself. She whispers into his ear.

'Alright. I'll be there in a minute.'

She leaves. I look at Conrad questioningly.

'A couple of people have died in the night,' he says. 'When that happens a group of us take shifts to guard the bodies until we can burn them.' He looks at me meaningfully. I catch on after a moment.

'Oh. You mean – people will – oh.'

'We're starving here. I'm not sure if we even should be stopping them. I mean, what good will it do?'

The girl appears again. 'We're stopping them because we're not animals. We have to try to keep a grip on that. They were people, our friends, not meat.'

I'm in danger of vomiting up the small amount of food I have left in my stomach so I start to walk away. The girl grabs my arm. For a second I have a clear image in my head: a hospital room. The girl, too, too thin, skin like paper, eyes hollow. I'm too shocked to move until she snaps me out of my thoughts.

'Hey! You don't get to judge them until you've been here for a while.'

I shake her off angrily and leave. As soon as we're out of earshot Ali says: 'We have to leave, don't we?'

I nod. 'We were always going to have to go, Ali. This just speeds things up.'

'When?'

'Tomorrow. So get as much rest as you can before then.'

Boy

'Sir.'

I can't get used to them calling me that. Makes me sound like a goddamn teacher.

'What?'

'Some of the men want to know when you'll be coming out. They – they need direction. Some of them think you've...'

'I've *what*?'

'Turned, sir. Gone to their side. Like the others.'

I stare at the nervous man in front of me. 'What others?' I say. He just stands there, fidgeting. 'Idiot,' I mutter, turning away. I hear him shuffle about. He leaves after what seems like an eternity.

The truth is, I have been distant lately. My head's disturbed.

Why couldn't I kill her?

It's like she's taken up permanent residence in my head. Moved in, rearranged the furniture. I need to evict her, and I can only think of one way to do that.

But whispers a small voice. *What if the same thing happens next time?*

Well, it won't. It can't. And to make absolutely certain of that, I'll have a back-up option.

I leave the tent. There's a group sitting nearby. They immediately fall silent.

'Don't mind me,' I say, friendly-like. They don't resume talking, all the same.

I'm looking for somebody specific. Large fella, Galen or Galek or something. Not over-burdened in the brain department, but pretty mean. He's sitting by the well eating what looks like half a pig.

'Hi,' I say. He grunts at me. 'I want to ask a favour.'

He looks at me but doesn't stop eating.

'I want you to be my back up,' I say. 'I don't know what happened back there. I think maybe their side is using some kind of mind-trick on me.' He looks at me, eyebrows raised, disbelieving. Bastard. 'Anyway,' I hurry on. 'If I get into a similar situation next time I want you to slit my throat,' I say. His eyes widen. 'And then go and kill the girl. Got it?'

He looks uncertain but he nods and grunts, then turns back to the meat. I'm guessing thoughts don't linger for too long in his head.

With the correct motivation I should be able to do it. And if not, well Galen will be doing me a favour, because I wouldn't want to be me when the boss turns up.

It's doing my head in. What's wrong with me? Why is my mind so fixated on the girl?

I go back to my tent, intending to take another nap. Preserving my energy. However, it is occupied. By the boss. She looks at me like I'm a large turd, as usual.

'Why are you wasting time?' she asks, grouchily.

I shrug. 'I was waiting for further instructions. I don't know where they are, your, erm… majesty?' What am I supposed to call her?

'I've been watching them. They're not so far ahead but you'll need to walk for two days at least to get pass the ravine. But I have some gifts for you. You'll find them outside the camp. Also, Niall, we have some new allies.'

'Mmm?'

'One of the others has agreed to donate some of their people to our cause. You'll reach their camp on the way. And to make certain you don't get lost, I'm sending Annabelle with you to lead the way.'

How had I not noticed the massive black bird in the corner of the tent?

Annabelle. Hmm. Seems oddly sentimental for her to name it. What's the word? Incongruous.

She reads my thoughts.

'Oh, I didn't name her,' she says, smiling thinly. 'She used to be a girl. She's more useful now. She will fly between you and her and report back to me, to ensure you don't wander off course.'

I stare at the girl-bird. That's pretty cold, even by my standards.

'How do you know she's on our side?' I ask. I figure if I'd been turned into a bird revenge might be on my agenda.

'She's seen what happens to people who get it wrong,' she replies. Then she's gone.

I go back outside.

'We're shipping out,' I say to the sitting group. 'Come on, get packed up.'

The surprise lasts for only a moment before it's replaced with resignation. They disperse. The nervous man from earlier stays behind. He has this weird tic when he speaks to me; he keeps pushing his sleeves up. I doubt he's noticed himself doing it but it's massively annoying.

'Sir.' Left sleeve. 'Where are we going?' Right sleeve.

I run through everything he needs to know. Then I go to look for the gifts she mentioned.

Excellent. She's left us some pack animals. They look a bit like donkeys.

A thought occurs to me. *Were these people too?* I stand in front of one of them and look into its eyes. Is there a human trapped inside there? The donkey stares back at me and then snorts a massive glob of snot all over me.

'You fucking little…'

I kick it which sends the whole lot a bit crazy. Some of the other people come over to see what's happening. A girl with blonde hair starts trying to soothe them, while glaring at me. I go over to the spring to wash off the mucus.

This should make a big difference. We'll still have to walk but if we don't have to carry all of our equipment we should reach the girl much quicker. Then… well, we'll see. I'm confident I can do it this time. I'm going to have to, if I want to survive. And surviving is what I do best.

Girl

That evening when we go to the fire there are eyes on us from all around, in the dark spaces where the firelight doesn't reach.

'Ignore them,' I say.

'Why are they watching us?' asks Ali.

'They don't trust us,' I say.

Conrad appears a few minutes later and my paranoia subsides a little. There's nothing to eat tonight so the fire is more of a ritual but it's warm at least against the desert cold.

'How long are you staying?' he asks. I tell him our plan. 'I think that's a good idea,' he says.

I hear the subtext plainly. 'They want us to leave,' I say, gesturing in a general way at the village.

'Not everyone. It's just, there's so little food some of them are wondering why we're helping you.'

I almost laugh. 'Helping us? By taking all of our food and equipment?'

'All the same, there's resentment.' He reaches over and takes my hand. This time I don't move away. 'You have to believe I'm sorry I behaved as I did. If I could make up for it...'

The firelight is flickering hypnotically. The evening feels ethereal. 'Perhaps you can,' I say. 'Come with us.' I feel light headed and reckless. 'I missed you,' I say.

'I missed you too.' His eyes reflect the orange firelight. 'I wanted so much to be a better man. To help you.'

Something softens inside me and I place my hand over his. 'It's OK.' We stare at each other and I wonder for a second if he's going to kiss me.

Then the girl appears. She glances at us then puts her arms around Conrad. 'There you are.'

Conrad gives me an apologetic look. I just look away.

Later that evening, while Conrad is talking to a group of men a few metres away the girl comes back. I guess that she isn't coming to check on our well-being and I'm right.

'You need to leave,' she says.

'We *are* leaving,' I growl back at her. 'What's your problem, anyway?'

She looks at me with loathing. 'He was doing better before you showed up. Do you even know what he's been going through?'

I want to laugh out loud. And I want to punch her stupid face. But I do neither. 'I'm pretty sure we're all going through stuff.'

'You don't know. He was hurting so badly when he came here. He wouldn't speak for days. He's finally started to come around. Then you turn up and undo it all.'

I roll my eyes. 'You don't know the full…'

'I know more than you think. I know what you are, what you're carrying. I don't care. I just want you to leave.'

'This isn't about his health, is it? This is about him. You think I'm going to take him.'

'Are you?'

'That's up to him.'

'But you want him to leave.'

'I don't know. But I don't want him to stay in a village full of cannibals and psychos either.'

'You don't deserve him. You don't care about him at all!' She launches herself at me like a crazy person. I find myself consumed by fury. I'm fighting back like a demon, fists and nails flying. Ali dives between us. 'Hey!' he shouts. 'Stop. Both of you!'

I haven't calmed down yet. I start shouting something incoherent and so does she.

'Hey!' he shouts again. He turns to her. 'Whatever you think, Girl's the bravest person you could ever meet. She's better than Conrad. Better than you. You couldn't do what she's doing. So just leave her alone. OK?'

The girl huffs away with one final glare in my direction.

'Hey! You protected me,' I say, laughing. But Ali doesn't laugh.

'What's wrong with you?' he says and stalks off.

'She started it,' I call after him.

I don't sleep well that night. I can't stop thinking. About Conrad and the girl. About the eyes in the dark. About what we have in front of us.

The next morning we get up early and pack away the few things we have left. There's no breakfast to be had and I don't want a fanfare so we just go.

Ali still isn't talking to me, which is just fine. I'm not in a chatty mood. I just want to walk and think.

Unfortunately it soon becomes clear that we're being followed. Two men. They're not making much of an effort to hide.

'What do they want?' asks Ali.

'I don't know. I don't want to find out either.'

There's not much on the landscape which could offer a hiding place. It's wide open. Our options right now seem to be allowing them to reach us in the hopes that they're friendly or out-distancing them. I like the second much better. We're in far better shape than they are.

The problem is that means we have to walk much too quickly in the desert heat and we can't stop until they do. We're soon struggling.

'I need to stop,' says Ali, about a hundred times.

'I know. But not yet.'

Eventually I look behind and they've gone. They must have given up. Now we just have to find shade, quickly.

'Look. What's that?'

Ali's pointing at something in the distance. It's a big structure about half a mile away.

'I don't know.'

We walk towards it anyway. It's our only option. My skin is burning and Ali's is too.

It's a stone monolith, smooth and tall. It doesn't provide a lot of shade but it'll do. We put the blanket over us and finish a flask of water.

'We'll camp here,' I say.

When the day starts to cool off I have a proper look at the monolith. Someone has carved names into it.

'What do you think it is?' Ali asks.

'I don't know,' I say.

We hear them a few hours after nightfall. I'm on my feet in seconds. I can't see anything but I can hear their feet.

'Girl! They've got me! They've got me!'

I run towards his voice with me knife outstretched. But I don't reach him. I'm grabbed from behind by the other one. I struggle against him and manage to land my knife on his arm. He loosens his grip enough for me to wiggle free but he has me again in seconds. He has a knife of his own and I feel it on my throat. I know it's over. I can't do anything. They're going to kill us and they're going to eat us.

So this is how it ends.

Boy

Evening. My least favourite time of day. We stop walking and we eat and then sleep. Some of them talk. Not me. Some of them do more than talk. Again not, apparently, me. Nobody approaches me unless they need something. They're afraid.

I don't mind the solitude. It's what I'm used to. Except for the memories. Sometimes I can't stop them and they're fucking unwelcome.

Tonight's horror show. 15 May. My birthday and the day I left home. I can see her face still. She's pissed and unpleasant, calling me all of the useless bastards under the sun. She's also sporting a massive bruise across her face from my other legal guardian. She always defends him. Why does she always defend him?

I've had enough. I'm not waiting for him to get back and beat another seven shades out of the two of us. So I pack my bag and come downstairs.

She begs me to stay. She's crying, sorry, sorry. Things will be better.

They won't though, will they, Ma? They never are.

Please, Niall. Don't go.

She's pulling me back in. And that's when I do it. I push her away, roughly, just like him. She's light and drunk and she falls over like a sack of spuds.

I'm so ashamed to see her like that. I loathe myself and I loathe her. I pick up my bag and go. Anything's better than this shit.

That's the stuff that comes back to me when things get too quiet.

My least favourite time of day. At least I get to rest my feet.

Girl

When I wake it's light. I put my hand to my neck instinctively. I have a cut but it's small. I sit up and look around. Ali. He's a few feet away.

'Ali!'

I jump up and run over. His chest is moving up and down. Thank god. Thank god. I shake him and he stirs.

'Wake up.'

He sits up, rubbing his eyes. 'What happened?'

'I don't know.'

I can see what looks like a pile of clothes a hundred yards or so away. I gesture for Ali to stay where he is and approach it silently, knife raised. The knife falls as I get closer.

'It's alright.'

The two men who were following us are lying there in a bloody heap. Now they're no longer a threat I can see them for what they were: skeletons with skin stretched so thin you can see through it. Living ghosts.

'What is it?'

'The men who were following us.'

'Are they alive?'

'I doubt it. They're not going to hurt us anymore.'

We're both thinking about the same thing.

'Come on,' I say. Maybe whoever did this has gone now. Either way we have to get out of here.

'Not that way.'

A new voice. We turn towards it, startled. A man's head appears from behind the monolith. 'It's impassable. You need to go towards the sunrise.'

We walk towards him, cautiously. 'Thank you,' I say. 'And thank you for helping us.' I gesture towards the bodies.

He shakes his head. 'No. No. One mustn't thank another for causing a death. No. No.' He returns his attention to the monolith. He's carving into it with a stone.

'What is it?' asks Ali.

'To remember. I have to remember them.'

'Who?'

The man doesn't reply. After a moment he looks up again. 'You have memories. The old world. Yes?'

I nod. 'Yes. How do you know?'

'I remember too. I'm like you, but not like you.' He holds out his hand. 'My name is Josef.'

I shake his hand. 'I'm Girl.' He raises his eyebrows.

'It's a pleasure to meet you, Girl.' He shakes Ali's hand too. 'And you are the protector, correct?'

Ali's still too frightened to talk. He just nods.

'Well, well. Come and eat with me.' He gathers his tools in a small bag and begins to walk. We look at one another.

'I'm really hungry,' says Ali.

We fall into step behind him. After a few minutes we come to a hut. Josef spreads out a blanket on the floor and gestures for us to sit.

We do as he says, uncertainly. He begins to rummage around various bundles and after a while produces some plates, which he fills with dried meat and biscuits.

'Are you sure you can spare this?' I ask.

He nods. 'In life, one of my pleasures was eating in good company. It's something I rarely get to do now. So, enjoy.'

We're so hungry the food is gone almost immediately but he doesn't seem to mind.

'Now,' he says. 'Tell me your story. How did you come to be a participant in this game?'

I look at him, startled. He makes a dismissive gesture. 'You first.'

I begin to tell him my sad little story. He nods along. When I come to the part where I'm still pregnant he doesn't look surprised, but he is very interested.

'Ah. So that's what they intend to do. I see.'

'Now you,' I say. 'What happened to you?'

'Some drinks, first,' he says. He's stalling for time. That makes me nervous. He hands us some wooden cups filled with water.

'I have a little well, back at the village,' he says. 'You must fill up your bottles, before you leave.'

I thank him. He gets up and walks over to the door where he just stands, looking out. He mutters something under his breath.

'Pardon?' I ask, looking at Ali in bemusement.

'I'm sorry. I've lived alone for a long time. I've forgotten how to be around people.'

He paces a few times. 'You have to understand,' he says, after a moment. 'It's not easy for me to remember. But I will, because I think you need to hear it.'

'Thank you,' I say.

He stops walking. 'I killed them all. All of the other people in my village. I murdered every one of them. I'm telling you this straight away because it's the most difficult part.'

I stare at the thin, sad man in front of us. 'But why?'

'I will explain, as well as I can. It's not a simple question to answer,' he says. 'Unlike everybody else I met here, I was brought here alive. I had a wife, two children. I was happy. I didn't die. I was simply *removed*.' He makes a snatching gesture. 'They wouldn't have known where I went. They might have assumed I just left them.' He goes quiet.

'I didn't know they could do that,' says Ali, forgetting to be scared.

'They did it because one or more of these gods-who-are-not-gods wants to break this toy of theirs. They've become tired of playing with their human dolls and now want to piss in the toy box.' He sits now, his head low. 'They thought that bringing a living man into this abomination might do the trick.'

I nod. 'That's why I'm here.'

'Yes. A live birth. I feel sorry for you, dear.' He draws breath. 'Anyway, for me it didn't work. They brought me here for no reason. And they wouldn't, or couldn't send me back. I was supposed to live here with the others, to join in. If I fought, I got food. If I did not, I starved. This is why I'm thin.'

'You wouldn't fight?'

He shook his head. 'I was angry. From the moment they told

115

me what my role was in this miserable business I just got angrier. But my anger was not with the other people. They were victims, like me. They thought they were fighting monsters. No. I'm angry at them.' He points upwards.

'So why did you kill them all?' I ask. It's abrupt but I'm rattled and impatient. I still don't know whether I can trust him.

'In the end it was a choice. I could see them dying in front of me anyway, one by one, in the name of their atrocious sport. I wanted to refuse to fight back, to deny them their prize. So I did the only thing I could think of. I killed each of them, quickly, as painlessly as possible.'

This actually makes a weird kind of sense. Only here could mass murder sound like the reasonable option.

'Were they angry?'

'Of course. There were thunderstorms for days and the food stopped entirely, for the other village too. *That* I regret. They didn't ask to be involved in my self-indulgent protest.' He looks pensive. 'The two men who followed you were not evil; they were desperate. You do what you have to do.'

I'm not sure about that. I'm still clinging to the idea that there are some lines I won't cross. But I'm not sure of anything.

'You're a hero,' says Ali.

He spins around. 'No I am not. I am absolutely not. I am a killer. They are opposite things.'

He stalks out of the hut and we're left staring at one another in confusion. We sit still and wait for him to come back inside. He doesn't. When I finally go to look for him he's nowhere to be seen.

We decide to take advantage of the relative safety of the hut and rest. We spend a day sitting around, talking, eating bits of dried biscuit, playing silly games.

He returns at the end of the day, smiling brightly.

'My friends.' He produces the carcass of an animal from his bag. 'Let's eat together. You are moving on tomorrow, yes?'

'Yes.'

We collect dry wood, something at least there doesn't seem a shortage of. The meat feels like a feast after days of hunger.

'How did you find it?' I ask. 'There's so little life here.'

'Yes. But there is usually some, if you know where to look and make sure not to take too much.'

We sit and watch the fire throwing up tiny dancing sparks.

'Where did you go?' I ask, eventually.

'Back,' he says. 'To the village. I visit them often.'

Boy

We've been walking for weeks now in desert. Every day is the same. Get up, propel ourselves forward until we're about to drop, then stop. It's boring. How was the afterlife, Niall? It was fucking monotonous, John.

That's why there's a buzz of excitement when finally, finally, we see something on the horizon. A village. We don't care who lives there, even. I mean, they're unlikely to be worse than us, anyway. We just want to look at something other than sand for a while.

But when we get there it becomes quickly apparent that there's something wrong with this place. Nobody comes to meet us. They've seen us; they're just watching from their huts with this hopeless look, like they've given up. Finally a girl approaches.

'You're not wanted here.'

'We're not wanted anywhere. We just need to stay for a night.'

'We have nothing to offer you.'

'You have shelter. That's enough.'

I'm not sure why I'm negotiating with her. We have the advantage after all.

'One night. That's it.'

'Yep. Scout's honour.'

She shows us to a couple of small huts. There are twelve of us left so it'll be a bit of a squeeze. Specially when I tell them I'm not sharing. I get a few filthy looks but no arguments, so that's that. The biggest and nastiest get the other hut and the rest can sleep outside.

We tie up the donkeys near to our huts. Some of the villagers are looking at them in a way I don't like so I decide to deploy a guard overnight.

At sundown a few of them gather at the fire. This is usually when the food gets passed around so I walk over but there's nothing. The girl from earlier is there and would you know it – that guy who led me to the resistance people. C – Connor. No. Conrad. He's looking at me like I'm bad news, which I probably am.

118

'Hey,' I say. 'Any food around here?'

He doesn't answer. He just sits, watching me.

'No food,' says the girl. 'Have you got any that we can share?'

'Nope.'

'Then we just sit and wait for the hunting parties to get back.'

'And they'll have food.'

'Probably not.'

She tells me this story about how everybody at another village died and now they've been abandoned and are slowly starving to death. I'm only half listening. I'm a selfish prick and all I can think is if they don't bring any food I'll be tempted to eat the donkeys myself.

Of course, they don't and I don't. I just spend a very frustrating night waiting for food that doesn't arrive and hardly get any sleep in my private hut.

In the morning I can't wait to get out of there. Before we leave I go to find Conrad. He doesn't want to see me and tries to walk away but there's nowhere to go.

'It's alright,' I say. 'I'm not going to hurt you.'

'I'm not scared of you,' he says. 'Not anymore.'

I don't believe him but I don't care to argue.

'I'm sorry for lying to you,' I say, although I'm not, not really. 'I've got a job to do.'

'That's how you justify what you did, is it?'

I shrug. 'Don't need to justify anything. We're all dead anyway. The way I see it, I did them a favour shortening their existence in this place.'

'That must be a great comfort to you.'

He's starting to become annoying. 'Do you know which way they went?' I ask.

'I'm not going to help you murder her.'

'How can it be murder if she's already dead?'

He doesn't answer.

'Oh well. I tried.' I turn my back on him and walk back to the others. 'Pack up. It's time to go.'

This place is really starting to creep me out. As we walk

through we're followed by the same hollowed out stares which greeted us. They've gone already, but their body hasn't realised it yet.

'Hey,' I call to Galen. 'Have you got any flint?'

A tiny spark is all it takes. Everything's so dry that within minutes there's a pretty good blaze going. The villagers are finally stirred out of their stupor, rushing about trying to limit the damage. I feel nothing.

Girl

We leave Josef the following morning.

'Goodbye,' he says. 'I wish you luck on your journey.'

We thank him and set off, more cheerful. Our bellies are full and we're rested. However, the baking sun quickly wears down our enthusiasm. It's already too hot and by the time we reach the other village we have to take shelter.

It's eerily like its sister. Everything is exactly how it was on the day everybody died. There are clothes hanging out to dry and a pot hanging over a long dead fire. The floors have all been swept and there's hardly any dust considering we're in a desert.

I imagine Josef coming back every day, cleaning, tidying. A daily pilgrimage to remember and be sorry.

We stay there for a full day. It's comfortable enough but it feels a little like camping in a mausoleum. Full of ghosts that we can't see.

It isn't until we're on our way out of the village that we see them. Neatly arranged rectangular graves in rows of eight. Tended with the utmost care. He knows which grave belongs to whom. There are small items like carved stones and dried plants placed on some.

He's the last one alive: their custodian.

'Girl. Are you alright?'

'Mmm. Leave me alone, Ali. I'm sleeping.'

'It's almost midday. We need to find shelter.'

I pull myself reluctantly out of my torpor. I haven't had a good sleep for months until now. I guess my body's making up for it.

'Come *on*. We need to get out of the sun.'

He's right. This place is deadly in the middle of the day. The sand is littered with the burnt up carcasses of creatures who got caught out. One day we stayed out too long and both got painful blisters all over our skin. We've been cautious ever since, until now.

'Sorry,' I murmur, grabbing my pack. 'I'm just so tired.'

Ali ignores my apology. 'Come on. I think I see something.'

There's always something, I tell myself. *Jane is looking after us*. We walk on. I can feel my skin starting to burn.

'Why did you let me sleep so long?' I complain.

'I couldn't wake you! Don't blame me because you're lazy.'

The heat's making us both bad tempered.

There it is. A small cave. It's still some distance away.

'Come on. We just need to keep going,' I say.

'My feet hurt.'

'Try to ignore it. We have no choice.'

By the time we reach the cave we're burnt all over, but especially our feet. Ali flops onto the floor and bursts into tears.

I sigh and turn away from him. I have nothing left to give him. It's taking all of my strength not to start crying too.

As I sit there I hear a tiny sound at the back of the cave. Suddenly I'm alert. *You always check before you go in*.

I tell Ali to move to the edge, which he reluctantly does. I pick up a stone and toss it into the cave. A mass of enormous black spiders come scuttling out. Ali screeches, I yell and both of us run back out into the scorching sunlight.

'What is wrong with you?' I scream, at the sky. 'Why are you doing this to us?'

The sun is beating down on us. We have no choice.

'Back in. Now,' I say.

'No! I'm not going in there.'

'You are, Ali, even if I have to carry you in. Spiders or death. Come on.'

We walk in slowly and perch at the very edge of the cave. We're both jumpy; every noise startles us. Thankfully the spiders seem frightened too and keep to the back of the cave. Ali's looking around nervously, his eyes wide.

'There's one. There's one,' he splutters. A spider as big as my head is walking towards us, slowly. I pick up my knife and bring it down fast, impaling it.

'Well, there's supper.'

'I'm not eating *that*.'

'You won't be saying that later.'

It seems an eternity till it's cool enough to venture outside again but as soon as it is we hurry away from the cave. My skin won't stop crawling. I'm compulsively checking my hair in case one of them hitched a ride.

I hate this world. I hate it so much.

'Are we still going the right way?' asks Ali, for the fourth time today.

'Yes. Look. The sun's over there, isn't it?'

'I hope we get there soon.'

'She said it might be months, Ali.'

It's night. We've made a fire and I'm eating a spider kebab. Ali is true to his word; he's eating yesterday's scraps.

'Hey, Girl?'

'Mmm?'

'I remembered some stuff. Some more stuff.'

'Did you? What stuff?'

'My family. My mum and dad and my sister. And my name,' he said, shyly.

'Well, what is it?'

He shakes his head. 'It's Ali now. That's who I am.'

'Like I'm Girl.'

He nods.

'Alright. Do you remember anything else?'

He grins. 'I used to be really good at video games. There was this one…' His brow wrinkles. 'I can't remember.' He looks upset. 'I can't remember the game.'

I raise my eyebrows. 'Whatever it was, it didn't make your aim any better, did it?'

He throws a cloth at me. 'Shut up and eat your spider.'

And then Jane is there, sitting by the fire as though she'd always been there.

'Hello,' says Ali.

'Hi, Ali. How are you doing?'

'We got trapped in a cave with massive spiders.'

'Yes, I saw. You were very brave.' She turns to me. 'Girl, I'm having some problems at the moment.'

I almost laugh out loud. She has the decency to look a little ashamed.

'Yes, OK, fair point. I'm not complaining, not really. But I need to tell you I may not be able to visit you for a while. My people are making things very difficult for me. They've restricted my access to the world. I've brought you as much food as I can, but after this I'm afraid you're going to be on your own for a while.'

I just stare at her, dumbly. Then I shrug. 'How much worse can things get anyway?'

She gives me a look which says *don't tempt them.*

'Keep going in the same direction. I'll guide you, one way or another. And I've made sure there are plenty of places you can find shade, when you need to. You'll have to find your own food and water, though.' She pauses. 'The other side are watching you – they're using a bird. Have you seen it?'

We both nod.

'Well, just ignore it. It won't harm you. If you can just make it to the haven I've created you'll be safe, at least for a while.' She looks at me, sadly. 'I'm sorry to do this to you.'

She thinks she's leaving us to our death.

'The haven is still about a month's walk away. Just keep going. Once you're there you should have a few more weeks before the baby is born, so you'll be able to rest. Focus on that. I'll come back as soon as I am able.'

I sigh, and nod.

'Good luck,' she says, and then she's gone.

Ali and I look at each other. 'Well, who needs her anyway?' I say, trying to smile. Ali just looks at me, worry etched into his face.

Boy

Walking again. And you know what? For once I'm actually enjoying it. It feels good to be doing something. Of course, it helps that the donkeys are carrying all of my stuff. And the animals are helping a bit too.

Haha. I'm a funny guy.

I only have to carry myself. It's definitely helping.

It's not as cold as it was either. I'm taking this as a good sign. Perhaps this place has seasons, and we're heading into summer. Things are looking up. I start to whistle. I'm picturing myself as that preacher guy in *The Night of the Hunter*. Or any other Robert Mitchum character. I'm so caught up in my fantasy that I completely fail to see the man materialise in front of me.

'Niall.'

I stop whistling.

'Who are you?'

'Rosaline sent me.'

'Who? Oh, *her*. Right. What can I do for you?'

'Stop for a while. I need to show you something.'

A different kind of whistle brings the front walkers to a halt.

'We're going to take a break. Make the most of it.'

They sit in a group a few metres away.

'OK. What is it?'

The man looks like an accountant, or a maths teacher. He's wearing an old jumper which has a couple of holes in and is sporting the worst comb-over I've seen in a long time. It's flapping about like it's alive.

A strange choice of costume for a god, but who am I to question?

'Sit down. Look at this map.'

The chart in front of him is much more detailed than the one I had before.

'You're here,' says the man. He points to a large area of nothing. Appropriate. 'She's here.'

He points to another empty area.

'What do those lines mean?'

'Heat. That area's desert, extremely hot. You'll enter that section in two or three days. Once you're there your travel will be restricted to early morning and evenings. Midday is too hot and night is too cold.'

I nod. 'Alright. Desert. That's new. Anything else?'

'We believe she's travelling to here.' He points to another place which has been marked with a tiny cross. In pencil.

'You use pencils?' I ask, incredulous.

The man stares at me. He chooses to ignore the question. 'If she reaches that place we're in trouble. It has a high level of protection. I think they're trying to get her there for the birth.'

Wait. What?

'The *birth*? Whose birth?'

The man frowns at me. His hair flops over his eyes and he pushes it away irritably. 'The girl's pregnant. Didn't you know that?'

My mouth falls open. 'No. I didn't know that.'

'That isn't a problem for you, is it?'

I think about it for a moment. 'No,' I say. 'We're all dead anyway, right?' A thought occurs to me. 'Why do you want to kill her? What did she do?'

'The correct question to ask is what *is* she going to do. And I've just answered that question.'

'The baby?'

He nods.

'If that baby is born it will be the end of all of this. In case you start to feel sentimental about the girl or her child, remember that she's been placed here as a weapon against all of us. If you allow her to live, you might as well have detonated a bomb.'

I frown. 'So, how does *that* work?'

The man looks at me. 'I know this world feels real Niall, but think of it as an immersive video game. The child is a virus. It isn't meant to be here.'

I suppose that makes a kind of sense. Well, no, it doesn't, but when did that matter? I look back down at the map. Another question occurs to me.

'What's here?' I ask, pointing at the edge of the map. I want to write 'here be dragons'. If I had a pencil.

'Nothing,' says the man. 'That's all there is.' He moves his face too close to mine. He has really bad breath. 'We need you to move faster. We'll delay them as much as we can too, but we can't break the rules.'

I shift backwards, away from him.

'Alright, I'll hurry them along. I'll try, anyway.'

'Do more than try. It matters. This is about more than a few small lives.'

He leaves. No more drama, he's there and then he isn't.

I sit by myself for a while. They don't want to sit with me and I sure as shit don't want to sit with them. I run my fingernails through the dust on the ground. It feels real. My fingers feel real. They're *my* fingers. I've bitten the nails right down.

I still have a scar on my chest from being stabbed with a compass by Ben Bailey in Year 10. The water I'm drinking tastes like water. Bitter and gritty but water, all the same.

It's making my brain sore. I stand up.

'Come on, chop chop. Time to go.'

There's a general groan and some muttering.

'We've to go faster,' I shout, to nobody in particular. 'If you bastards value your crappy little existences you'd best get a wiggle on.'

Girl

I can't do this anymore. I can't. It's too much. I'm in pain just about everywhere. The food is running out. The sun is relentless. I'm sorry Jane, but I can't do it.

'What's wrong with you?'

Ali appears in front of me, frowning.

'I've had enough, Ali. I need to stop.'

'Don't be stupid,' he says.

'I'm not being stupid. I can't do it. They're going to have to find someone else.'

'Sit,' instructs Ali. I'm too tired to argue. He hands me the water bottle. I take a mouthful then hand it back. 'Wait here. I'll try to find food.'

This is what we do, now. We spend our days alternatively melting down and picking one another up. It's so hard. But somehow we keep going.

He's gone for about an hour and when he comes back he's carrying a large reptile. We don't need a fire; we leave it out in the midday sun and it cooks a little too well.

'I'm glad I've got you,' I tell him.

'I'm glad I've got you too.'

Once we've eaten we rest and wait for the hottest part of the day to be over.

'We need to find water, soon,' I say.

Ali looks thoughtful. 'I used to play this game on my Xbox.' His eyes are focused on something faraway. 'Do you remember Xboxes?'

I roll my eyes. 'Water, Ali. Focus. We need to work out what to do.'

'Shut *up*. I mean, this game was like a survivalist thing. And you got water by drilling into trees.'

I nod. 'I think I saw something like that once. We haven't got a drill though.'

'We could try to use your knife.'

'I suppose.'

When the heat subsides we set off again, looking out for plant life.

'Everything's dead,' I sigh.

All of the trees are white and skeletal.

'I'm so thirsty,' complains Ali.

'We'll find something,' I say, with conviction I don't have.

The day just seems to get longer. We're starting to feel the effect of heat and dehydration. I'm dizzy and nauseous and Ali is starting to ramble.

'I had this teacher called Mr Norris; he had these massive ears. Do you remember him, Mum? Lug Norris. Do you remember?'

'I'm not your Mum, Ali.'

'Oh. Right. Where are we going, Girl?'

'Just keep walking.'

Eventually exhaustion and darkness force us to stop. We put our canvas up quickly and lie together, shivering.

'Girl?'

'Mmm?'

'Is this it? Are we going to die now?'

'No. Jane will find a way to help us. Go to sleep.'

I dream. I'm back home again. Mum is there, and so is Ali. They're sitting together playing on the Xbox. When I walk towards them she looks up. *The bird*, she says.

I wake up abruptly. There it is; the black bird. It's sitting on Ali's pack, watching us.

'Ali.' I shake him.

He looks up.

'What's it doing?' he asks.

'Just watching.'

There's something strange about it. I can't work out what it is. We've seen loads of creatures in this world but this one is different. It's intelligent.

'Do you want food?' I ask.

'What are you doing?' says Ali. 'It's on their side. We should kill it and eat it.'

'I'm not sure it *is*, exactly.'

'Is what?'

'On their side.' I offer the bird some crumbs of leftover reptile. It eats them quickly. Then it flies up and away.

'There you go,' says Ali. 'Off to report where we are. And you fed it.'

I shrug. 'It probably won't make any difference anyway.'

We settle back down to sleep. Ali immediately falls into a semi-coma but I'm awake now. I wrap myself up in my blanket and sit at the edge of the tent.

The sky is completely black, as always.

I start to think. I think about being ten years old. That was a good age to be. I got my first smartphone and I thought I was really cool. I had a lot of friends.

Thinking about being ten years old me makes me sad. I feel like I let that girl down. I could have tried harder. I just couldn't see my way out of the darkness. It was suffocating. If I had found a tiny pinprick of light...

Hey. Wait a minute. I shake Ali awake.

'Look. Do you see that?'

'What?'

'A star. I saw a star. Look.'

We stop and stare at the sky.

'You must have imagined it.'

'No. Keep looking.'

'There!' Ali points. A tiny, barely visible point of light in an otherwise bare sky. 'What does it mean?' he asks.

I start giggling. Ali looks at me like I'm crazy.

'Maybe it's a joke. She's making a kind of joke. It's like a biblical reference.' I know I'm making no sense at all. 'Yes! That's it. We're supposed to follow the star. It'll take us to the safe place.'

'How do you know?' Ali looks worried. I think he thinks I'm losing my mind. Maybe I am.

'I don't. But it makes sense. I think it's her way to help us, from... wherever she is.'

'I wish she'd send water instead,' grumbles Ali, turning over.

A loud *caw* makes him sit bolt upright in his bed.

'It's back!' I say.

The bird has returned. It's holding something in its beak. It's...

'A flask! Water! It's got water!'

The bird drops the bottle.

'How do we know it's safe?' I wonder. 'I mean, they sent it, after all.'

'You said they're not allowed to poison us. You said that!'

'Didn't stop them before.'

'Oh, I don't care.' Ali grabs the bottle and takes a big swallow. I shrug and take one too.

'Tastes so good,' he says.

'Thank you,' I say, to the bird. It rises up and flies away.

The water won't last long, but it's given us breathing space. Follow the star. Look for food and water. Stay alive.

Boy

We're in a desert. Flat, empty apart from a few dead animals. Hot, obviously. Whoever designed this place knew what they were doing; it's making me want to kill things. The landscape has been crafted to put its inhabitants in a really bad mood, and it's doing a stand up job.

According to the map we've got over a month of this type of terrain before we get back to grassland.

I wonder how she's faring. I mean, I have guys to look for food and animals to carry everything. She has a kid and a big belly. She doesn't have a protector anymore. Will there even be a job for me to do at the end of all this? Bit of an anti-climax if I finally reach her and she's dead already from thirst or heat or whatever.

Hmm. What is that?

I'm having a disturbing feeling. I want to shove it back into my subconscious where it belongs, but it won't stay there. The thing is, I don't want to kill her. I don't. That's why I couldn't do it last time.

I'm going to, obviously. I have to; it's her or me. I'm always going to choose me. But I don't *want* to do it. I prefer her not-dead.

She's been in my thoughts a lot; too much. Not much else to think about around here. That would be OK if I was thinking about ways to kill her and suchlike. But I find myself thinking about her eyes; they're dark and angry and they look at me like she hates me but finds me a little bit intriguing too.

Whatever it is, it's irrelevant. I've a job to do, and if I don't do it this time there won't be a me to fail again.

I wonder if she's figured out I'm having doubts. Rosaline. She hasn't been around for a while but she keeps sending the other, maths teacher guy to check up on me. He's been asking me a lot of questions.

'Do you have a strategy this time? For when you reach her?'

'Yep. Going to kill her.'

'Don't be facetious.'

'Don't ask stupid questions.'

And that fucking bird is creeping me out no end. I think I'm alone, and I look up to see Annabelle staring at me, unblinking.

'Shoo! Fuck off! Aren't you supposed to be spying on *them* not me?'

I think Rosaline is using it to keep her eye on me. I'm tempted to put an arrow in it. I'd probably be doing her a favour, anyhow. Except then maybe Rosaline'd turn me into something. She's a bit unpredictable.

For example, she's just appeared a few metres away and made some poor guy walk into a donkey.

'Niall.'

'Do you have to call me that?'

'It's your name.'

'It's disconcerting. No-one calls me Niall.'

She looks around the group. The others hastily kneel. She beckons for me to follow her.

'Niall, please don't think you're more important than you are,' she says, once we're away from the rest of the group. 'You must be respectful. I've been patient with you, but that won't last forever.'

I touch an invisible forelock. 'Right you are.'

She glares at me. Then before I even have time to think I'm lifted off my feet and suspended in the air, in full view of the whole group. And that's when it starts.

My entire body is shot through with excruciating nerve pain. I've never felt anything that comes close to this. I feel like I'm being ripped apart really, really slowly. I just want it to stop. I just want it to stop.

And it does. I'm dropped to the ground, where I curl up in a pathetic little ball, whimpering like a sad puppy.

'Now do I have your respect?' she asks, calmly.

I just nod. She carries on talking as though one of us hadn't just tortured the other.

'Niall, I have some good news.' *Really?* 'I've heard a strong rumour. The other side are worried that their girl isn't going to make it. She's become quite sick. So you may not have a job to do, after all.'

I want to say: 'Why are you telling me, in that case?' Actually I just want to tell her to fuck off. But I say neither, which seems to please her.

'Anyway, the sickness means she can't go anywhere for a while, which gives you the opportunity to find her. If she isn't already dead, she'll be sick. It'll be the easiest job you've ever done. And Niall.' She pauses, something unpleasant in her expression. 'If you start having unwanted thoughts again, remember the pain. Think about what I'm capable of doing, if you disappoint me.'

Then she's gone, and I suddenly find that I have a new clarity of purpose.

I sit there for a few minutes, trying to process everything that has just happened. Some of the others approach tentatively. Are they worried about me?

'Leave me,' I bark. They back away.

The pain is completely gone, but I can't shake the memory of it. I'm suddenly nervous, anxious.

And how did she know what I was thinking?

Girl

'I'm sorry,' says Ali, again.

'It's not your fault. We both drank it. We were too thirsty.'

'But I drank it first. You said no.'

'I would have anyway, Ali.' I close my eyes, hoping the nausea might subside. It does a little.

'Girl, are we dying?'

'I don't know, Ali. But we're together. That's what matters.'

Ali groans, and retches loudly.

We've been like this for almost a full day, in the heat of the desert, with no more water. There's no other way to look at this. We've come to the end. Full stop. We're no longer walking. We've found shelter and we're staying here, until… well, we're staying here.

'We should have known. Why would the bird help us?' says Ali.

'I just had a feeling,' I say. 'Hey. Who's that?'

A figure is approaching us.

'Who's what?'

I point.

'I can't see anyone. Where do you mean?'

I can see her face now. 'What are you doing here?'

'Who are you talking to? You're scaring me!'

My mum looks at me with tears in her eyes. 'Ro. My poor Ro.'

'No, I'm alright Mum. Don't cry. I'm fine. This is Ali, we're friends, and…'

Ali is staring at me. 'Stop it, Girl. There's nobody there. It's just us.'

'I shouldn't have left you,' says Mum, taking my hand. Hers feels cold against my hot skin. I start to shiver.

'I wish you hadn't,' I say.

'That's when it all went wrong,' she says. She places her hand on my round stomach. 'That's my granddaughter.'

'A girl? I *knew* it was a girl.'

'She looks like you. She *is* like you.' She looks down. 'I have a message for you. They sent me to tell you something.'

'Who?' Then I realise. 'Them. *They* sent you.'

'Yes.'

'Why are you listening to them, Mum? They want to hurt us.'

'I'm not here for them. I'm here to help you.'

'How?'

'I want you to stop fighting, Rosie. It isn't your fight. It's theirs. You're just hurting yourself.'

The words feel like a release. I feel my body start to relax. I'm really tired.

'Girl. Look at me. Wake up. It's not real. Wake up.' And then: 'I can't survive without you!'

Reality washes over me. Mum is gone. Ali is by my side, crying.

'Sorry,' I say, hugging him.

'I thought you were going. I thought…'

'I'm OK.'

We curl up together, feverish, exhausted.

Not this time I think.

In the first light of the next morning we're disturbed by a loud cawing from outside the shelter. The bird is back.

'Go away!' shouts Ali. He throws a stone at it. The bird hops out of the way but doesn't fly off. 'Why is it watching us?' he says. He reaches for his bow.

'No, don't,' I say.

'Why? It's food.'

'It's not just a bird. It's intelligent.'

'So? It's spying on us.'

'Maybe it has to.'

The bird hops towards me.

'Is that right?' I ask. 'You have to watch us.'

It moves further towards us. Ali and I look at one another.

'Er… OK. What about the water? Did you know it was bad?'

The bird jumps away from us.

Ali's frowning. 'I mean, it's probably just walking about,' he says. 'And even if it is trying to talk, why should we believe it?'

It turns and flies up, landing on the branch of a dead tree. It caws, loudly.

'It's making fun of us now,' huffs Ali. He picks up a stick and lobs it towards the bird. The bird swoops down and catches the stick with a deft movement, then flies away.

It returns a short while later, still carrying the stick, which it drops in front of Ali.

'Want to play catch again?' says Ali. He's half smiling. Then he notices something. 'Hey – Girl. Look.'

I turn my head towards him. He's brandishing the stick towards me.

'What?'

'Look at it. It's damp.'

I look and it's true; the end of the stick has recently been immersed in water. We both turn towards the bird.

'What if...' Ali begins.

'Did you find fresh water?' I ask, at the same time.

The bird flies up into the air again. This time Ali follows it, carrying one of our water pouches.

'Stay there,' he shouts.

'Be careful.'

'I will.'

I pull the blanket up and try to get comfortable while I wait for him to come back. I'm really cold, although I can see the hot air shimmering already this morning. Fish does a small, sluggish wiggle. She's been quiet lately. I want to worry about her, to be that kind of mother, but it's taking all of my effort to keep myself alive. It's every girl for herself. Still, I'm glad to feel her move.

Do you know you're special? I ask.

She does a backflip in reply. *How am I going to do this?* I wonder. For the first time I'm starting to think about actually having this baby. If I survive the sickness and the drought, that is. I'll have to give birth, soon, and then I'll have another small human to care for, at least until she brings on the apocalypse.

God, I wish Mum was here.

Wait – maybe she is. Maybe it wasn't just a fever dream.

'Mum? Are you there?' I call out. Nothing. It was just another way for this place to mess with my head, I suppose.

Ali returns a while later. The canteen is full and he's grinning broadly.

'There's a spring! And you know what, Girl, we're nearly out of the desert. There are hills! I saw them in the distance, from where the spring was. The bird's helping us, I don't know why, but it is. I'm going to keep going back to it every morning until you're well enough to walk again...'

I let him chatter away until he finally runs out of power.

'Well done Ali,' I say, smiling. The water tastes fresh, and clean.

'I think we can do this, Girl.'

'I hope so, Ali.'

That night Ali falls asleep as soon as he lies down. I lie awake for a while as usual, staring at the single point of light in the sky.

What will happen to us?

I eventually drift into a restless sleep. After what seems like five minutes I'm startled awake again by a noise.

'It's alright, Rosie.'

My mum is sitting by my side.

'It *is* you. I thought it was a dream.'

'I'm here. I need to help you. You're my little girl.'

I hug her tightly. She smells just like she used to; I inhale her scent.

'Can you stay?' I ask. 'I really need you.'

She shakes her head. 'I don't belong here. Neither do you. You need to leave.' Her voice is soft, the voice she used when I was sick, or sad. 'The place where I am... it's so beautiful. All of the things I used to worry about, they're all gone. Apart from you. I can't rest until I know you're safe, too. Please come with me, away from here.'

I look towards Ali, fast asleep nearby. 'I just can't, Mum. I have to finish something first.'

She grabs my wrists. Her eyes are pleading. 'Rosie, I'm

worried. If you do this, they might not let you come to where I am.' Her voice changes slightly. 'You're making them angry!'

I reach out and touch her cheek. Her skin is soft, as always.

'You're not her,' I say.

She draws back. 'Don't be silly, Rosie. Of course it's me. I'm trying to save you. You don't know what you're doing.'

'No.' I'm sure of it now. 'My mum is the bravest person I've ever known. She got sick and she fought it as hard as she could, with nobody to help her. She kept it away from me for as long as she could. She was amazing. She would never say that to me.'

'Death changes a person,' she said, in a hard voice.

'I know,' I reply, standing up.

October 12 2023. The day my Mother died. She'd become ill a few days earlier. I'd been told to prepare, and to call family, but there was only me. I sat by her bedside for four days. On the second day in hospital she woke up briefly, and she knew. 'I love you,' she said. I didn't say it back. To say it would be admitting she was leaving me. So I didn't. 'You're amazing,' she said. 'You can do whatever you want. And you can get through this. I know you can.' But she was wrong about that.

She stands up too, and for a moment we're just staring at each other. Then, just like that, I'm looking at the other-Jane.

'Humans are so flawed,' she sighs. 'Can't you see, I'm trying to help you? Do you want to cause the end of the world?'

'It shouldn't exist in the first place,' I reply. I'm not afraid of this woman. 'I'm just setting things right.'

She rolls her eyes. 'Oh, very honourable. I suppose Jane has filled your head with lots of rubbish about you having a noble purpose. But I expect she hasn't told you that she could have done this without your assistance. She could have used herself as the trigger, just as easily. Morally virtuous Jane would still rather use an expendable human than put herself into danger.'

I frown. 'That's not true.'

She laughs, unpleasantly. 'I'm not capable of lying, Rosie. That's one of the things which make my species superior to yours.'

Her voice is grating on my every nerve. A tiny seedling of anger starts to grow inside me.

'Even if that's true, it doesn't matter. I'm not giving up. This place needs to be destroyed, and I'm going to do it.'

The other-Jane smiles this smug little smile. 'Mmm. I wonder,' she says.

I stare at her questioningly.

'Have you ever thought about what this noble quest might cost you?' she says. 'Might cost... him?' She points to the sleeping Ali.

'What do you mean?' I ask, fiercely.

'When Jane told you the boy was going to be your protector, I'm afraid she had a very specific purpose in mind for him.'

Suddenly a scene begins to play out in my head, like a memory. Ali and I standing in a steep canyon, surrounded by dark grey rock. The boy is there, and some others, all armed. The boy looks nervous. A large man pushes him out of the way and lunges towards me with a knife, but instead he stabs Ali in the stomach. And I watch as my best friend crumples in front of me, a stream of blood rushing from him.

'No! I won't let it happen!' I shout, tears running down my face.

'That's his purpose, Rosie. I thought you ought to know what you're signing up to.' The woman smiles at me nastily. 'I'll be watching you. Think about it. If you want to spare the boy an agonising death, end this. I promise I'll keep him safe.'

And then she's gone.

I spend the rest of the night sitting next to Ali, watching him sleep. *I can't do this. I can't.*

When he wakes up he knows there's something wrong.

'Why aren't you asleep?'

'I had a bad dream.'

'Oh. Do you feel any better, yet?'

I nod. 'Yes. I think I might be able to walk today.' I've made a decision. 'Ali, you have to stay here.'

'*What?*'

I nod. 'Yes. Jane visited me in the night. She said that it won't work, if you're with me. She said you should stay here, where you can find water. Then when it's all finished I'll come back and find you.' *If the world still exists.*

He looks perplexed. 'Girl – I'm not staying here,' he says.

'But…'

'No.' This isn't the same timid, frightened boy I started this journey with. He's looking at me with a self-assuredness I haven't noticed before. 'I'm staying with you. You're having a baby, you're going to need someone to help you. I'm not leaving.'

I'm not sure what to do. We're staring each other down, until finally he breaks off, laughing.

'What's got into you?' he asks.

I can't hold it in anymore. I'm angry at myself when the tears start up again but I can't stop them. Ali puts an arm around me.

'What is it? What's wrong?'

I start to tell him about what had happened in the night. When I get to the bit about the vision his eyes grow round for a moment, and then he shrugs.

'We're all going to die, here. What does it matter?'

'I won't – I can't…' I can't get my words out.

'Well, I can. And it's my decision,' he says. 'Besides, how do we know she's not tricking you?'

'She said she can't lie.'

'That could be a lie! And even if it isn't, it doesn't mean it's set in stone. Anything could change, especially now we know about it. We have to carry on, Girl. Both of us.'

I know he's right. But I can't stop thinking about what I saw. I have to stop it from happening, somehow.

Boy

I'm sitting by the campfire. Galen is on the other side, eating something noisily, his chops dribbling and slurping. It's like watching one of the donkeys eat.

'What?' He's noticed me watching him.

I shrug. 'Just wondering what you were thinking.'

'I'm thinking you should mind your own business.'

We're not friends, Galen and I. We have established a situation of mutual tolerance. That's why our arrangement will work; he can't wait for an opportunity to stick a knife in me. He'd do it now if he thought he could get away with it.

I'm hungry. There's still a bit of meat left. It's different from our usual fare. Looks like chicken.

'What is this?'

'Bird,' says Boris. He's a monosyllabic sort of guy. It takes me a minute to work out what he means.

'The girl-bird?' I push the dish away. There are some lines I won't cross, then. I've lost my appetite. 'I thought she was spying for us. What happened to that?'

Galen shrugged. 'Tastes good,' he said, lifting up another chunk of Annabelle and shovelling it into his mouth.

'You're disgusting,' I say, standing up. I have to get away from him.

I walk away from the camp. Not too far; I wouldn't want to give the impression I'm reneging on the agreement. I just need to be away from those people.

I haven't thought about my former life much while I've been here, apart from to think *I'm glad that's over.* But tonight I guess I'm nostalgic. For convenience food, and TV, and a hot shower. And Jamesons. God, I'd murder a whiskey right now.

'I'll murder whoever you like for an Old Fashioned,' I shout into the night air.

I wonder if I was chosen for this gig because I spent four years sleeping on the streets. Or if they fucked my life up deliberately to train me for this shit.

Perhaps they just saw something in me that they could use. I've always been pretty cold.

'What are you thinking about?'

Oh. The maths teacher is here. It doesn't take long before they start checking up on me.

'I'm just thinking. About before.'

He sits. Can't they leave me alone for once?

'You had a difficult life, didn't you Niall?'

I don't answer. I don't want sympathy.

'Oh, I don't feel sorry for you,' he says. 'Human life is a different sort of game. It's really not much different from Afterwards. Just a lot more difficult. You did pretty well, given that you had the worst start.'

'Pretty well?' I spit the words out. 'I was homeless when I was seventeen. I was on drugs since I was fourteen. And I was kicked to death before my twenty-first birthday.'

'You did quite well to survive that long, I think.'

Mr Comb-over is annoying me. 'Whatever you've come here to say, get on with it and leave me the fuck alone,' I growl.

He raises his eyebrows.

'You're sensitive about your old life, aren't you?' he says.

I want to swing for him at this point, but I content myself with turning away.

'The girl is recovering,' he says. 'They're going to start walking again. However, the illness has gained us some time. You're only about a day's travel from her current position. Another delay and you'll reach her.'

'What happened to the bird?' I ask.

'She betrayed us,' replies the man, simply. 'Listen, Niall. The girl is almost ready to have the baby. I know you know what will happen if she does. It can't happen. So this time you have to act. Kill her, or your miserable little life on Earth will seem like a beautiful memory compared to what will happen to you here.'

I yawn, loudly. It irks him.

Funny word, irk. Sounds like a small creature, a rodent or something.

'You would do well to take this seriously, Niall. Rosaline…'

'Isn't here.' I'm taking a gamble that this guy isn't the torture type.

'Listen. Things are going to change rapidly. Once she goes into labour both sides are going to have to act. We have to be quicker, and more effective. Oh, and one more thing.'

'Mmm?'

'There's a man living alone in a village a mile or so from here in that direction.' He points. 'You'll pass the village tomorrow. Kill him.'

I raise my eyebrows. 'Who is he?'

'Does that matter?'

I shrug. 'Not really. But I'd like to know.'

'He's a killer.'

'Oh.' *Aren't we all?*

He moves on to giving me this long and boring run down on the route ahead, as if we've just been making small talk instead of ending a man's life. Then he's gone.

After a moment I feel a familiar rumbling coming from the ground. We haven't had a quake for a little while. I decide the smart thing to do is just to sit here and see what happens. Sand is shifting about all around me; I'm in danger of being engulfed. She won't let that happen. Hopefully.

I can hear shouting from the camp. They're panicking.

It's a strange thing; it isn't like a sandstorm. There's no wind blowing the sand up into the air. It's just churning and sliding all around me. I'm swimming in sand, trying not to drown. In the moments I'm not in mortal danger I watch the movement and it's like watching water. It's kind of beautiful, and strangely silent. Then it shifts underneath me and I'm crapping myself that I'm going to be buried alive.

Finally it's over. I walk back to what's left of the camp. Someone has been gobbled up by the sand; one of the mutes. A couple of the others are trying to dig him out.

There isn't too much damage, other than that. Our stuff is made to be taken apart and put back together, so it's fine. The donkeys look a bit spooked and one of them has run off.

'Hey! Gather,' I shout. The two who are trying to dig their friend out look at me, then at each other. Then they shrug and walk towards me. Life is cheap.

'There's a man hiding out nearby,' I tell them. 'He's our next job. We have to find him, assuming he isn't underneath six foot of sand by now. As soon as we've got him we'll be on our way. You, and you,' I point at a couple of the knuckle-draggers. 'Start getting the donkeys loaded up. Everyone else fuck off and pack up. We're off to kill a man.'

Girl

I feel different. In the last week something has changed in me. Lots of things, more accurately.

Physically: Fish suddenly seems enormous. Up until this point I've just been me, with this weird bowl shaped thing stuck to me like it doesn't belong. But all of a sudden it's like I've become all belly, and I'm exhausted. We're still in the desert because I can only walk a couple of miles a day. It's slow, painful progress. Everything hurts. And people do this by choice?

Perhaps I'd feel differently if I was back at home scanning through baby goods online with my feet up on the sofa.

I long for cushions and some crappy TV.

But something else is different too. Since I saw the vision of Ali and we made the decision to continue, it's like something has snapped inside me. I know what I'm going to do. I have to keep going, and have this baby. I know that; it's a physical inevitability. But I'm no longer willing. I'm doing this because I have to, and I'm on the side of us. The weak, the dead, the enslaved. Ali and me.

I'm angry. Really, really angry. At those who did this to us. But at Jane and her allies too, for allowing it to exist at all.

I'm not a virus; I'm a time bomb.

'What's up with you?'

'I'm angry, Ali.'

'You're a grumpy pregnant woman. My auntie was like that.'

'Have you remembered more?'

He nods. 'I think I remember it all, now. My mum and dad, my little sister, my aunts and uncle.' His face clouds. 'I think I did something stupid.'

'Join the club,' I reply.

'I think I know how I died, Girl. I caused it. I had an accident.' He's faraway now, back in another skin, another world. 'I was messing about with some older kids from school. We were on bikes. I was showing off, on the road.' He trails away.

I place my arm around his shoulders. 'I bet most of the people here have got a story of colossal stupidity. I've got loads.'

He's looking down. 'All this, from one small mistake. I didn't deserve this.'

'None of us did.'

'Do you think it *is* a punishment?'

'I don't think they care enough about us to punish us,' I say.

Ali is silent. After a moment he stands up and walks away.

'Are you alright?' I ask.

He doesn't reply.

I'm trying to decide whether to go after him when he comes back. He looks unhappy.

'I made one mistake and this happened to me,' he says, angrily. 'They don't care what else we did. Like all the times I helped my grandma when she couldn't walk very far. Or all of the time I spent with Yana, my baby sister.'

'I don't think they care about us at all, Ali. I think we're just useful to them.'

'What are they? Gods? Aliens? What?'

I shrug. 'I don't know. But I don't think they're as all powerful as they want us to think they are. They don't seem exactly… in control.'

Another day and we should reach the hills. If I can walk at all. I'm starting to feel like Ali's grandma.

'Come on. We have to try,' I say, more to myself than Ali.

It's early morning. This is the best time of day for walking. We should get a good couple of hours hobbling in before it gets too hot.

'I don't even know why we're doing this anymore,' says Ali.

I look at him. 'We're doing this for us. Jane said the place we're heading to is safe. That's why.'

'OK.'

There's a sort of harsh beauty about the desert at certain times of the day. The morning half-light is pale and streaked with blood, as though death has painted the landscape.

We walk, slowly and carefully, through soft sand. After about half an hour I have to stop.

'What's wrong?' Ali is wide eyed with concern.

'Nothing,' I lie.

He gives me his *I-don't-believe-you* look.

'Really. I just need to rest.'

I'm in pain. Fish feels like she's burrowing downwards and I'm cramping like crazy. *Not yet* I tell her, silently. It isn't time.

'Are you scared?' asks Ali.

'No. I have you. Why would I be scared?' We both know that's horse-shit but it feels good to say it.

'I mean of having the baby. Are you?'

I think about this. 'No. I'm really not. I'm more scared about what happens afterwards.'

'Hey. Look!' Ali is pointing, excitedly. 'We're nearly there. Look!'

The sand is thinning out and here and there are patches of brown dirt. There are a couple of trees with actual leaves on them.

'We've made it through the desert!' Ali is almost jumping up and down.

Somehow I know it isn't going to be that easy. Almost as soon as he's finished speaking a low rumble begins.

'Quake!'

Ali's eyes grow frightened. 'What do we do?'

I can tell already that this quake is stronger than the others we've had in the desert.

'What do we *do*?' repeats Ali. I need to think.

'We stop,' I say.

He looks at me questioningly.

'Well, we can't tell where the ground will break, so this is as safe as anywhere. And at least if we're still we're less likely to get hurt.'

We huddle together in the sand as the ground churns nauseatingly.
Crack

The noise is all around us. It feels as if the world is splitting in half.

'Girl! Look! What is that?'

He's pointing into the sky. At first I can't see anything. Then I notice it.

There's a line.

If you put your head this way and tilt it slightly, it's just about visible.

We're just staring at it. The ground is still shaking around us.

'Did it… rip?' Ali asks.

I can't answer because suddenly the ground is shifting beneath us. I grab Ali and hold on as tight as I can. Sand is in my mouth, my eyes, my nostrils. I'm coughing and choking and I'm not letting go of Ali. He's shouting my name over and over.

The quake lessens, and then stops. A tiny rumbling continues for a few moments, then that stops too.

Ali is next to me, coughing up sand.

'Are you alright?' I ask.

He's too busy coughing to answer, but nods.

I lie on my back in the hot sand, and spread my arms and legs out like I'm making a sand angel. I'm staring at the line in the sky which might just be the very beginning of the end of the world.

'Girl?'

'Yes, Ali?'

'I'm hungry.'

We start walking again as soon as we can. We have to get out of the desert quickly now before the hottest part of the day. It takes all of the energy I have to keep going but we do, and after about two hours of walking we're finally on dirt ground again. The trees are increasing in number too, and it looks like we're headed into another wooded area. We decide to set up camp where we are.

Ali goes off to try to find a water source and food. I sit and nurse my sore, well, everything. He's gone for hours. He doesn't return until the light is starting to fade. But he's carrying two weasely creatures and has filled up our bottles.

'I had to track them for ages,' he tells me. 'Like a proper hunter.'

I skin the creatures and we eat them raw. They taste pretty good, and the water is fresh and cool.

'Look at that,' says Ali. The line in the sky looks different in the dark; it's illuminated. Or rather: light is coming from within it.

We're both staring at it, thinking the same thing. *What's behind the sky?*

'Do you think that's how it's going to happen then?' asks Ali. 'The world will just tear apart?'

'How should I know?' I snap.

'Yes. That's how it's going to happen.' Jane is here. 'I haven't got long. I'm not supposed to be here.'

'What's on the other side?' I ask.

'Our domain,' she replies. 'Now listen to me. You're nearly there. The haven I made for you is about three miles away.' She points in the direction of the star. 'Your baby is getting ready. It won't be long now.' *No shit.* 'The other side are going to try every trick in the book to stop you getting there. You need to be really careful from now on. Do you understand?'

I face her. 'When were you going to tell me that Ali's going to die?' I ask.

Her cheeks blanch. 'I... I wasn't going to. Why would I?'

'And is it true that you could have done this yourself? But you chose to use me and Ali because it's more *convenient*?'

She looks worried. Then her face changes to a look of irritation.

'Yes, theoretically I could have put myself in the world. One of our own being placed as a competitor might have had the same effect. *Might.* But what if I had been killed, and it didn't end the world? Who's left to fight the battle?' She looks at me, sadly. 'I know it's hard. But try not to listen to the things they tell you. They're the bad guys.'

'You all are,' I reply.

'That's fine,' answers Jane. 'Just get to where you need to go and don't let them stop you. It might seem you've run out of options, but there's always something. You're strong, Rosie. You can do this, I know you can.'

She turns away and then vanishes. Ali and I huddle together and stare at the sky, with its gateway to another world, until eventually we both fall asleep.

Boy

A line. There's a line in the sky. What the actual fuck.

It's glowing white. Like someone took a star and stretched it out. But I don't think it's that. No.

I think it's a tear. A break. In the fabric of wherever the hell we are. I think the world is breaking apart. And I think she's causing it.

I'm sitting there just looking at it when a shout goes up. One of the hunting parties has found the man. They've brought him back to the camp. He's tied up and a bit battered but he's calmer than any of us. Just sits there in the dirt, like the Buddha of the fucking desert.

May as well get this over with. I feel unnecessarily nervous.

'So you're the secret weapon?' he says to me. He's kneeling in the sand, hands and feet bound. 'You're the tough guy they sent to kill the pregnant teenager.'

'I'm no tough guy,' I say, a bit too defensively. My hands are shaking. Why are my hands shaking? 'Untie him,' I say to the guy at the back. He frowns but follows the order anyway. The man doesn't move.

'Get up,' I say.

'No, thank you.'

'Get up!' I repeat, holding out the knife.

'No.'

I'm panicking a little. 'Leave us!' I bark at the others. They glance at each other and walk away. I tell myself I don't care what they're saying about me.

'I'm going to kill you,' I say. I'm not intending to be menacing. I'm saying it to myself. Problem is, I don't believe me.

'Yes, I imagine so.'

'Don't you care?'

He sighs. 'Sit down, for a moment.'

'Why?' I ask, suspiciously.

'There are some things I would like to say to you, before my death.'

I sit opposite him.

'What's your name?' he asks.

'Niall,' I say. 'But nobody calls me that anyway.'

'Well, Niall. I'm Josef. And you're not a killer. However, you are going to kill me.'

I swallow. 'You're wrong. You don't know what I am.'

He holds up his hand. 'Maybe, maybe. I just don't see it in you. In a fight, yes, perhaps. In cold blood? I don't think so. Why were you brought here, Niall?'

'To kill the girl.'

'Yes, of course. But why you?'

'My life was a mess. I was kicked to death on the street in Manchester. I suppose they thought that might make me angry.' *Why am I telling him this stuff?*

'And are you?'

'Absolutely fucking fuming.'

'At whom?'

'At everyone.'

'Of course you are. And you should be. I am going to give you a gift, Niall.'

'What?'

'My death. In a moment, you will take that knife and you will cut my throat. I will bleed to death in front of you.'

I'm very wrong-footed. 'You – you're asking me to kill you? Do you want to die?'

'Actually, yes. I'm tired. So you are going to do both of us a favour and kill me, in cold blood, in front of all of these people. And then you will be a killer, that thing that you aspire to be.'

'Er – thanks?'

'Don't thank me. I've been what you wish to become for a long time now. I can't live with it anymore. But my release will come at a cost, to you.'

I shrug. 'I won't be agonising over you, if that's what you think.'

'I hope not. But if you do, remember, whatever choice there is in any of this, I choose to die.' He got back onto his knees. 'But,

Niall, please think about this: no matter how powerful these beings think they are, there is always a way to win.'

I stare at him. 'This is how you win,' I say. 'By choosing to die. By wanting to die.'

He nods, slowly. 'Now kill me, please.'

I'm paralysed. He's watching me. 'Go on. It's difficult, I know, but you must.'

And so I do. And it's the worst thing I've ever done.

The others come back over and take the man's corpse away. A couple of them speak to me but I can't, not yet. I've got ringing in my ears and I'm fighting the urge to vomit.

Some killer.

Girl

There's another camp in the distance. We're going to try to avoid it if we can, but the baking sun might make that impossible.

'How many do you think there are?' wonders Ali.

'I don't know. Lots, probably.'

'Do you think they'll see us as monsters?'

'How should I know?'

'But do you *think*?'

'Perhaps. And even if they don't they'll probably still try to kill us.'

He's quiet for a moment. 'So what do we do?'

I sigh. 'I don't know, Ali.' I look around. 'There's a cluster of trees over there, do you see it? If we can get as far as that they'll give us some shade and then we'll be nearly at the hills.'

'OK.' Then: 'But do you think it's safe? What if there are other things in the trees?'

I groan. 'No. It's not safe, Ali. Nowhere is.'

'Alright, alright. Just saying.'

'Well don't. I'm doing my best, that's all.'

He goes quiet. Then: 'You're in a bad mood.'

I stare at him without speaking until eventually he laughs and says: 'Sorry.'

Village or trees. Village or trees. Humans or unseen monsters. Impossible. We start to walk towards the trees. The sun feels hotter than ever. We're being cooked where we stand.

We've walked for half an hour and the woods look no closer. I'm starting to feel sick. We stop and have some water.

'How is that possible?' says Ali.

'What?'

'The village is closer but the woods aren't.'

It's true. We can see the perimeter fence clearly now. We look at one another and sigh. 'I hate this stupid game!' I shout, to nobody. 'We're going to the trees.'

Ali rolls his eyes. 'There's no point!'

'Yes there is.'

We begin walking again. After ten more minutes the trees appear further away, if anything.

'Fine!' I snap. 'We'll go to the village like good little participants. Come on.'

Ali is watching me, half amused and half scared.

We reach the village in minutes. It's empty. Unlike the last empty village we visited this one is falling apart. The wooden shacks are all rotting and filled with sand. The fence has fallen away in places. It looks like it's been silent for a long time.

Still, it's safe enough. Perhaps someone is trying to help us, after all.

'There are no bodies,' says Ali. There's no relief in his voice. Where are the people?

'They might be buried,' I say, thinking of Josef. Could he have travelled this far?

But there's no burial site that we can see. 'Well, it doesn't matter,' I say. 'We stay here for one night and then we carry on.'

'What happened to them though?'

'I don't know.'

My skin is crawling but that's become pretty normal so I ignore it. We choose a hut and spread our stuff out. Make ourselves at home and eat.

We hear it at nightfall. A pitiful cry, like an animal separated from its pack. Another and another. We look at one another in fright. What now?

'Don't worry,' I say. We have weapons. It'll be fine.

'I wish we hadn't come here,' says Ali.

'We had no choice.'

'I know. But I don't like it.'

We sit there and shiver as the light gets less. The wails are getting closer.

'Can we light a fire?'

'It's too late now. Ssh.'

He moves closer and I put my arms around him. We sit and wait.

The first one appears a few minutes later. A small screaming ragged thing, screeching through the centre of the village and then gone.

'What is it? What is it?' Ali's eyes are round.

'I don't know.'

'Was it a person?'

'I don't know.'

Another one. Like the first. Moving too fast, crying into the night as it goes. And then another. But this one runs at us. Ali tries to aim his bow but he's shaking too much. I push his arms down.

'It's OK. Let's see what happens. I'll deal with it if I have to.'

It runs straight at us and then stops. A boy, Ali's age or perhaps even younger. His face is stretched out into this permanent scream of fear. He isn't making any noise at first and then he starts howling like an injured animal. I reach out to him but I don't think he's really seeing me. I touch his arm. He feels cold. He looks down at my hand for a moment, then screams again and runs away.

'What are they?' says Ali for the hundredth time.

We spend a horrible sleepless night in the village, listening to the screams pass by like sirens. None of the others approach us but we're too unnerved to rest.

In the early morning we're gathering our stuff together wearily when I'm pulled to my knees by sudden sharp pain in my side.

'What is it? What's wrong?' His eyes are wide.

'I'm OK. Just pain.'

I breathe it out. After a couple of minutes it subsides. I get to my feet, shakily.

'What was it?'

I don't have an answer for him but I can feel it building again.

'Is it...' He points at my bump.

'I don't know, Ali.' I'm trying not to snap but it's hard. I've had no sleep and I'm hot and exhausted and I want to cry but I can't.

'Why don't you look for some food?'

He looks relieved to have something useful to do and I'm happy not to have to talk. What's happening to me?

156

Just rest. It's going to be OK. Breathe.

I place my hand on my belly. Fish gives a half-hearted wiggle.

The pain is going now, leaving behind a dull ache. I force myself to sit completely still.

Ali comes back much sooner than I expect. He doesn't have any food but his eyes are alive with new information.

'Are you alright?' he asks.

I nod. 'What is it? What have you found?'

'Can you walk?'

I stand, carefully. 'I think so. Not far though. What is it?'

'Come with me.'

I follow him through the beaten up village. At the end is a large hut. Ali gestures for me to be quiet and points inside.

It's dark. At first I can't tell what I'm looking at. It's like a pile of clothes is stacked up at the back of the room. Then I realise it's the people from last night. There are six or seven of them, all sleeping on top of one another like a pack of wolves.

I realise with a jolt that they're all children. Some of them look as young as eight.

They look peaceful now, nothing left of the howling banshees from last night.

We're about to leave when one of them raises her head. We stare in rising panic.

'What do we do?' whispers Ali.

'Just wait.'

'But—'

'I know. But they're just children. And they could have hurt us last night but they didn't.'

The girl sits up. Gradually the others are stirring too. They're looking at us with curiosity. I'm trying to decide if they plan to eat us. I know Ali's thinking the same thing. But if we run it might kick off some sort of prey drive. Better to stay calm.

The girl approaches us. My hand is hovering over my knife. She circles us and then stops in front of me. Her hands reach out to my belly. Ali steps in front of me.

'It's alright,' I say.

The others are up now. They gather around us. Nobody speaks; they just stare at me like they're trying to understand me. And then they take it in turns to touch my belly, curiosity filling their eyes.

We leave the village later that day. Ali's nervous; he keeps glancing over at me and asking if I'm OK. I promise to tell him if I have any more pain and that's a lie; I'm full of pain, but I want to keep walking. It's the only thing that stops me from over-thinking.

'What do you think they are?' asks Ali, after a while. 'The children. Why are they like that?'

'I don't know. What do you think?'

He pauses, like he's trying to put his thoughts in the right order. 'I think – I think they're just too scared. They don't know how to stop being afraid.' He stares at me. 'I would have been like that too, if I hadn't found you.'

'They were the first ones to come here.' Jane. 'When they started this place up they were going to use children only.'

We stop walking. 'That's barbaric!' I'm horrified. 'Why would they do that?'

'Children are very impressionable. And they do what they're told. Plus, they can be pretty cruel.'

'But it didn't work.'

'No. They didn't fight. They just became… well, you saw what they became.'

I feel nauseous.

'Now do you understand why I'm so determined to destroy this place?'

I think about this and subconsciously my hand goes to my belly. An uncomfortable thought is rising in my mind. What if the world *doesn't* end? What if my baby has to live here, in Afterwards?

That thought is enough to make me want to give up right now.

Boy

'Hey.'

A large form blocks the light from the tent entrance.

'What?'

'We need to go. You getting up?'

I turn over.

'Get up. We need to go.'

I'm not moving. I don't have—

'Hey!' The tent is pulled away, then the blanket. I'm left in the sand, curled around myself like a baby. Galen is looking at me scornfully.

'What?' I growl.

'I don't care what you're supposed to be,' he says. 'You're not it. They got it wrong.'

He spits on the floor, right in front of me, then walks off. Something flashes in my head and suddenly I'm leaping on him and wrestling him to the ground. For a massive guy he falls like a sack of shite.

Unfortunately once he's recovered his senses he turns out to be stronger and faster than me. All I have is sheer anger although I have plenty of that. I don't care that he's punching the crap out of me. It's like a release.

By the time some of the others half-heartedly pull us apart I look like a busted couch and he looks… well, normal. He gives me this look like next time he's going to finish me.

'Right! Let's get going,' I say, brightly. Blood is dripping from my nose and my left eye is swelling up. The others are looking at me like I've completely lost it.

Later that day the scouting party comes back to say there's another village in the distance. This news doesn't fill me with joy. More collateral damage.

We reach it in the afternoon. At first glance it seems to be abandoned, which suits me perfectly. Shelter, a night off from pitching the tents.

We haven't been there for an hour when a shout goes up.

I don't get up. I figure if it's something important someone will tell me. This strategy works a treat; by the time I know anything about the group of children they've found sleeping in one of the houses, they've been disposed of, leaving me morally untroubled.

Someone builds a fire. I sit next to it and chew some dried meat silently, staring at the white slash across the sky.

You don't belong, I tell it. Just like her. Just like me.

Another shout goes up. They've found someone else hiding out in one of the houses. This is turning out to be an eventful day.

Girl

When the sun comes up the next day something is different. The sky; it's brighter. I look at the shimmering line in the sky; it's bigger. It's widened overnight and light is spilling out of it.

'It's really bright!' laughs Ali. He spreads his arms out wide, basking in the light.

Even at the hottest part of the day in the middle of the desert the sky stays this twilight grey. All of a sudden it's like someone's flicked a switch. An uneasy feeling is growing inside me, but I push it down and smile at Ali.

'I know.' I look at him in mock-horror. 'Is that what you look like? I'd never have stayed with you all this time if I knew.'

'Hey!' He throws a pebble at me.

'Oy! No throwing stuff at the pregnant…' My voice trails away.

'What's wrong?'

'I feel strange.'

Ali is on his feet. 'Is it the baby? Is it time? What do I do?'

'No, I don't think it…'

I never finish the sentence. Everything goes dark around the edges. The last thing I hear is Ali calling my name.

I open my eyes. At first I can't focus; the light is too bright.

'Has it widened even further?' I ask. Then my eyes adjust.

At first my brain can't interpret what I'm seeing. I stare around nonplussed until it catches up.

I'm in my bedroom.

I'm back home, in my own bedroom. It looks exactly the same as it did on the day that I died. It smells the same. There are dirty clothes on the floor. There's a patch on the wall where the yellow paint has flaked away. And next to my bed, near my pillow I've written my name and his.

I lie down on my bed and bury my face in my pillow. It smells musty and familiar and cosy. I pull the duvet around me. I don't know what's happening but I just want to be here, now, in this place.

'Hello, Rosie.'

Her.

'What do you want?'

She sits on the end of my bed. I don't want her to be here. She doesn't belong in my world.

'We've given you a gift, Rosie. A gift nobody has ever been given, in the whole history of Afterwards.'

I turn over and cover my head with my pillow. Her voice becomes muffled but I can still hear it.

'Don't you want to know what it is?'

I lie there wondering what to do. I just want her to go. But I need to know what's happening. I sit up, reluctantly.

'Go on.'

'We've given you another chance, Rosie. A chance to undo the bad decision you made. A chance to have your life back.'

I swallow. 'So this... is real? I'm not just dreaming?'

She smiles. 'It's entirely real. This is the day you died. You have the chance to make a different choice this time.' She walks over to the bookshelf and picks up my old notebook. 'You had dreams, didn't you Rosie? You wanted to be an artist, and a poet. You can still be those things. You will be. Just be braver this time.'

She tosses the notebook over to me, and then she's gone. I open the book. Inside is filled with drawings and verse. They're pretty good. Maybe I *could* do those things. Maybe.

All of those months of regret and longing for a life stupidly discarded; all of it can be undone. I can have my baby here, where she was meant to be. I don't need anyone else. I can do this.

I'm trying to ignore the word that's shouting in my head, over and over.

Ali.

What will happen to him? How will he cope without me?

The answer to those questions sit like a lead weight in my stomach.

My future is in front of me, bright and shining, like I've just picked it out in a shop and brought it home. Rosie Smith, poet and artist.

Where did you get the inspiration for your work, Rosie?

When I was sixteen I went somewhere far away, and didn't know how to get back. But I finally found my way home.

And perhaps eventually I'll start to believe it was all a dream. Perhaps.

But it wasn't, was it?

Afterwards *is* real.

Suddenly the room doesn't feel cosy anymore. I throw off the duvet and go downstairs. The house is quiet. Mum died about a month ago. The house is always quiet.

There's a stack of mail near the door addressed to Mum. I didn't get around to making any phone calls after she died. I kick them aside and open the door.

The cold air wraps around me. I breathe it in. It smells odd: chemical. I look up into the sky. It's grey and damp. A plane is flying over.

'Are you alright?'

A man is staring at me. I suppose I must look odd, out on the street with no shoes on gazing at the sky.

'I'm fine. I've just been away for a while. I forgot what it was like.'

It's too bright, for a start. It's hurting my eyes.

The man walks away. I go back into my house and put my trainers on. They feel wrong on my feet; scratchy, uncomfortable. But I don't want to draw any more attention.

I know where I'm going. I grab my coat and leave the house.

I still remember the way. I pull my hood as far down as I can over my face and walk on ground that is too hard, too manmade, until I reach the place where you climb over the small fence. I scramble down the hill, avoiding the broken bottles and cans and dog shit.

I'm here. It feels like I remember. It feels like Afterwards. I can still hear a faint drone from the motorway, but if I sit here for long enough maybe it'll be like I'm back there.

Don't get me wrong. I'm not nostalgic. I know the place is just slow death. There isn't much to love about it.

I suppose I'm just so used to being trapped in a cage that being free is terrifying. The world is too big. I've forgotten how to live in it.

I sit for a while and just exist, alone. After a few minutes my thoughts begin to slow down and I can start to untangle them.

Perhaps Ali will be alright without me. He's grown up since we started walking. He has more confidence, and he's good with that bow. Perhaps he can lead a new resistance, without me. Jane will help him. I don't owe anybody anything. I deserve my life back. Mum would want me to take it, I know she would. To live, have my baby, become someone. Not somebody important, just a person living their life, doing good stuff and bad stuff and being in the world. I want that. It's mine.

There's somebody nearby. I hadn't seen him at first. He looks homeless; he's wearing an ancient khaki anorak and a beanie with holes in it. Sometimes they come down here. He's watching me.

It's funny; before I would have been scared of him. Now he just looks like someone trying to survive.

Even so I don't want to chat. He comes over anyway.

'Hello,' he says, sitting down.

'Hi,' I say, looking away.

'What are you doing here, by yourself?' he asks. 'Shouldn't you be at home watching Love Island or something?'

I smile. 'Probably.'

'So, something on your mind?'

I nod. 'A lot.'

'Well, I can spare you a few minutes in my busy day, if you'd like to tell me about it.'

I frown. 'Do you believe in life after death?' I ask.

He raises his eyebrows. 'I was expecting boyfriend troubles, not existential questions. But OK. No, I don't. We're here, and that's it. Thank Christ. I don't want to go through all this again.' He pauses. 'Do you?'

I nod. 'I didn't. But something happened which made me think differently.'

'Somebody close to you die?'

164

I nod. 'My mum.'

He looks away, towards the motorway bridge. 'I had a near death experience, once.'

'Did you? What happened?'

'I used to ride a motorbike. Came off it here, in actual fact. That's why I come here sometimes. Someone saw me and saved my life. A girl, about your age.'

I stare at him. This has to be more than a coincidence. 'It was me. I helped you. I thought you were… dead.'

He looks astonished. 'No. You? Really? You know how long I've been coming here, hoping to run into you?' He clasps my hands. 'It's great to meet you. What's your name?'

I don't answer.

'Well, you don't need to tell me. You probably think I'm a weirdo. And you're probably right. But thank you, all the same.' He grins at me. 'Maybe I can repay you by helping you solve your problem.'

'What problem?'

'The problem which makes a gorgeous young girl sit outside by herself on a cold day in November. Go on, what is it?'

I frown. 'I went somewhere for a while. It was horrible, but I made a friend. And now I'm here, which is good, except I can't help them now. And I can't go back unless I do something terrible.'

He accepts all this much more easily than I expect.

'I've been there,' he says.

'*Have* you?'

'Two years at Her Majesty's Pleasure. Made a few mates. Felt bad and good when I had to leave them. They're OK though. Nobody's ever as important as they think they are.'

I half-smile. A thought occurs to me. 'Did you see anything? When you nearly died?'

He answers immediately. 'Nope. No white light. Didn't see my mam or my old dog waiting. Nothing.' He gives me a searching look. 'You don't look like a jail bird to me. So where is this place? And what do you have to do to get back?' He seems to be joining the dots in his head. 'Why this fixation on death, anyway? Have you had a near death experience?'

'Something like that,' I reply.

He suddenly looks concerned. 'Look – whatever you think you experienced, it was just a dream. Just your brain flashing up random thoughts, and euphoria caused by a lack of oxygen to your brain. It isn't real. So don't be tricked into anything stupid, hey?'

'Perhaps you're right.' *You're so wrong.*

'So what did you see? Was there a light?'

'No. Not much. I think it was Hell.'

The man looks troubled. 'Just a nightmare, darlin, that's all.'

'No.'

'Excuse me?'

I'm talking more to myself now. 'It wasn't a nightmare. I was really there. In Hell. And I have to go back, but I really don't want to.'

The man opens his mouth to speak but doesn't seem to know what to say. I decide I've had enough conversation. I stand up and hold out a hand. 'Nice to meet you. I'm Rosie,' I say.

'Rick. Look after yourself, Rosie. And listen – you don't have to do anything. Nothing's decided. You can decide your own future, OK? And no more talk of Hell, right?'

I leave him and begin to walk into town. It's busy with shoppers wandering around the Christmas markets. It's loud and full and I can smell ten different things. It's making me feel nauseous so I leave quickly. I just keep walking. I instantly feel calmer. I don't know where I'm going and I don't care.

I find a park. It's big and open and quiet. I sit on a bench facing a pond.

Something moves in my pocket.

Shit. My phone. I forgot it even existed. Mum used to complain about me being surgically attached to it.

I take it out of my pocket and stare at the screen. I can barely remember how to use it. I place my finger on the sensor and it unlocks.

I feel like a different person, but my fingerprints are the same.

I have a new message.

It takes a moment for me to realise that's odd. At this point in my life I've lost contact with all of my friends. I have no living relatives that I know of. Nobody calls me. Nobody speaks to me. And nobody messages me.

I tap on the screen and the message pops up.

It's time to go back, Rosie.

Boy

It takes me a minute to recognise him. He doesn't look the same as he did a few weeks back. He's thinner and the guys who caught him have made a mess of his face. It's even worse than mine.

He knows who I am immediately. He's shaking.

'It's alright. You don't need to be scared.'

He's white as sheet but he says: 'I told you last time. I'm not scared of you.'

I raise my eyebrows just enough to show him that I see through him.

'Alright.' I sit down. 'Why are you here?'

He shrugs but says nothing.

'What happened to you?'

'You mean after you burned the village to the ground?'

I nod. 'Yes. I suppose I do.'

He frowns into the distance. 'Why should I tell you?'

'Because there's no reason not to. Look, I'm sorry, OK? I'm sorry I don't play nicely. But that place was a—' I flail about for the right word. 'It was abhorrent. It made me feel sick.'

Conrad gives me a look of pure contempt. I decide to change the subject. 'There's some debate about what we should do with you, you know? Some of them want to kill you, some of them want to set you loose.'

He closes up again. It's like talking to a rock.

'Me, I think we should keep you with us for now. I think you might be useful to us.'

'I won't help you hurt her.'

'No, maybe not. But we'll see. Anyway,' I stand up. 'I can't promise the other guys are going to be very nice to you. Some of them want you dead. But I'll try and keep you alive.'

Nothing.

Two days later and we've almost caught up with them. They're about a half day's ride away when Rosaline appears and brings us to a halt.

'There's been a development,' she says, like she's talking about a business transaction. 'The girl isn't there anymore.'

I'm the only one who groans externally but I can tell from their faces the others are equally thrilled.

'Why? Where is she?'

'She's just… gone. She's no longer in the world.'

Oh. This isn't so bad then. At least we can stop walking.

I'm ignoring the other feeling.

'Right, then. What do we do?'

'Keep going anyway. Find the child and kill him.'

Cold.

'Then what?'

'I expect she will be back before long. At which point we will continue with the original plan. And if not, well, things can go back to the way they're supposed to be.'

There's something about the way she looks at me when she says that. The truth hits me in the face: there's no place for me in the world once the girl's gone. I've been put here as an assassin. I'm an anomaly. Redundant, is the term. Can't be a killer if there's no one left to kill.

'I'm next, is that it?'

'We haven't decided what to do with you, Niall. But if you make yourself useful, there could still be a place for you here. A position of power, even. And on the other hand, if you become a liability, we won't hesitate to remove you.'

My future is laid out in front of me, starkly. Kill the girl and the kid, do what I'm told and I get to live like a good little middleman. Deviate and die.

As soon as she's gone I turn to the others, who all have that frightened rodent look they get after a visit from Rosaline.

'You heard her. Let's go. We've a child to catch.'

When we've been walking for a couple of hours we reach their camp. It's in a wooded area and it's empty.

'Hello?' I call out. 'Hey, kid, come out. We won't hurt you.'

An arrow zips past my ear and lodges itself in the chest of the man behind me. He falls to the ground. The rest of the party ignore him; they're not a sentimental group. We spread out, looking into the trees in the direction of the arrow.

'Hey, come out. We just want to talk.'

Another arrow. This one doesn't connect.

'Listen,' I shout, from behind a large trunk. 'We can just wait. I imagine you've got maybe ten arrows left, tops. There are twenty of us. So however you look at this, there's no way out, kid. Best option is to surrender.'

Another arrow. It hits Galen in the arm and he cries out in pain.

I may as well get comfortable; I think this will take a while.

Girl

A few seconds later another message appears.

Come to the bridge.

I stare dumbly at the phone for a few seconds. What bridge? What does it mean?

There's an old lady by the pond, feeding the ducks.

'Excuse me. Is there a bridge near here?'

She nods, smiling. 'You must mean the old viaduct. That way, about half a mile.'

'Thank you,' I call as I walk away.

'You're welcome, Rosie,' she replies.

I turn back, but she's gone. I start to have that prickly sensation at the back of my neck.

I walk in the direction she indicated. After about ten minutes it looms in front of me. *How have I never seen this?*

It's one of those huge bridges that look like they've grown alongside the landscape. There's a path to take pedestrians and cyclists up to it. As I walk towards it I see a series of signs.

Your life is precious. Don't throw it away.

Things will get better. Talk to somebody who will listen.

As I approach I see him.

'Hello again.'

The man from the street. Is it a coincidence?

'I sent you the message, Rosie.'

No, then.

'Who are you?'

'Somebody who knows what you need to do.'

'Did Jane send you?'

'I sent myself. But yes, we're working for the same thing.'

I'm in the middle of the viaduct now. I look through the wire grille at the landscape. It's pretty, even on this November day.

'You need to go back, Rosie. You must know that.'

I turned around to face him.

'Why must I know that? Why do you people always assume you know what I'm thinking?'

The man placed his hand on my arm. 'I know it's difficult. They wanted it to be difficult. They want you to give up.'

'But – don't you see? That's what I did in the first place. I gave up. I don't want to do it again. I *won't* do it again.'

'Don't you care about Ali?'

'Of course I do.' The tears are streaming now. 'But I can't kill myself. Not again.'

'Perhaps you don't have to.'

'What do you mean?'

'The rules don't apply here.'

The conversation just stops. We stand there looking at each other, with the wind whipping about us.

'I'm not going back,' I say.

'I'm sorry, Rosie, but you are.' There's a tiny change to his tone. It's barely there at all, but I hear it. He looks taller, suddenly. He reaches towards me and I back away, bumping into the barrier.

'Keep away from me.'

'It'll be quick. I know you're frightened. But you're too important for us to lose.'

'No! I don't want to be. I want my life!'

'This is how it has to be.'

He places a hand on my shoulder and suddenly I'm on the wrong side of the barrier. He's standing next to me.

'We can do this together if you want. I'll hold your hand.'

'I won't!' I'm reaching about behind me, trying to get hold of something, anything, trying not to look down. I can hear someone shouting nearby. I move my foot fractionally.

It happens quickly.

I'm not sure if he pushes me or I just slip. I have a brief sensation of terror and that's it.

Boy

I'm getting really bored now. It's been almost a full day. Why can't we find him? The woods aren't that big.

He seems to move around. Arrows have been coming from four different directions. They've stopped now, so I think he's run out, finally. I have no way of knowing for certain if he's even still here. I think he is though. He's probably hoping she'll come back.

I wonder where they've taken her. Is she dead? I mean, deader? That has to be it, I suppose. Except, if they could do that, why wouldn't they have done it earlier? They're a tricky bunch, my lot. Not to be trusted. Clever though.

'Why don't you just leave him? He's just a kid. What harm can he do?'

Conrad. He's like an annoying conscience.

'I have my orders,' I say. Truth is, I'm not thrilled about it either. I wish they'd find me a mark I actually want to kill.

Like Conrad, perhaps.

He no longer shakes when he sees me. I've been spending a bit of time with him because frankly, I need someone to talk to who isn't a knuckle dragging psycho or a mute. That doesn't mean that he doesn't irritate the bejeezus out of me most of the time.

'Hey. How are you?' I ask.

'How do you think I am?'

'OK. Let's skip that bit.' I make myself comfortable. 'Tell me about the girl. What's she like?'

He stares at me. 'Why are you always asking about her?'

'I want to know what I'm up against.'

'I won't help you.'

'You don't have to tell me her weak points. I'm just interested. What's she like?'

'She's brave. She knows what she needs to do and she doesn't hide. She's better than me.' He frowns. 'What's this really about?'

'Nothing. I told you, I'm just interested.'

'It's more than that. You have this weird obsession with her.'

I jump up as if I've been bitten.

173

'Don't be stupid.'

'No, it's true. You only ever want to talk about her.'

I start to walk away. Then I stop. 'She's gone, did you know?'

'What do you mean?'

'Rosaline told me she's no longer here.'

He looks at me. 'She's dead?' He doesn't sound upset. He sounds relieved.

'I don't know. She's been taken somewhere else, I think.'

A shout goes up around us. I think they've finally found him.

'On my way.'

He's in one of the smaller, denser trees, near the top. We send some arrows up but there's too much foliage in the way. He's wedged himself in behind some branches.

Galen starts trying to make a fire underneath it.

'No, no, no. Everything's dry. The whole area'll go up.' His hand is still twitching but I'm not sure if he wants to continue with the fire idea or reach for his knife. For me. 'One of us is going to have to go up,' I say. Nobody moves. I roll my eyes. 'Alright.'

I haven't climbed a tree since I was ten. It's harder to do when your limbs are long and you're not too supple. I get about half way up and stop for a minute to catch my breath. 'You could just come down,' I shout to the boy. 'It'd save me a lot of effort. We're going to get you in the end.'

I receive a blow to the head from something like a large acorn.

'You're starting to annoy me.'

I move up another couple of branches and stop again. I'm scratched everywhere.

'Why don't you join us? The girl's gone. She left you. We'll protect you.'

'I'm twelve, not stupid.'

'Fair enough. Well, we're going to get you anyway. It's just a matter of time.'

'I don't mind. I'll wait here.'

Frustrating little—

'She didn't leave me,' he adds.

'Oh. Are you sure? I mean, it looks like she did to me.'

'She was taken. She wouldn't have gone if she had a choice.'

'Right. No, course not. Only…'

'What?'

'Well, I don't think they're allowed to kill her. And I don't think this place allows us mortals to just disappear and reappear. That's their thing. So, it's strange. I just think…'

'What?'

'She killed herself once, right? I think she did it again. Couldn't take it anymore.'

'It's not going to work. I know she didn't do that. She vanished in front of me.'

Stubborn little shite.

I'm trying to figure out how to get past the twisted branches in front of me when suddenly this gets pushed down in my list of priorities. There's a tremendous cracking sound and everything starts to shake. I cling to the tree with everything I have. I think I have a better chance up here than falling fifteen feet onto the ground. I glance up at the kid. He looks petrified.

'Bet you wish you got down now, you little shit,' I shout, but my words disappear into the noise and chaos.

Then everything becomes dust and sound and bright, bright light and I feel myself falling while still clinging. I think I'm knocked unconscious at that point. I wake up a few moments later, still in the tree, but the tree is now uprooted and resting precariously against one of its brethren. Every part of my body hurts. I don't think anything's broken though.

'Hello? Anyone there?'

I climb out from between the branches awkwardly. I see Galen and a couple of the others, picking themselves up. There are two, no three people just lying there amongst the debris. I look around for the kid but he's gone.

'Dammit!' I shout, to nobody. 'Why are there still earthquakes anyway? I thought she was causing them?' Something clicks. 'Does this mean she's back?'

'Yes. She is.' Rosaline.

I climb down the trunk, wearily. 'Well, where is she?'

Rosaline smiles. It's a strange sight. I'm reminded of that creepy arsed Japanese bird sculpture that was all over the internet a few years ago. She looks like she's about to devour something. Possibly me.

'She's close. Very close, in fact.' She pauses. 'Things are going exactly as I had hoped. She's losing faith in her side. It's time to capitalise on that.'

She outlines her strategy. It's clever. I can tell she's not telling me everything, though.

'Do you think you can do your part in all of this?' She sounds weary.

'Yeah. Fine.'

'Good.'

And she's gone. I wonder what happened. And if I'll ever find out.

This place is beginning to lose its novelty. I'm weary from the constant walking and I'm becoming seriously tired of Rosaline's bad tempered face looming over me when I least expect it. It'll be over soon, one way or another.

I'm asleep when the cry comes. Suddenly footsteps are everywhere. I get up slowly. There's never anything that urgent.

I walk over to the place the others have gathered. Oh, OK.

'I don't know how he did it,' says Galen, pathetically. 'I was here the whole time.'

'Well, somehow he did,' I say, enjoying this immensely. 'Maybe you fell asleep?'

He gives me a really nasty look.

Conrad is gone. All that remains is that old cloth he was using to stop the bleeding from his leg wound.

'Anyone else see him go?' I ask. A couple of the others shake their heads.

I send a couple of them out to scout around. 'He might still be close. He's pretty beaten up. He probably can't walk fast.'

Galen is still standing at his guard post, looking miserable.

'I was here the whole time,' he repeats.

I almost feel sorry for him. Almost.

I go and sit by the fire and get some food. I sit there alone, chewing on a piece of meat, thoughtfully. I'm realising something. Perhaps I'm starting to get the hang of this place. I'm finally understanding how it works.

This whole episode has a definite whiff of them about it. I'm sure Galen is telling the truth; he was standing guard all night. And yet Conrad is gone.

The question is, did our side take him or theirs?

I poke the fire with the tip of my boot and a piece of wood falls into the ash, causing a cloud of smoke to rise. I'm barely seeing it. I'm thinking.

Girl

I wake up screaming. In my head I'm still falling. After a moment I realise where I am. The screams turn into sobs.

I don't want to be here.

But, here I am. I cry quietly for a minute or two and then it just stops. Numbness, weary resignation replaces anger and frustration.

I suppose my body is now at the bottom of the bridge. I'll probably make the local newspaper.

I'm naked. This isn't such a problem here; it's much warmer than the place I first woke up in, all of those months ago. And I'm alone, apart from Fish.

Hello again.

I look down at my enormous stomach. My belly button is sticking out. Ugh. Fish does a wiggle and I see ripples under my skin. I stroke my skin, gently.

After a couple of minutes I start to look around for my pack. I find it pretty quickly. There are some clean clothes in there, and a few days' rations. Overall, re-death has worked out quite well for me. Except.

Two things. First, I don't know where Ali is. I know I have to find him before I do anything else.

Second, when I do find him I'm going to have to deal with the crushing guilt that comes from knowing that I didn't want to come back to him. That I was prepared to leave him here, alone. I chose my life over Ali. There's no way to avoid it; it's a big, ugly fact.

Anyway, I'll deal with that when I come to it. Firstly I need to find him. I need to make sure he's safe.

I have no way of knowing where I am, until someone turns up and tells me. Do they place us where we wake up or is it random?

We had just reached the woods when they took me. I can see some woods in the distance, but who knows if they're the same? There are no landmarks. But the air is warm. I think that's a good sign.

I know I can't stay here. It's too open. Once I'm dressed I decide to walk in the direction of the trees, just to have a purpose. As I walk

I begin to feel a familiar rumbling beneath my feet. I drop to the ground.

There's a loud cracking sound above my head and everything begins to shake violently. Fissures are forming in the ground all around me. I can see trees being uprooted in the woods. I crouch on the ground, arms around my belly, head down, just waiting for it to stop. Just stop.

It does, but not before I'm thrown over. I land heavily on my back and just lie there, like a tipped cow.

There's a huge rip in the sky, now. Behind it is white light. As I stare at it I think I can see things moving inside it, but I can't be sure.

I try to stand and remember it's not that simple. I roll onto my side and perform a sort of scrambling movement and pivot myself upright. Ali would be falling about laughing if he could see me. Actually, he would probably have helped me to stand.

It isn't that I didn't want to come back for him. I did. I just couldn't face what I needed to go through to get back here. Somehow that distinction doesn't help my conscience.

'Hello, Rosie.'

Jane.

'You're back,' I say.

'And so are you.'

I look down. I didn't want to come back.

Jane sits, and gestures for me to join her.

'I wanted to make sure you're alright,' she says. 'What you've been through must have been tough.'

I raise my eyebrows. 'No. I'm not alright. But thanks for asking.'

Jane looks concerned. 'Well, I suppose I deserve that. I suppose we all do. But you do understand, don't you? Why we had to bring you back?'

I don't answer. Jane takes hold of my hand. 'Let me ask you something. Why do you think they did it? Gave you your life back?'

I frown. Why did they? 'To get rid of me.'

Jane shakes her head. 'Think about it Rosie. As a strategy, it wasn't very effective. They knew we'd bring you back. They were counting on it.'

'What do you mean?'

'I mean, I highly doubt they were even allowed to send you back there. If we hadn't retrieved you they'd have been in terrible hot water. But they knew you were too important for us to just leave you there.'

'Retrieved me.' I spat the words out. 'You killed me.'

'We had to, Rosie. There was no other way.' She paused. 'Aren't you curious as why they'd go to all that trouble, if they knew it wasn't going to work?'

I shrug. I'm acting like a sullen kid and I don't care.

'For this, Rosie.' She gestured towards me. 'They want you to be angry at me. At us. It's their best hope. If you're no longer on our side, they have a chance. They've split you apart from Ali, made you betray him, and made you hate the cause you're working towards. I'd say they've done a terrific job of putting a spanner in the spokes.'

I stare at her, rearranging the past few days in my head. It's true. They never intended to give me my life back. They just wanted to make me really, really long for it. And it worked. I walked right into their trap.

'You have every right to be angry,' says Jane. 'But it's misdirected.'

'Is it?' I turn to her. 'I think it's directed exactly where it belongs. All of you. Not just them. You're all manipulative. You turn up here and give us instructions and expect us to follow them, because you've decided that's what's best. You're right, I am angry.'

I turn my back on her.

'I'm sorry,' says Jane, softly. 'But your job is more important than your life. I thought you understood that. You need to get to the place, and soon Rosie. The baby is going to come, and you have to be… just make sure you're there.'

'I…' I turn back to her but she's gone. However, in the distance I see a different figure.

'Ali!'

He breaks out into a run when he sees me. I can't run. I stand, with my arms wide. He comes flying towards me, crying and smiling and shouting.

'Girl! I thought you were, I thought...'

We hug and hug and I'm crying too and I can't tell him why.

'Where were you? Where did they take you?'

I tell him as much as I can. I tell him about my room, and the world being the same.

His eyes are wide. 'I can't believe it. How did you get back?'

He's just assumed I found a way back to him. It hasn't occurred to him that I wouldn't have tried to return.

'They killed me. Jane's people. They found me and killed me. She said that that was their intention all along. The other side. They wanted to mess with my head.'

'I'm so glad you're back. I really missed you! But you should have seen me, Girl. I shot arrows at that boy and all of his group. They couldn't find me because I kept climbing between the trees...'

I let him chatter on. My heart feels like a lead weight in my chest. I can't tell him. Not ever. It would break his heart, almost as much as it's currently breaking mine.

We go back into the woods to look for somewhere to camp. The boy's around here somewhere so we're constantly vigilant. The place we settle down in is surrounded by dense bramble apart from the small gap where we got in, so we should see them immediately if they approach.

I'm thoughtful. The events of the last few days have been emotionally exhausting. I'm tired of being batted around in their games.

We eat, and Ali goes to sleep. I get the feeling he didn't sleep much while I was gone because he's flat out and snoring a few seconds after curling up next to me. I stay awake and stare at the white wound in the sky.

I sit there for hours, thinking about them and us and how we've been manipulated, and about how, despite their power, everything they have built rests on one human girl and her baby. And I think about my mum.

She and her parents had arrived in Manchester from Lebanon when she was four. They had nothing, but she'd studied and worked. When she got pregnant with me, that could have been the end for her career but she'd refused to let anything, even me, get in the way. Somehow she'd found the time and the energy to be an amazing nurse and a great mother. A really great mother.

When she first felt ill, she'd been working night shifts. She assumed she was working too hard. Besides, she didn't have time to get checked out properly. She took something and forgot about it. This happened more than once. By the time she realised there was a real problem – well, you know the rest.

I'm tired. Of trying to do the right thing. Of toeing the line. Of doing what other people expect of me.

A noise from the woods makes me suddenly alert. It sounds big. Is it an animal or a human? Is it the boy?

I shake Ali gently, and gesture for him to be quiet.

'What is it?' he whispers. I place a finger to my lips and point towards where the noise came from. We both reach for weapons and just watch, silently.

My mouth drops open as I watch Conrad, bloody and disorientated, stumble into the clearing. He sees me and the blood drains from his face before he collapses in front of us.

Boy

We're walking again. Forwards on cut feet through dust and exhaustion. We're reaching the end of the road in more than one sense. Everyone's had enough. Nobody's talking anymore. We're just zombies, walking because that's the only thing we can think to do.

The landscape is rocky here. There are hills in front of us. Rosaline says that's where the girl's heading, to have her baby. I don't like the look of the landscape, although it's hard to put my finger on why. The hills are dry and dead, like the bones of an army of huge animals that've been left to bake. A few wiry trees and some scrub here and there.

We reach a valley by nightfall and decide to set up camp. There's no reason not to. There's a tiny mountain spring where we can refill our flasks and we have room to spread out. Still, I'm uneasy. I just don't know why.

It's hard to trust your instincts when you live under constant threat.

The last of the light disappears over the hills and then we're left with the crackling firelight. Nobody's speaking. We're sitting apart from one another, eating whatever we each have left of our rations, some of us by the fire, some in the shadows. I'm stuffing this dried tasteless cracker stuff into my mouth and trying not to think about how meaningless it all is, when there's a shout. One of the men, in the dark. He isn't saying words but the sound that's coming from him is terrifying.

In seconds we're all up and gathered round him. One of the others has had the intelligence to grab a branch and light it, so we can see him pretty well. His leg is stuck in the ground – he can't pull it out and from the sound of him he's in agony.

A few of the bigger guys start pulling him and eventually with a sickening scream they get him out, or at least most of him. The flesh has been eaten away from his foot, leaving only bone, flapping uselessly. The guy is screeching like a banshee. We all stand about uselessly for a minute or two and then one of the guys who pulled him out breaks his neck in a single movement.

We fall back into eerie silence and this time nobody's eating either.

Moments later another man starts screaming.

'They're underneath us! They're everywhere!'

This time there's no running to help. Every last person grabs their pack and sprints out of that pass. The man who shouted is the exception. He doesn't move. The last time I see him he's covered with what looks like a grey blanket. He's being eaten.

It isn't until we're at least half a mile away that I remember the donkeys. They have all of our stuff, including what's left of the food. And we left them there, with whatever that was.

Girl

Ali rushes over to Conrad. 'You're hurt.' He's bleeding a lot from a wound on his leg and he looks like he's taken a beating.

'Where have you been?' I ask. He shakes his head but doesn't reply. The food Ali has brought sits there in front of him, untouched.

'How did you find us?' He ignores this, too.

'Let him rest,' Ali says. I take the food off him. No point in wasting it.

He just sits there, in the middle of our camp, with a haunted look on his face. I don't like looking at him.

I wish he hadn't come back. He made his choice.

Ali's a nicer person than me. He's taking care of Conrad, cleaning his wounds and giving him water. And gradually he seems to come back to himself. He still isn't talking, above saying thank you and yes and no, but he looks less intense. Except every now and again he looks at me and it's there again. The look of fear.

Ali takes it all in his stride. He spends his days hunting and caring. I think he's actually enjoying it.

After a couple of days of Ali's kindness, Conrad finally speaks.

'When you left the village they came,' he says. 'A day later maybe. Marched in there, expecting to be fed. And then when they saw we had nothing – they set the place on fire. Some of the others didn't even run. They just sat there, let the fire consume them.' He shivers. 'I left. I don't know how I stayed alive. I don't remember eating anything. I didn't hunt. I just walked.'

'How did you get hurt?' asks Ali. Conrad winces, whether from real or remembered pain I can't tell.

'I met a group of mutes and we stayed together for a while. We were attacked, by an animal. I survived again, somehow. The rest didn't.' He takes a breath. 'I just remember walking in desert with blood dripping from me,' he says. 'I found shelter. A village. But then they found me.'

An alarm bell rings somewhere.

'Who?' I ask.

'The boy. His people. They found me and brought me to their camp.'

'Why would they do that?' I wonder.

'Did they hurt you?' asks Ali.

He nods. 'They beat me. But the boy… he didn't hurt me. He wasn't what I expected.' He raised his head. 'He kept coming to me, just to talk. About you,' he says.

I scoff, incredulous. '*What* about me?'

'Just you. What you're like. He wanted to know everything I knew about you.'

'So it's easier to kill me.'

'No. It's more than that.'

He stops talking. I can tell he's exhausted.

'You should rest,' I say.

He takes a few deep breaths.

'I had a dream, the night after you left the village. It was really strange.' He pauses. 'She showed me. What we are.'

He's staring at me with such intensity it's frightening.

'And what are we?' I ask, warily.

He sighs. 'We're nothing.'

Ali and I glance at each other.

'What do you mean?' I ask.

'I mean, we're nothing. Our lives, they don't matter. We're empty vessels.'

I place a hand on his arm but he shrugs it away. 'Conrad, whatever you think she showed you…'

'No. It's true. I saw it. I'm nothing. He's nothing.' He points at Ali. 'We don't matter because we're not really here. We're just shadows '

'No.' I raise my voice. 'That's not true. You can't trust her. She twists things.'

'She explained to me. They were helping us, the empty ones, giving us a last chance at life before our spirits were gone. Nobody really got hurt because there was nobody *to* get hurt.'

I stand. I've had enough of this conversation. 'Get some rest,' I say.

'Don't you understand?' he calls after me. 'You're destroying the world for nothing.'

186

I daren't risk the woods in the dark but I have to get away from Conrad. Ali too, if I'm honest. A few months ago I'd have climbed a tree but I guess that's out now that I'm the size of a hill. There's a space behind a tree at the back of the clearing where I can sit for a while. I rest with my back to the trunk. I can't see the sky from here, but you can't have everything.

Even if what Conrad says is true, it doesn't change anything, I tell myself.

Except it does. It changes me. It changes Ali.

She's just trying to mess with your head. I know that. The problem is, it's working. My head is in a mess.

Is it true?

I stare down at my huge belly. 'What do we do, Fish?' I ask. She does a flip, in reply.

'Girl?'

Ali appears in front of me. He looks like he's been crying.

'Girl, is it true? Am I just… a ghost or something?'

I put an arm out and give him a hug. 'You feel real to me,' I say.

He seems comforted. 'I… I can feel my body. I can think. So I must be real, right?'

I nod. 'She twists things. Whatever we are, all of us, it's different from what we were before. But that doesn't mean we're not real.' I bite my lip. 'And Conrad… he's damaged. He's scared. Try not to worry too much about what he says.'

Ali looks a bit happier. After a while he goes back to the clearing to try to get some sleep, leaving me with my thoughts.

My mind casts about for something different to think about and it fixes on what Conrad had said about the boy. It seems clear to me that he's not right. There's a strange neediness about him, despite his bravado. I don't understand him at all. A year ago I might have thought he was harbouring a secret crush on me, but not here, not now. And not while I look like Moby Dick.

No, it must be something else. I remember reading stories of assassins becoming obsessed with their mark. Like a reverse Stockholm syndrome. It must be that.

Boy

There's virtually nothing left of any of them when we return in daylight. Whatever was eating them has done a thorough job. I see a metal buckle and a few tin plates which had been in the donkey's packs. They've been devoured.

Here and there on the ground are the dried out corpses of insects. I pick one of them up, carefully. It's tiny, about the size of an ant. There must be millions of them, waiting under the ground for someone to come by. I shudder, despite myself.

She's nearby.

We moved on from the valley immediately. None of us wanted to become the next meal. So we picked up what we had left and walked on, tired, demoralised.

We're near the end, at least. This is important. I can't mess it up. I fucked up pretty much everything in my actual life, but I think it would have ended up that way no matter what I did. Here is different. I hope, anyway.

We have a plan, of sorts. We know where they are, now. They're in a clearing about half a mile north. Surrounded by foliage. It'll be hard to get in there without them seeing us, so we're going to…

'Hi.'

What. The. Fuck.

She's here. She's standing in front of me.

I look around. The others are nowhere to be seen.

'They're dealing with Ali,' she smiled. 'He's getting good at being evasive.'

'Don't I know it,' I say. I'm bemused. 'Why are you here?'

'You were going to come to us, weren't you? To attack us? I thought I'd save you the effort.'

'Erm – thanks? But why?'

She sits. My god, she's massive. That baby's going to pop out any second.

'I wanted to meet you. Without either of us trying to kill the other.'

188

'Really.'

I'm in a tensed up hunch, like a nervous meerkat.

'Why don't you sit?' she suggests.

I do, and immediately regret it. I don't want her to think she's the one in control. So I stand again. She looks puzzled.

'What?'

'I… I'm just more comfortable standing,' I say. 'What do you want? I mean, really.'

'I just want to find out who you are,' she says.

'Hell of a risk, isn't it? Just to get to know me better.'

She shrugs. 'Everything's risky.'

I wipe my sweaty palm on my hair and hold out my hand to her. She looks at it warily.

'I'm Niall,' I say.

She shakes my hand lightly. 'I'm… Rosie. But nobody calls me that now.' She stares at me, this really direct, unnerving stare. I stare back, hoping she can't see me sweating.

'So what do I call you?'

'Girl.' She takes a breath. 'Are you going to kill me, Niall?'

I nod. 'That's the plan. Kill you, save the world. That's how it's supposed to go. Heroic, when you think about it.' I'm gabbling. She looks unimpressed.

'What were you in life?' she asks.

'Why do you want to know?'

She shrugs. 'Conrad told you about me. Seems only fair I find out about you.'

'I was nothing in life,' I say, moodily. 'This place is working out better for me though.'

'I'm very happy for you,' she says. 'Did you kill yourself?'

The question takes me aback for a second. 'No. Kicked to death. You?'

'Yes. I killed myself. I think we've all caused our own deaths in one way or another.'

I consider this. 'Yep. I suppose I did. Been killing myself slowly since I was a kid. Just took some bastards to finish me off. So… that's why we're here? Like a punishment?'

189

'Who knows? It's a game! Did you know that?'

I nod. 'Yeah, she said something about that.'

'Doesn't it bother you? That we're doing all of this for their amusement?'

I shrug. 'Not really. It's an improvement in my circumstances. At least when I die here someone will notice.'

She gives me a sour look. 'So that's all you care about? Someone giving you some attention?'

'More than I had before.'

She stands, with some difficulty. 'Alright. I just wanted to find out who we're up against.'

'So, that's it? Truce over? Next time we see each other...'

'...One of us will die,' she finishes. She smiles. I smile back. It's weird, but it feels pretty good.

'Alright then,' I say. And she leaves. I sit there for a couple of minutes, more conflicted than ever. And then...

'Niall.'

Uh-ho.

'You're thinking of betraying me.' It wasn't a question.

I brace myself for pain but it doesn't arrive. Instead she hovers over me with that weird Momo smile on her face. She touches my cheek, gently.

'Humans. You're odd little creatures. That's what makes Afterwards so interesting for our people. We can never quite predict how you will react to things. For example, nobody in my world expected you to develop feelings for the girl. It makes no sense at all.'

'Wait,' I say. 'Are you saying that people watch us? I mean, other people besides you?'

'Of course. What would be the point, otherwise? It's mainly for the fighting, but sometimes the more sentimental among my kind become interested in your little affairs. It may interest you to know that you're something of a hero, among certain members of my species.'

'What are you?'

'We are just a different kind of being. Think of us rather like a more evolved version of yourselves. We exist on a different plane, and have learned how to manipulate the universe around us.'

'Are you gods?'

'To you we are.'

I fold my arms over my chest. 'Not to me.'

She smiles, coldly. 'I see.' I'm push down onto my knees.

'The thing I think you don't understand, Niall, is that you're lucky. You're already on the only side that can possibly win. What do you think will happen, if the girl has her baby?'

'The world will end.'

She inclines her head. 'Yes. The world ends. Does that mean the end of Afterwards?'

Realisation dawns on me. 'You're just going to start it up again, somewhere else.'

'Precisely. But better, and with fail-safes to prevent this kind of thing happening again. The game will go on, regardless of the opinions of my opponents.' She laughs, drily. 'So, choose your side well.' She pauses. 'And just in case you're tempted to any form of rebellion, remember this, Niall—' I'm pushed flat, face down in the mud. I feel like I'm being ground underneath the heel of somebody's shoe. 'It would be entirely futile. You can't fight a god and win.'

Girl

I return to the clearing and wait for Ali. Conrad is just sitting there, staring. He unnerves me. It's like he's broken. I make no attempt to talk, just walk by him and flop heavily by a tree.

Ali gets back around an hour later, his face flushed and full of excitement.

'You should have seen their faces. At first I shot from behind them, and then I climbed across this thick branch, to… hey, what's wrong?'

The pain must be written across my face. 'Nothing. I just…' The suddenness of the pain makes me stop.

'Are you… do you think…?' Panic fills his eyes. 'What do we do?'

'Be calm. It's alright. It's gone now.' I shift myself about to make sure. I breathe out. 'It's gone,' I say again, more to myself.

Ali is looking at me nervously. 'Sit still. I'll get you some food.' He's back in mother-hen mode, his excitement forgotten. He brings me the remnants of a couple of squirrels he caught earlier that day. 'Eat.'

I divide the meat into three. Conrad takes his share without a word but Ali shakes his head. 'No. The rest is yours.'

'Ali, I'm fine. You need to eat too. How will you look after me if you get sick?'

He reluctantly accepts a small portion.

'You're all bones,' I say, poking him in the ribs. He squirms away. He still looks worried.

'I'm alright, honestly,' I say.

I'm nervous though. I wish my mum was here. I haven't got a clue what to expect.

'You need rest,' Ali says.

'I need a tub of Ben and Jerry's,' I say.

Ali laughs. 'And a pizza.'

'Mmm. Yes. With tuna.'

'That must be a pregnancy thing. Nobody normal would put tuna on a pizza.'

192

'Hey! It's good. Don't knock what you haven't tried.'

Our bellies seem even emptier with all of the food talk but it still feels good, so we carry on.

'Chips and cheese,' he says.

'What? You weirdo. Who eats chips with cheese?'

Our fun is interrupted, as always. Suddenly Jane is standing in front of us. Our smiles die on our faces as we take in her expression.

'What is it?'

She turns to me. 'I know you know how close they are, so I won't bother telling you. And I also feel sure you must know how dangerous your little adventure was. Why would you take a risk like that?'

I shrug. 'I wanted to know who we're up against. He knows all about me. It seems only fair.'

Jane shakes her head. 'I will never understand your species. Why take such an unnecessary gamble? He could have killed you there and then.'

I fix a level gaze on her. 'Well, perhaps I'm past caring.'

Her eyes narrow. 'You have to be more intelligent than this Rosie. You know what's at stake.'

Fury wells up in my chest. I have to bite it back. 'Well, I'm still alive. To destroy the world another day.'

Jane takes a breath. 'Whatever issues you have with me or your job don't matter a jot. This is bigger than either of us. It's important, Rosie.'

My job. Makes it sound like a Saturday shift at McDonalds.

She's drawing something in the dirt. A map.

'You haven't got much time left. The pain you're having is a sign.' She points at a stone on the ground. 'This is where you are now.' She draws a long line. 'That's the way you need to go.' She squints upwards, towards the streak of unnatural light in the sky. 'You can follow that thing,' she says. 'It's directly over the place I need you to get to. The centre of the world. Once you're there, you'll be safe, until… the end. But until then I expect them to throw everything they have at you.'

She turns around and looks at Conrad. 'You can't trust him,' she says.

Conrad looks at her without looking at her. His eyes are empty.

'What's wrong with him?' I ask.

'This happens sometimes. He's been here for a long time. The candidates are only supposed to be around for two or three years. When they survive longer than that, well sometimes…'

'The *candidates*?' I stand up painfully, spitting the words out. 'You designed this place so that if it didn't kill us it would eventually drive us insane? What are you? What is wrong with you?'

Jane gives me a solemn look. 'Hold on to that anger, Rosie. Remember that's why we're doing this. It's time for the game to end. Only you can do that.'

I roll my eyes. 'Lucky me.'

Jane places a hand on my shoulder. 'I know it's hard. I don't know if it makes a difference to you but one of the reasons we picked you is we saw a rare strength in you. Very few people could have done what you've done.'

'I'm not strong,' I snap. 'I'm surviving. That's all.'

Jane gives me a sympathetic look which irritates me all the more. 'That's all you need to do. Just keep going.' She pauses for a moment, thoughtfully. 'Pass me the backpacks,' she says.

I do it without question. Maybe she's going to give us some more supplies. That would be nice.

'Thank you.' She stands. 'You'll do this last part without them. That way I can be sure you won't waste any time getting to where you need to be. If you go there directly and find water on the way you'll be fine.'

'You must be crazy!' I explode. 'My weapons are in there. Blankets for the cold.'

'Like I said. Motivation to hurry to the checkpoint. I'll give you all of this and more when you get there.'

'You're leaving us defenceless!' I fume.

'I would never do that, Rosie. And you're resourceful. More than you know.' She gazes at me for a moment, her eyes thoughtful. 'Rosie, I need you to remember something. It's important.'

'What?' I growl.

'Just this. When you get stuck, which you will, try looking beneath the surface of things.' She says this part very deliberately.

I frown. 'I don't know what you mean.'

'No. But you will.'

And then she's gone, leaving us with nothing but the clothes we are wearing.

After she leaves I sit by myself for a while. There are two reasons for this. The first is that my body feels like it's covered in lead weights. The second is that it's a small victory, in my head. I will go to the place where I will die. But I'll do it in my own time, thank you.

The problem is, she's right and I know it. This baby isn't going to wait till I'm good and ready. So after maybe half an hour I stand, painfully.

'Come on, then,' I say. 'We'd better go.'

Ali stands. Conrad sits uselessly staring into nothing.

We begin to walk in the direction Jane has sent us. It's still hot, even though we're no longer in desert, so we take our time and keep looking out for water as we go. Every now and again I get a pain throughout my abdomen, like someone's squeezing it. It's not so bad, so I keep it to myself.

We walk throughout the morning, continually looking up into the sky for reassurance. The long white streak sits above us, a constant reminder of our purpose. *Who's behind there*? I wonder. What do they do? Do they live ordinary lives, like us? Does everybody sit around in togas drinking wine from goblets? And what do they think of humans? Most likely they don't think of us at all, otherwise how could they do these things?

After a few hours we find a brook and decide to stop for a while to refill our flasks. Ali goes off in search of an animal he's spotted, leaving me alone with Conrad. I don't plan to speak to him and am settling down to rest when he says, 'Girl,' in a soft voice.

I open my eyes and look towards him without speaking.

'What do you think comes next?' he asks.

'What do you mean?'

'After this place. Do you believe in Heaven, or Hell?'

'I don't know,' I say, truthfully. 'I suppose there must be something. And it has to be better than here.' I stare at him, suddenly nervous. 'Why?'

'We're nearly at the end.' He looks away from me. He's got this small red thing in his hand, a fruit I think, and he starts tossing it up and catching it like a ball. 'What if it's worse?'

That's the thought we all have, in the back of our minds. That's the thought we're blocking out, because if we didn't we'd go crazy. Maybe that's what's sent Conrad over the edge. He isn't lying to himself anymore.

I shrug. 'I'm concentrating on the here and now,' I say. 'That's all I can do. Getting through each day.'

He looks at me then, this strange expression on his face. 'Do you ever wonder if you're on the wrong side? If you're one of the bad guys?'

I shrug. 'You're talking like I was ever given a choice.'

He tosses the fruit over to me.

'What's this?' I ask, immediately wary.

He shrugs. 'I found it. I don't want it. You can have it if you want.'

I think he's trying to make peace. 'Thanks.' I put the fruit in my pocket.

I've had enough of Conrad, messing with my head. I decide to stretch my legs, just far enough to put a couple of tree trunks between me and him.

Maybe I am one of the bad guys. I mean, good girls don't blow up the world.

I'm too exhausted to think properly. I haven't got the energy to debate anything with myself at the moment. It's all I can do to keep going forwards.

I take the little red fruit out of my pocket. It looks innocent enough. I take my knife out of my pocket and cut a slice. It smells like an apple. I take a bite.

'Girl?'

God, he's persistent. I ignore him and close my eyes. I try to conjure up Mum's face but it's hazy. Why is it hazy? Am I forgetting her?

'Girl, don't eat that.'

I sit bolt upright.

'Why? What did you do?'

His face is white. 'They gave it to me. Told me to give it to you. To stop you… you know.'

I place my hand on my stomach. 'So it was supposed to do what? Kill me? Or my baby? Or both?'

'I… I don't know.'

I've eaten some of it. I put my fingers into my throat to try to bring it back but I get nothing but yellow stuff. No bits of apple.

'Conrad, I think I…'

The edges of everything are becoming blurred. I can't concentrate. I can hardly see.

'Jane.' I can't even be certain I'm saying her name out loud.

I'm in my bedroom. It's night but that doesn't matter anymore. I never leave the house so it's all the same. I'm in pain. I'm in the kind of pain that makes you feel like tomorrow is impossible. Another day like this one would be unbearable. I can't. I hate my bedroom. It feels like it's shrinking, like the house is shrinking around me. I hate my house. I hate everything else even more. I just want it to stop.

'Girl. Can you hear me?'

I take a mouthful of vodka and stare at the tablets in front of me. I'm not even thinking, really. It's just one thought. Obliterating this life.

'Girl. Girl!'

Where is that voice coming from? Who is that? I reach for the first pills.

'Rosie.'

This voice is different. I turn around. 'Mum!'

She looks past me at the bed. 'Rosie, what are you doing?'

197

I don't want her to see me like this. 'Mum, I...'

'Rosie, why do you have my tablets?'

Mum doesn't get angry that often. But when she does I know about it. She bears down on me like a demon, sweeping the tablets off my bed.

'You stupid, stupid girl! Why would you do this?'

I place my head in my hands.

'Mum, I'm so, so sorry. But... it's too late.'

'What do you mean?'

'I did it already. I'm dead. I'm dead, Mum, and so are you.'

It isn't until that moment that I realise that's true. For a moment we stare at each other. Then all the fight seems to leave her. She sags, and sits on my bed.

'Oh, yes. I'd forgotten.'

I stare at her. My mum. I want to drink her in, keep her safe in my memory where I won't lose her again. Warm brown skin, freckles, the best smile. Those glasses which fell off her nose all the time. Her laugh, the loudest cackle I have ever heard.

'I miss you,' I say.

'I miss you too, chicken,' she says. She touches my face. 'I'm proud of you, Rosie. Did I tell you that?'

'Only every day.' I laugh. She smiles.

'I'm even more proud now. What you're doing... it's very brave. I couldn't do it.'

I have a troubling thought. 'Mum, how do I know it's you? Not just some trick?'

She looks at me steadily. 'I suppose you can't ever know that,' she says. 'But I'm not here to tell you what you should do. That's up to you. I only want you to know I love you.'

'I know. I know that.'

She hugs me. It feels warm and perfect and exactly how it used to be. 'Rosie,' she says. 'You have to go back. It's going to be difficult. But you can do it. Things don't always go as you expect them to.'

'I don't want to go back. I don't want to leave you again.'

'I already left, Rosie. Neither of us can change that.'

She kisses me on the forehead. 'That's for you,' she says, and kisses me again. 'And that one's for my grandchild.'

'Girl. Wake up!'

I open my eyes to see Ali and Jane standing over me.

'Oh, thank the Lord. You're back.'

'Girl, what happened? Where's Conrad?'

I shove them away just in time to avoid them as I'm violently sick.

'She's been poisoned,' says Jane. 'Here. Give her this. I'll be back soon.'

I feel pretty awful. My head is spinning. My stomach is crunched up inside.

And I don't know whether I dreamt her.

And that's the moment it hits me. The full force of almost a year of grief, which has been shoved down and shoved down because it's been the least of my troubles. It hits me like a tidal wave.

I slump against the tree and cover my face with my hands, listening to the sound of my breathing. In, out.

Somewhere in the distance I can hear Ali. *Are you alright, Girl? What's wrong? How can I help? Can you hear me?*

I can, but I'm not ready to come back yet. I need a bit longer to sit with my grief.

I had almost forgotten her. Without even a photograph to look at she was becoming hazy in my mind, a jumbled up collection of things which I couldn't piece together into a whole; a smile, a hairstyle, crinkled eyes. Now I've got her back, just for a bit. Until I forget again.

The earth shifts underneath me. A quake.

'Girl. We need to move. The tree could fall.'

Ali takes both my hands and starts trying to pull me to my feet. The sight of him struggling is enough to bring me back to reality.

'I'm not *that* heavy,' I say.

Relief floods his face. 'You are,' he says. 'It's like trying to lift a truck.'

'Hey!' I punch him, softly.

'Are you alright, Girl?' he asks, as another quake starts up.

I nod. 'Ali?' I'm speaking loudly, over the noise of the quake. 'Yeah?'

'Please will you call me Rosie?'

The quake vanishes into nothing halfway through the sentence, and I'm still shouting. We both laugh.

A little while later I'm still sitting by the same tree. Ali has cooked us some small unfortunate creature. I'm hungry now; really hungry. My portion of rodent looks pitiful. I know Ali would give me his, but there's no way I'm letting him go hungry.

'Where did Conrad go?' asks Ali. 'Did he have anything to do with it? Your sickness?'

I explain about the apple. Ali scowls. 'Why would he do that?'

'He's not in his right mind,' I say. 'And they're good at tricking people. It's what they do.'

A little while later still: 'Rosie.' It actually feels nice to hear my name. Especially coming from Ali.

'Yes?'

'I'm glad you're OK.'

Boy

They can't have been gone long. The fire is still warm. I reckon they probably moved on this morning.

'We're too late. Again.'

Galen is looking at me with an ugly sneering expression.

'Doesn't matter,' I say, quickly. 'Half a day's travel at best. And believe me, she's not going to be moving fast.'

I gather the group together. They're a strange looking lot. The new fighters we've got from the other tribe are different from ours; better, if I'm being honest. Strong looking, healthy and well trained. Make our guys look like amateurs.

'We're not going to be here long,' I tell them. I point at a couple of the newbies. 'You two, have a look around for their trail. And you—' I point to a red-headed girl. 'Look for water. They must have had some here. We can refill before we start up again. The rest of you can take five.'

Galen is muttering something to himself.

'Yes?'

'You're wasting time,' he says.

I stare him down. 'How? Do you have a better idea?'

He nods. 'They went that way,' he says, pointing to a gap in the trees.

'You know that for certain?' I snarl.

'Yep.'

He doesn't elaborate. The thing is, I know he's right. There doesn't seem any other obvious route they could have taken and I've been doing this long enough now to spot the broken twigs and squashed leaves where human feet have been. I'm stalling.

'Well, I'm the one in charge.'

'Not for long,' he says, with a grin.

What does that mean?

'You know what, there's a reason she chose me over you, Galen,' I tell him. 'It's not all about being able to hit things.'

In order to prove me wrong he swings for me. I duck out of the way and in seconds I'm behind him with my knife to his throat.

201

'It would be really easy to kill you,' I say. 'And satisfying too.'

I move the knife away slowly, watching him. He gives me a look of pure loathing.

'One day she'll be done with you,' he says. Then he turns his back on me.

'Hey!' I shout after him. He doesn't turn back. This really annoys me. 'I should have cut your throat,' I mutter.

The two men I sent to find their trail come back and confirm what I already knew. But they do have some surprising news: they've found two full packs, complete with arrows, knives, food, everything. Now why would they just abandon everything they have?

There really can only be one explanation: because they don't need it anymore. They must be so close to the place they're heading for that it doesn't really matter.

A churning sensation begins in my stomach. It's almost time to decide.

'Alright, lock and... hey, what's going on?'

The men are all crowded around something. It's... oh. It's the redheaded girl. She's convulsing.

'What's wrong with her?' I ask.

One of them holds up a flask.

'She was drinking from this.'

'Where's it from?'

One of them points in the direction of a tiny brook.

'Did anyone else have any?'

Nobody answers for a moment. Then one of the men at the back says: 'All of us. We all had it. You, too.'

Aw, shit.

Minutes later and we're all lying around the clearing in various states of distress. The redheaded girl is worst hit; she was walking around fighting with invisible things until she accidentally hit Galen and he clobbered her. Now she's lying in the corner convulsing and shivering.

It takes a few minutes to take hold of me. Then I start seeing little demons creeping out of the trees. Ugly little fuckers, twig-limbs and wooden grins and within minutes they're all over me. I know I'm hallucinating but that doesn't stop my skin from crawling.

'Niall. Drink this.'

One of the demons is standing over me holding a small bottle of something. This one is even uglier, weird staring eyes and… oh, OK. I take the vial.

Rosaline is watching me grimly. 'Better?' she says.

I look around. No more demons. I nod. 'I still feel like shit though.'

'That'll pass. Give the others the medicine.'

I start to hand around bottles. Some of them take it off me without a fight but I have to wrestle with a couple of them to get the stuff down their throats. When I reach Galen he's just sitting there, normal as Galen ever gets.

'You OK?' I ask.

He shrugs. 'Guess so.'

'Didn't you have any water?'

'Yep.'

Perhaps the poison doesn't work if you don't possess the capacity for abstract thought. 'Well help me to pass these out, will you?'

'I will, once the fire's gone out.'

OK then. 'You'd best take this,' I say. 'Just in case.'

He looks at it for a second, then knocks it back.

'Don't know what started it,' he says. 'We didn't have a bonfire.'

I'm distracted by an unfamiliar voice. I turn around to see the other Rosaline, their Rosaline, standing in the clearing, looking at ours.

This is going to be interesting.

'You poisoned my men.'

'You poisoned my girl.'

'Is this how it's going to be? You broke the rules.'

'Never seems to stop you.'

'You're fighting dirty, Jane.'

'So are you.'

The two women – god – beings are slowly circling each other. It reminds me of a wildlife show I watched when I was about twelve, where these two tigers were fighting for dominance in the pack. They're practically growling at each other.

Everyone is coming out of their poison fugue now and we're all watching them.

'You won't win, you know.'

'We'll see.'

'They'll never let you win. They like the game too much.'

'Perhaps you underestimate them.'

Then suddenly Rosaline flies at her. Literally flies. She's on the other, giving her an almighty whack around the head. The earth starts trembling under our feet.

The other one is sent tumbling backwards but she recovers quickly and then she's on Rosaline, who defends herself by clawing at not-Rosaline with long, talon like nails.

The tremor is increasing in intensity as the two figures tear at each other like wildcats. Then suddenly they're not there anymore and the tremors have stopped.

I look around at the others. I suppose I'm checking that I didn't hallucinate the whole thing. But they're all standing around open-mouthed, like me.

I think we just saw a god-fight.

Rosie

So we're going to do this. One day's travel, I hope. Follow the crease in the sky. We're nearly there. This nightmare is nearly done.

I *can* do this, Mum.

One foot in front of the other. That's all it is. A series of single steps.

The terrain is dry but there's vegetation here and there and Jane's right, water can be found pretty easily. Well, of course she's right. She probably helped design the place.

As I walk I'm thinking about the journey and about all of the people who this place has tortured and killed. All of those who thought they were fighting against demons. Did they know, in the end? When they were dying, did they see through the mask?

I'm doing this for them. Jane and her kind can go to Hell. And when they do I hope it's like Afterwards.

'You're not very chatty,' says Ali.

'No.'

And there's Ali. Whatever is going to happen to him, it will be soon. His fate and mine are wrapped up together. Maybe I won't be able to stop it. But I'm going to try with all I have, pregnancy or not.

Every bone in my body aches. But we have to keep going. If we don't and they catch us we're defenceless. Jane has well and truly stitched us up.

The pain is increasing now. Every now and again I have to stop and breathe it out for a minute or two. Ali looks at me like a rabbit in front of a truck.

'Are you alright?'

I let out a long breath. It hurts, but I just say, 'I'm fine. I just need to catch my breath.'

Ali still has his bow and arrows. He never puts them down, these days. But it doesn't matter much because there's nothing to catch here. Food is another thing which is going to have to wait till we get there.

One foot in front of the other.

It isn't far now. I can see something in the far distance. A change to the landscape. It goes from greeny-brown forest to dark grey hills with no foliage. A dead place. Not very inviting. But it's all we have, so we have to keep going.

Then I see something else.

'Is that… water?'

We're squinting into distance at a line of glinting light. It's almost a mirror image of the line in the sky.

'I think it is,' says Ali.

'How big do you think that is?'

I'm not really asking. I already know the answer. If we can see it from here then whatever it is must be massive. And the hill we're trying to get to is behind it.

'Maybe there's a bridge.'

'Mmm.'

It's possible, I suppose. I mean it would be stupid of Jane to create a safe haven for a heavily pregnant girl behind an impassable lake.

All the same, I have a bad feeling about it. I know Afterwards by now.

As we approach my fears are confirmed. It's wide and deep. We can't wade through it.

'I can't swim,' says Ali, crestfallen.

'Neither can I, right now.'

We sit, and decide to think it through for a while. The water is still and glassy, reflecting the white gash in the sky eerily.

'At least we have a water source,' I say.

But even that turns out to be a false hope. When I bend down to scoop up some water in my hands Ali says, 'Stop!'

I pause mid-scoop.

'Look at the water. And around it.'

There are dead insects all around, floating on the water and lying around the bank.

'What is this place?' I shout. I'm so thirsty I want to cry. 'No water, no food. What are we supposed to do?'

I throw myself down onto the floor a little too violently, and a pain shoots through my middle. I cover my head with my hands and sob.

Ali approaches cautiously. 'We'll work it out,' he says. 'Jane made this place. Right?' I nod. 'So the water isn't supposed to stop us. It's supposed to stop them from reaching us.' Another nod. 'Which means there must be a way for us to get across.'

He's right. Perhaps if we look around there'll be something here to help us. Perhaps we can build a raft.

But there's nothing. We left the trees behind a mile or so back. There's no way Jane would mean for us to walk back to them. It would take half a day at least.

So… what? What else did she say? She said we'd get stuck, and that I had to remember her words.

Which I can't remember.

Look for… look under…? What *was* it?

Ah. Suddenly it comes back to me. *Try looking beneath the surface of things.*

'I think there's something hidden in the water,' I say.

We split up: I go right, Ali goes left, examining the edges of the water. After a couple of minutes Ali shouts me over.

'It's a boat!' he says.

It's submerged about a foot down and partially covered in dead reeds.

'Do you think we just reach in?' he says.

I'm watching a fly scooting over the water. It thinks it's found a drink and dives down. The second its body hits the water it's stone dead.

'No, then,' says Ali, wide-eyed.

If only I still had my backpack with my tools.

But she told me we could manage without it. So.

Ali has found an old branch on the bank. We hook it into a metal loop at the back of the boat and use it to pull it closer, but the branch breaks.

'Hey, look. There's something here!'

There's a metal chain buried in the ground. It looks like it's

207

attached to the boat and someone has concealed it under the mud of the bank.

We wrap the chain around our arms and pull with everything we have. But we're weak. The boat hardly budges at all.

'Can I help?'

Conrad.

Ali stands in front of me. 'Get away from us.'

Conrad holds up his hands. 'I know. I wouldn't trust me either. But I told you, didn't I?' he said. 'I told you before you ate the whole thing. I've been following you. I want to help.'

He looks stronger now. And the craziness has gone from his eyes.

'Let him help,' I say. 'What choice do we have?'

The three of us pull together and the boat slowly emerges.

'Can we even touch it?' says Ali.

'I don't know,' I say. 'But we need to find a way to patch it up. Otherwise we'll all finish up like that fly.'

'There's something in here,' says Ali.

He's right. Inside the boat is an oilskin.

'OK,' I say. 'It's pretty hot. I say we give the boat an hour to dry off. And then we'll see what we can do.'

The sun is baking. Conrad has a small amount of water in the flask he keeps around his neck. He offers it to us, but we're wary.

'How can we trust him?' demands Ali.

Conrad takes a small sip. 'Look at my lips. They're wet.'

I'm so thirsty I don't even care if it's poisoned. I take the flask off him and drink a mouthful, before handing it to Ali who drinks, reluctantly.

The boat dries off quickly. We examine it for damage; it's fine, as far as we can see. I empty the oilskin onto the ground. It contains a toolkit for repairing the boat.

'We'll have to be really careful,' I say. 'We can't let the water touch us.'

There are oars in the bottom of the boat.

'Well, we'd better try I suppose,' I say.

We push the boat to the edge and climb in carefully. Then we start to row, gently to avoid splashing.

208

It isn't far. We get across in a matter of minutes, and climb out onto a steep bank. We push the boat under some overhanging grass to conceal it and wrap the chain around a trunk to secure it.

We're nearly done. The rent in the sky glistens above us, a raw wound. The place Jane has prepared for us must be close.

I hear voices. I turn back to see the boy and his people on the other side of the bank, looking across at us. One of them steps towards the river.

'It's toxic,' I shout. It's not that I care if they die. But I don't feel like watching it happen.

The man steps back and they begin a frantic conversation. I turn away.

'Come on. Who knows how long it'll take them to find a way across? We'd better move.'

A pain crunches through my body and at the same moment the ground begins to shake.

'Drop down,' I instruct Ali and Conrad. They lie flat and I curl into a ball as the world around us oscillates violently. I can hear tapping; pieces of slate are tumbling down from the hill. There's a deafening crack and a fissure appears which goes straight through the river. Water immediately begins to drain into it.

'Come on. We need to go!' I call to the others.

'But what about the quake?' asks Ali.

'No time.'

We battle against the moving ground. I'm dimly aware that the sky is brighter still.

'Keep going.'

We scramble up the hillside, pieces of rock falling like confetti all around us. My hands and feet are bleeding. Ali's too. I'm fighting internal and external pain and all I can think is keep going, keep going.

We reach the top of the hill and suddenly the landscape in front of us changes.

Oh no. We're looking at a canyon, of dark grey rock. I've seen this place before.

Boy

We're walking again when Rosaline reappears. She's looking less god-like than ever. Like she's taken a beating. I decide not to comment.

'You're close,' she says. 'Keep going. About a mile further on you'll find a lake. It'll seem impassable but I can help with that. Then you'll get your chance. Are you up to this, Niall?'

This wasn't really a question.

'Of course,' I say. 'Trust me.'

She looks down her beak-like nose at me. 'Trust is earned, Niall.' Then she's gone.

We walk on. I've got this tension in my stomach that I can't shake. Everything is irritating me. The others sense my mood and stay away.

We reach the lake pretty quickly. They're over on the other side, watching us. Galen moves towards the lake but the girl shouts, 'It's toxic.'

Shame she warned him.

It seems obvious, now we're aware of it. There's nothing living around it. It's a dead place.

So now what?

We start to debate our options when suddenly it becomes redundant. The ground starts to shake again. Is this what she meant by helping us or just another random quake?

We drop to the ground to wait it out. I look over at the girl. She's still walking, through the earthquake, up the hill. She's nothing if not committed.

'Look! The water!' shouts one of the men.

It's draining into a crack which has opened beneath the lake. So this *is* her doing.

It takes no time at all for the water to drain enough to shrink the lake and create a path. Rosaline reappears.

'The lake is corrosive,' she says. 'You'll have to wait until the ground is completely dry to follow them. I'll delay them on the other side. As soon as you can go, you must run. Understand?'

I nod.

The sun is strong. We sit by the lakeside and wait. I can hear my heart pounding away in my chest. Kill her. Don't kill her. Kill her.

Finally Galen shouts, 'It's dry.'

I swallow my thoughts and stand.

'Let's go,' I shout. They all look up at me. Can they sense my reluctance? Do they all know? 'Let's kill the bitch.'

Galen raises an eyebrow and laughs nastily. 'Let's do that,' he says.

Why couldn't it have been my job to kill *him*? That I could do. We start to run.

Girl

I freeze.

'What is it?' asks Ali, impatiently. 'We're practically there. Come on.'

I try to steady my breathing but I'm fighting back tears.

'Ali. This is – this is the place. That I saw. Where you…'

Ali's face goes from total incomprehension to sudden understanding. Fear.

Then he just shakes it off. 'We don't know what's going to happen,' he says, softly. 'And even if I die, what does it matter? We're on our way to start the end of the world.'

I suppose he has a point. But still.

'It matters. To me.'

'Come on. Let's go,' he says.

I look down at the ravine, then back at the boy and his group. They're a good way back and they look like they're unable to cross for now. Perhaps we can be across the ravine before they reach us.

'Alright.'

We start to make our way down the hill. Suddenly Jane's here, walking alongside us. 'Keep going,' she urges. 'You're very close now.'

I ignore her. At that moment a cramp hits me; stronger now, more urgent. It stops me in my tracks. Ali doesn't notice at first; he keeps on walking down the hill. It's Conrad who calls him back.

'Ali. Wait.'

He looks round and sees me doubled up in pain.

'Rosie!'

I try breathing through the pain. It does absolutely nothing. Then it just eases, by itself.

'Are you alright? What's wrong?'

'Nothing.'

I start to walk again, my face set into a blank mask. Just keep going.

'Do you think it's time?'

'Yes. But we have to keep moving. It isn't safe here.'

That's the moment I hear it: a low pitched growl. No: more than one. All around us. 'What now?' I groan.

From all around us they come: large wolf-like creatures, baring their teeth.

'Ignore them!' hisses Jane. 'They won't kill you. She's put them here to slow you down.'

That's easier said than done when they're all around you, wanting your blood.

'They might not kill *me*. But what about Ali?'

'I don't think they're here for that. They're just a deterrent. Keep walking.'

The creature at the front leaps at Conrad. 'We're defenceless!' I shout. 'You made us leave our weapons behind. So help us!'

'Just keep going!' she shouts again. 'They're a distraction! Nothing more.'

'That distraction is about to tear pieces out of us!' I yell. I shove at the nearest wolf. It's like pushing a hairy wall. With teeth.

But after a moment it becomes clear that they're not trying to maul us. They're trying to drive us back, using their body weight to push us backwards. Problem is, it's working. I'm not strong enough to fight them.

Then Ali's next to me and Conrad too and together we're pushing back, forcing our way through them, trying to ignore the snarling teeth.

'That's it!' shouts Jane. 'Don't look at them if that's what it takes. They're nothing. Just another roadblock.'

I close my eyes and keep moving forwards, using my shoulders to push through them. They're not attacking us even though they could rip us apart with those teeth and claws. Nothing about this place is ever what it seems to be.

Then the animals evaporate and we're left stumbling over one another in a thick fog. I can't see the others. I can barely see my own hands.

'Where are you?'

The pain is starting again and I sink to my knees. I suddenly feel really alone, like I'm the only person in the whole world. Then I hear Jane's angry voice cutting through the cloud.

'Oh, this is getting ridiculous. You're desperate. It's embarrassing.'

'I just need to slow them down. You know that. My boys will do the rest.'

'Keep walking!' The voice is in my ear and suddenly Jane is next to me, taking my arm.

'You can't do that!' screeches the other voice. 'You're not allowed to lead them. You know that.'

'I'm leading nobody,' replies Jane, calmly. 'I'm helping her to stand, that's all.'

And I'm back on my feet in a world of agony, stumbling forwards and downwards. My feet slip time and again on the gravel. I can't see anything.

'Ali?' My voice vanishes into the fog as if it had never existed. This feels like true death. I'm nowhere, I'm nothing. Just a single voice in my own head. I walk forwards or maybe sideways through greyness. I feel like I'm stumbling through my own despair. This is what I've reached. I've walked for miles across hostile land. I've fought people and the landscape and my own body and this is where it's taken me. I give up. I give up. I stop walking and allow the pain to take me over. I don't want to do this anymore.

'Rosie?'

I look up and Ali is standing over me. Something's wrong. He doesn't look like himself. He looks angry. Furious. I feel an overwhelming panic rising inside me.

'You were going to leave me. You weren't going to come back, were you?'

I feel cold all over. 'I… I wanted to. I couldn't. I couldn't, Ali. I wanted to.'

'You didn't!' He's shouting now, his words vanishing into the cloud like everything else. 'You were going to leave me here! You lied to me.' There are tears in his eyes which are much, much worse than the anger. I slump, defeated and allow the pain to envelop me. Then Ali's face changes and suddenly he's my mum.

OK. So I'm hallucinating. That knowledge should make me

feel better but terror still fills my chest. It's Mum's turn now to stand over me.

'You're such a disappointment. You could have been anything. You gave up. I don't know why I bothered with you.'

I know it's not, but it *feels* real. It's what I believe. I gave up. I let her down.

'Rosie!'

This time when Ali says my name it's different. His voice is soft, gentle. And he's there. Really there. 'It's OK. You're hallucinating. It's not real. You're safe.' His arms are around me. I feel safe. I can keep going.

I have to, for him.

Somewhere behind us I hear Jane's voice saying: 'That's what my girl has. That's why she'll always be stronger than your mercenaries.'

And the other voice: 'We'll see.'

Boy

We've almost reached them. They're in the middle of this dense fog – Rosaline's doing, presumably. It looks really strange. You know those cartoons where the character has a raincloud above their head?

We'll be on top of them before they even know we're here. It seems too easy, somehow. Even if I did want to kill her it'd be a bit of an anti-climax. As it is, I have no idea what I'm going to do when I get to her.

I just want it to be over. Funny, I didn't notice till now how fucking sick of it all I am. That's why I don't mind knowing Rosaline's going to kill me. I'm sick of being wrong-footed every time I see the girl. Sick of being someone's dog. I just want it all to stop.

As we approach them we get caught up in the same fog that's slowed them. It's like everything's paused. It's nice. Like a small holiday. Until the hallucinations start.

Starts with my dad. He looks just like I remember; thin, angry, unshaven, a can of Stella in his hand. Looking at me like I'm something he just shat out.

'You're a fucking waste of air, Niall. You ruined my life. You and that fat bitch of a mother of yours.'

He goes on like this for a while. I know it's not real and it doesn't matter anyway. It's irrelevant now. After a minute or two I shrug and tell him he's a twat and a useless dad and then he's gone and out of my head, forever.

Then it's Mam. But she's not much better than him.

'You'll have to do better than that,' I shout, into the air. 'Go on. See if you can find someone I fucking care about.'

It's pretty depressing, seeing a moving slideshow of all of the people in my life and realising I don't give a fuck about any of them. Also kind of liberating.

And then I see him: Josef. He isn't berating me for killing him. He's just sitting there, blood pouring from his neck, looking completely serene. Then he drops and the whole thing replays itself

216

again and again like a bad dream. I can't deal with this. I close my eyes but I can still see him.

'Fucking stop, will you? Fuck off!' I'm yelling uselessly into the air.

Then, unexpectedly it does. The mist thins out and I realise we've mingled. Her people, my people. We're standing a couple of feet apart from each other. Everyone has the same stupid expression for a moment and then the chaos starts. People running and shouting everywhere. Panic. Anger.

Everybody apart from me and her. We're not moving. She sits. Right there, in the middle of all of the confusion. She's sitting down. The kid is in front of her, looking petrified but refusing to run.

She looks like she's in pain. She hasn't even noticed me.

Conrad's there too. He's finally picked a side. Good for him. He's giving some of my men a run for their money.

The kid's watching me. He looks terrified but I don't know if it's because of me or her.

'Get on with it,' growls Galen. He pushes me towards her. I shake him away, grouchily.

I know what I'm supposed to do. But I can't do it. I know that for sure, now.

Suddenly she looks up and sees me. I meet her eyes and am filled with a wave of panic. I realise I'm not even panicking about Rosaline, or what's going to happen to me. I'm worried about her. And I'm worried about what she thinks of me, standing here like a total loser.

She's laughing. She's about to die and she's fucking laughing her head off.

And then suddenly I'm not there anymore.

'Hey! Where am I?'

I say it because that's the thing you say when you're spirited away. But I know where I am. I'm back on the street, in Manchester. Suddenly all of my confidence drains from me. I'm back to being that scared kid trying to stay alive. The kid I was the night I died.

Until I remember: I'm not that kid now. I'm a killer. I see that I have a knife in my hand.

217

They're walking towards me. The ones who killed me. I'm going to get my chance to set things straight.

It doesn't occur to me to think about why I've been put here. It doesn't occur to me that maybe I'm hallucinating again. I don't question it. I just know that this time around it's going to end differently.

I stand there and wait for them to get close to me. I'm having trouble seeing them. I keep losing focus on them, like I'm six pints in. Then one of them lunges. I attack him with ferocity I didn't even know I had. I'm fucking angry. My death has really pissed me off.

I feel a sharp pain on my shoulder. It's wet with blood. I didn't know these guys had a knife.

I'm still struggling to focus on them. They keep morphing into something else. I can't see them. I'm lunging about wildly with a knife until I feel a fist make contact with my face and I'm sent flying across the alley.

No. Not the alley. I'm in the ravine.

I groan. I haven't moved from here.

I look around. My own guys are lying there, dead or dying. Did I do that? Conrad doesn't look in great shape either. Only Galen is still OK. And the girl and the kid.

'Great job,' says Galen. I run at him and try to punch him in the face but he blocks and shoves me away. He approaches the girl, knife in hand.

'You can't kill her,' I call.

'Watch me,' he growls.

He rushes at them. Ali is still standing in front of her, brave as a lion. Galen is within inches of them when he disintegrates.

Shit. I wasn't expecting that.

There's nothing left of him. Just dust.

Their version of Rosaline is there. She looks as spooked as me. 'You need to go,' she hisses at me. 'Unless you want the same thing to happen to you.'

No, I do not. I leave, stepping lightly over the bodies of my companions.

Girl

The mist disappears and suddenly they're right there, in the middle of us. We all stare at one another for a few seconds like none of us can trust our own eyes yet. And then they move to attack us. Ali jumps in front of me holding the knife Jane gave him like it's toxic. His hands are shaking.

'Ali, go! Get out of here!' I shout.

'No! I have to protect you!'

'Go!'

We've got no chance. There's about fifteen of them against the three of us. It's pointless.

The realisation of this makes me weirdly euphoric. I start laughing. I can't stop. Tears are streaming down my face.

Ali glances back at me and the sight of his worried expression sobers me. 'Sorry,' I say. I want to hug him again.

That's when I notice the boy. He's staring at me with this frightened expression. Then he looks away at something I can't see and suddenly goes crazy, lunging about with his knife, attacking his men and Conrad indiscriminately. Some of them run, some of them fall.

The only one who doesn't do either is a huge man with a nasty look. He says something to the boy and then he's coming towards us, knife out. Ali's trembling all over but he doesn't move.

'Stay back!' he shouts.

The man laughs.

'Run, Ali!' I shout again, even though I know he won't. 'I can't watch you die!'

The scene is playing out exactly as I saw it. I know what happens next.

'Then don't watch!' says Ali.

So I look up at the sky. And right there above us is a tiny patch of blue.

It's never blue. It's grey or black. It doesn't go blue. What does it mean?

That's when the ugly man with the knife turns to dust in front of us.

We're left staring at the dust in the air. Then I grip Ali's arms, reassuring myself that he's still there. 'You're alive. You're OK.'

Ali looks like he's about to faint.

The boy is glancing around like he has no idea what's just happened either. Four of their people are bleeding on the ground. And Conrad. Then the boy's gone too and we're left here wondering what just happened.

Ali's still shaking. 'We're alright!' he keeps saying, over and over.

Jane approaches us. 'You need to finish your journey,' she says. 'It isn't far. Just on the other side of the ridge. Think you can do it?'

I don't want to move and I tell her so.

'It's important. You have to try,' she says.

I open my mouth to answer but then I'm floored by another cramp.

'Rosie, it's started. Your baby is coming.'

'No shit!' I mutter, grimacing against the pain.

'Rosie, listen to me. On the other side of that ridge is safety. It's hidden, it's protected. You need to get to it.'

I am fighting another rising pain so I ignore her.

'We haven't got much time. You need to keep moving…'

'No!'

I scream this. It's as much about letting out the pain as it is answering her.

'No, I'm not leaving here. I'm not…' My words are taken away by crippling crunching spine crushing agony. *Oh my god, how do people do this?*

Then it's gone and I'm OK again. 'I'm not moving,' I say, once my breath returns. 'I'm staying here.'

'Rosie. You don't have a choice.' Jane's voice is firm.

'No. I never have a choice. We never have a choice. Well this time I'm choosing. I'm staying here.'

'No, you're not.'

'Yes, she is.'

Ah, Ali. I love you so much. He's standing in front of me, a fierce warrior boy, bow in hand.

'I won't let you touch her.'

Jane looks at him with something like sympathy on her face. Then with a swipe of her hand, she pushes him aside.

'Believe me, I am sorry. If I had a choice…'

She approaches me, hands outstretched. I feel like a wild animal that has been cornered. I think I'm baring my teeth.

'Get. Away. From. Me.'

'I'm sorry Rosie. It's time to go.'

'No! No.'

She reaches towards me. I brace myself. And then she stops. But before I can begin to wonder what's happening the pain starts again. Tears are streaming down my face. Ali picks himself up and puts an arm around me, tears on his cheeks too.

'I can't do this. I can't do it. It's too much.'

'You can! You can. My mum had four kids. You're way tougher than her. You can do this.'

'I can't. You don't know.'

The pain gradually lessens. I'm exhausted.

'I hate this.'

Then I remember Jane. She's still standing there. She's just staring at me.

'What are you doing?' I ask.

'I can't touch you,' she says, quietly. 'I don't know who's doing this, but I can't transport you.' She looks defeated. 'Just come with me. Please.'

Is she right? Should I go with her?

No. I can't. I've survived this long by trusting my instinct. And right now it's telling me loud and clear that I need to have my baby and keep it safe.

More pain is on the way. I feel like I'm dying. Again. Perhaps I am. Perhaps the baby's coming out wrong.

Oh god oh god oh god oh god.

'It's OK. You're doing great. Keep going.' This is Jane.

'Why are you still here?' I scream at her.

'Because I want to be,' she answers.

As my pain reaches its crescendo I realise that the shaking isn't just my overworked muscles. The ground has started to shake violently all around us.

'It's starting,' says Jane. 'The world has realised your baby is on the way.'

All I can do in reply is scream. If the world were to end at this moment I'm not sure I would care.

Boy

I walk for about half a mile and then stop and sit down by a tree.

My situation has changed. In the space of five minutes I've lost everything. All of my men are dead or gone.

The thing is, I don't care about that. They never felt real to me anyway. It's like they were my shadows. All except Galen and I'm glad that fucker's dust.

But what am I supposed to do now? What's my purpose? It's going to take some consideration.

I begin sharpening my knife on a stone when the first one starts up.

Uh ho. Here we go again.

I follow the normal drill: find open ground, lie flat. It lasts about five minutes. I look up, to discover that I'm in a completely different place.

'Hey! What's going on?' I shout.

Rosaline appears in front of me. Then comb-over guy. Then two more. Pop. Pop. Pop. Pop. A real gathering. How fun.

'Hey. Why am I here?'

Rosaline glares at me. 'We have use of you. Be quiet until we speak to you.'

Speak when I'm spoken to like a good little boy.

Hey. Wait. They're having an argument. This might be entertaining.

'How could you let this happen?' This is from another female, and it's directed at Rosaline. Heh.

'Oh, come on. You knew the situation. This was always the most likely outcome.'

'No, I don't accept that. It should have been dealt with long ago.'

'I explained to you everything that happened and how they sabotaged my attempts to eliminate her. I fail to see how I could have approached anything differently.'

'By getting a more effective assassin.'

'Hey! I...' I find my voice has disappeared and I'm mouthing silent words.

'Be quiet!' snaps Rosaline.

Comb-over speaks. 'None of that matters now. We're here to decide what to do next. The baby is going to arrive at any moment.'

'So? She isn't at the epicentre. Nothing will happen.'

'Maybe not immediately. But while that child exists the world will become less and less stable, and eventually it will disintegrate. It can't change what it is.'

The third woman speaks. 'I can't help but wonder if perhaps we should let this world go. Start again, in a new arena. New world, new set of rules with fail-safes this time.'

The other three turn to look at her. 'Do you know how much has been invested in this world, Diana? Time, resources. It would be disastrous.'

'But perhaps inevitable,' replies Diana. 'The longer we postpone it, the more costly it becomes.'

Rosaline holds up a hand and Diana vanishes.

'I can't be bothered with whiners,' she says. She looks around at the others as if to say, 'Anybody else like to join her?' Bond-villain-esque.

'Alright,' says Comb-over. 'So we need to find a way to destroy them both. Do you think your assassin is up to the task?'

Rosaline stares at me. 'He's been... different from how I'd hoped, I must admit,' she says. 'He thinks he's in love. Such a tiresome concept. It always complicates things.'

'But quite entertaining, don't you think? Our ratings have never been better.'

'Mmm. Imagine what they'll be like when he finally betrays her.'

I sit up. She glances over at me. 'Oh, you will, Niall. Whatever you might believe about yourself, I know who you truly are. You're an assassin with a keen instinct for a self-preservation. Even so-called love won't surmount that.'

The other female looks unconvinced. 'Do we have a back-up plan?'

Rosaline looks at her like she's just spat in her glass of Chardonnay. 'No. And you know why. But it won't matter.'

'I see. Rule 26?'

'Yes. He's the only other true mortal in the arena, therefore our only option.'

What?

'Well, just make sure he knows what's at stake,' says comb-over guy. 'There have been too many complications already.'

Rosaline gives him an impressive death stare. He's unruffled. Then, with further pops all except Rosaline vanish again.

'Niall. I have some things to explain to you,' she says. 'Sit.'

I'm forced to sit. I mean, that's rude. I was going to anyway.

'I know you heard all of that, so I won't bother to repeat myself,' she said. 'What I need to check is that you understand the seriousness of your position.'

I hold up a hand, like I'm in school.

'Can I ask a question?'

'Is it relevant?'

'To me it is.'

She nods.

'What did you mean when you said we're the only true mortals here?'

She looks even more irritated than usual. I wasn't meant to hear that.

'Well, I don't suppose it matters now,' she says. 'Neither you nor the girl ever fully died. Instead, you were removed at the point of your death and placed here. That's why you can remember your life. You're still living it, in a sense.'

'*What?*' I stare at her, open-mouthed. 'But – I don't understand. I remember my death. I got the shite kicked out of me in Piccadilly. And then when I got here, all of the pain was gone.'

'Yes. We can manipulate mortals too. We wanted your arrival to be the same as everybody else's. They did the same with her.'

'And that's why she's still pregnant?'

Rosaline nods.

'So what about everyone else? What are they?'

'Souls, spirits, the leftovers of a life. Their physicality is an illusion, like so much else here.'

'My mind is… I mean, it's a lot to take in.'

Rosaline sighs. 'Niall, I really don't care if you're finding it hard to comprehend. That's for you to deal with, or not. I just need to know you're ready to set things straight. Are you going to kill her, and the child?'

'No.'

'No?'

'No.'

Simple, really. After all of the agonising it now it seems so easy.

She doesn't seem angry. Why isn't she angry?

'I need to show you something,' she says.

She places a hand on my shoulder and suddenly I'm watching a scene play out in front of me. She doesn't speak, just makes me watch it to the end. Then it vanishes and she's looking at me expectantly.

'OK, fine. I'll do it,' I say.

'I thought you might,' she says.

Girl

I feel like my body is being pulled apart. I can't do this. I can't.

Somewhere in the distance I can hear Ali saying words of encouragement. But the fear in his voice makes them sound hollow, or maybe that's my own fear. I'm screaming again. The earth is shaking underneath me and all I can think is I want the pain to stop.

I'm in a bubble of pain and noise and nausea.

I try to speak but I'm crippled by another wave of pain. It feels as though everything is ending. Perhaps it is.

I've been doing this for a long time now. Hours. The night has come and gone and I barely even noticed it.

Everything around me has disappeared into a blur. I'm distantly aware of Ali and Jane and the shaking ground but I'm lost in my own private hell of pain and sweat. I don't know what's happening to me. I don't know what to do. I hurt so much this can't be right. I'm going to bleed to death right here.

The pain recedes again but not completely this time. I vaguely register Ali standing with me, rubbing my arm, my back, looking petrified.

And then it's building again and there's a different pain in my back and my stomach and I need to push down but I'm exhausted and I want it to stop.

Why am I doing this? There are bodies strewn all around me. Death is everywhere. Nobody will care enough to bury them – they'll just lie there until they're picked apart. Why am I bringing a child into this?

And then everything else disappears again as I go back into my pain bubble. My body screams as I push down with all of the strength I have left.

'That's good. She's coming. Keep going.'

Pushpushpush

ohGodit'sagonymakeitstop

'That's it! One more push!'

I want to punch Jane's stupid face but I use the energy to make one more push and I feel the baby leave my body in one wet movement. Moments later there's a thin wail and I know that I can rest.

It's over.

The pain is gone. I'm lying on the ground, unable to move, a confused heap of person. The earthquakes have stopped. The world hasn't ended.

I haven't even looked at her. I can't look at her. I just want to lie here and stare at the sky.

For the first time since I got here the sky has turned completely blue. Actual blue. I barely remember the colour. Any colours, other than brown and grey. And now the sky is blue. I don't know what it means, and I don't care. For now I just want to look at it.

'Girl. She's so beautiful. She looks like you!'

It sounds like Ali is already in love.

I don't know how long I lie there. Ali doesn't pester me, apart from to ask if I'm alright a couple of times. I don't know if he's sensed I need some time, or if he's just too distracted by the baby. Either way, it's fine by me.

If I lie here it's almost like I'm back home. I could be anywhere. I could be not here. As soon as I look at them it'll disappear, and I'll be back in Afterwards, surrounded by death. So I'll keep looking up.

A sound brings me back to reality. A thin, shrill noise which doesn't belong here.

'Girl, she's hungry. She needs you.'

I sit up. I feel dizzy, and nauseous. 'I… I don't know what to do.'

Ali is looking pretty terrified. I roll my eyes and reach for the small, mewling thing in his arms.

He's right. She does look like me.

I'm not going to say there's a rush of love, or whatever you're supposed to feel. I think I'm too exhausted for anything that intense. But what I feel is: I want to protect this very small person. I want to help her. And for now that means figuring out what the hell I'm supposed to do to feed her.

228

'Hello, there,' I say, softly. 'Let's see if we can work this out together.'

How hard can this be? I mean, it's what we're designed to do.

Ali is looking uncomfortable. 'Why don't you go for a walk?' I say. 'Just until we've both got used to it all.'

He looks very relieved. 'I'll try and find some food,' he says.

'Do you need help?' asks Jane. 'I'm no expert, mind you.'

'Not at the moment,' I say. The baby's crying is making me feel stressed. I self-consciously lower my top and let the tiny mouth find my nipple. She slurps at it, greedily.

'See, you did it!' grinned Jane. 'You're a natural.'

'I doubt that,' I say. I watch the tiny being attached to my chest, feeding, oblivious to the trouble she's caused. 'She's so...' What? Perfect? No, I don't mean that. '...Natural.' She's not full of anxiety or pain or anything like that. She's just hungry.

There's a noise from the other side of the clearing. Jane glances over. 'I'll just check on him,' she says.

Conrad's still alive, but he's in a bad way. He's bleeding from a chest wound and his face looks like it's been pummelled. But nobody hurt me, or Ali. I don't understand why. When I ask Jane she's evasive.

'Something protected you,' she says.

'*Something*,' I repeat. 'Not you?'

'Not this time. Against the rules.'

'And them?' I gesture at the bodies. 'What happened? Why did he kill them?'

'I think he was hallucinating. I suppose it backfired. And then there was the other one.' She frowned.

'The one who... vanished?' I ask.

She nods. 'But he didn't just vanish. He... disintegrated,' she said. 'I've never seen that happen. Ever.'

I try to make sense of what she's saying. 'Somebody wanted me to have this baby,' I breathe.

She nods.

'But who?' I ask.

'I have no idea.'

'But you must have a theory. You do, don't you?'

'More of a feeling,' she says.

'And?'

'I'm wondering if it was the place itself. The world. Protecting you.'

'Afterwards?' I wrinkle my forehead. 'How does that work?'

'It doesn't. I told you, just a feeling.'

After a while Ali returns.

'Has she finished?'

I nod. 'A while ago.'

He grins. 'She's beautiful, isn't she?'

I smile, wearily. 'She is. You're right.'

He goes to pick her up but she's fast asleep in my arms, so he hesitates. 'No, go on,' I say. I need to sleep too.' He takes her from me and she starts to grizzle but he rocks her and she settles right down. I'm not sure whether to be jealous or happy that he's already got such a good bond with her. I'll settle for just getting a nap.

I don't know how long I'm asleep but it's dark when I wake up.

'Girl! You're awake. She's hungry again.'

This is my life now. I'm a dairy cow.

Ali is about to leave again but I stop him. 'Just get used to it. It'll only be weird for the first couple of times. You can't just leave whenever she wants a snack.'

So he sticks around, looking hugely uncomfortable. And then it's done and things are back to normal for a while.

'What's she called?' asks Ali.

'Fish.'

He gives me a look.

'Just for now. I haven't thought of a name yet.'

'What about Lydia?'

'No. Why?'

'That's my mum's name.'

'Oh. No, sorry.'

'OK. What about Yana?'

'No. I'll come up with something. Just be patient. She doesn't care.'

'I just want to know what to call her.'

'Fish.'

'Fish.' He just sits there, looking at her.

I stand up, and it's then that I remember just what my body's been put through in the last twenty four hours. I feel like I'm about to break apart. I hurt everywhere. And there's blood.

'I think I'll stay here,' I say.

'Good idea,' says Ali. 'I caught a squirrel. I'll make a fire and cook it now.'

He busies himself, humming. He sounds happy. Happier than I've known him to be the entire time we've been here.

'You're good at this,' I say.

'What?'

'Being an uncle.'

He grins. 'I know.'

We tuck into roasted squirrel and I begin to feel tired again. I'm starting to wonder if my new life is just going to be feeding Fish and sleeping when the boy appears again.

'What do you want?' This is Ali. He's standing over the two of us, holding a sword towards the boy.

'Hey. Easy now. Just a visit. No hidden weapons, see?'

He holds out his coat to show that it's empty.

'Alright. But stay over there,' says Ali.

The boy raises his eyebrows. 'Can I see it?' he says.

'*It's* a she,' I say, tiredly.

He looks embarrassed. Do psychopaths even get embarrassed?

'Sorry. She. Can I see?'

Ali looks at me. I can tell he doesn't want the boy anywhere near Fish. But instinct tells me he doesn't want to hurt her. Nonetheless…

'You can see her but not hold her. And no sudden movements.'

He holds his hands in the air and walks over to Ali. He smiles, which looks weird on his face. 'She looks like you.'

'I know.'

He suddenly looks like he's in pain. 'Can I speak to you?'

'Go ahead.'

He glances significantly towards Ali.

'I'm not leaving,' he says, firmly.

The boy makes an exasperated sound. 'I'm not here to hurt anybody, OK? I just want to speak to *her* without an audience.'

I stare at him. What's he up to now? Curiosity gets the better of me. I nod towards Ali. 'Take her,' I say. 'But stay close.'

'I will,' says Ali, glaring at the boy.

When he's gone the boy suddenly looks nervous. He keeps looking at the ground and just glancing up to meet my eyes.

'I'm Niall,' he says.

'I know. You already told me,' I say.

He looks like I've slapped him. His face clouds. 'I'm just trying to be friendly.'

I sigh. 'Look. *Niall.* I gave birth less than a day ago. I'm drained. This is time I could be sleeping. So whatever it is you've come here to say, say it, and then go and crawl back underneath your rock.'

Something changes in his expression. The hard glint returns to his eyes.

'You're mortal,' he says. 'They told me. You and me, we're still alive. Your little friend over there...' He shakes his head. 'Not him. But us, and the baby. We're still ticking.'

'What?' I shake my head. 'That's not true. I remember... I remember...'

'Dying? Yep, me too. Turns out we were both still just alive enough to matter.'

I stare at my hands. They look no different, of course. 'That's why... I was still pregnant.'

'Yep. And here's the thing. We can kill each other, but no one else can hurt us. That's why they brought me here.'

I nod, thinking it all through. 'To kill me.' I turn on him. 'Why are you telling me this? What's in it for you?'

He shrugs, not meeting my eyes. 'I just don't care anymore. About any of it.'

I stare at him. 'I'd love to have that luxury,' I say, eventually, glancing over at Ali.

He sits in the dirt. 'So what's next? Do you have a plan?'

'If I do, I'm not about to share it with you. Not until I know where you stand.'

He scoffs. 'You don't have a plan. You're making it up as you go along. Like me,' he adds. 'We're both as shit-scared and useless as each other.'

A tiny smile works its way into the corners of my mouth.

'You're the only person who doesn't think I'm some kind of hero,' I say.

'And you're the only person who speaks to me like I'm a person,' he says. He's scratching at the ground with his fingernails, distractedly.

'Back there, when everyone was fighting. You were there, looking at me. And then you weren't. You were somewhere else.'

'You want to know what happened to me?'

I nod. 'If you want to tell me.'

'I thought I was back on the street. The guys who killed me… they kicked me to death. I thought I was back there. So I did what my instinct told me to do.'

'You mostly killed your own men,' I said.

He looks grim. 'I know. I don't think they care about that. The ones who brought me here, I mean.'

'Do *you* care?'

He shrugs, again. 'Probably not as much as I should.'

'Well I care,' I say. 'You also hurt Conrad.'

'That guy had it coming, believe me.'

'How can you be so cold about it?' I snap. 'Whatever you've told yourself, however you justify it, these are real people.'

'They're not, that's the point.' He sounds impatient. 'Anyway, that's not what I came here to say.'

'Then say it and leave.' I cross my arms over my chest.

For a moment he's silent. I watch him without speaking. When he looks up there's hopelessness in his eyes. 'I have to kill you,' he says.

I roll my eyes. 'Again?' I say.

He frowns. 'No. You don't understand. It's different now. And I'm going to do it.'

Boy

I still have to kill her. Whether I want to doesn't come into it, I've discovered.

There isn't much Rosaline could have said or done to make me change my mind. I had made my decision and I didn't care enough about my own death to listen to threats. She could have done whatever she wanted to my mam and dad too, with my blessing. But she's clever, that one. She figured out the one thing she could do to make me go through with it.

She showed me the girl's future.

It isn't pretty.

The longer she lives here the harder it'll get, for all of them. The world will break apart. But it'll be uninhabitable long before that happens. The food will dry up. The water will go bad. And they will die. The choice was only ever between a slow death or a fast one.

That's why I'll do it, for real this time.

And that's why I'm back here on their doorstep, shuffling my feet like a kid trying to get up the nerve to talk to a girl. I'm trying not to think about what I need to do. I don't think I have the courage to do it. But I have to. I have to.

They're sitting next to a fire, eating. The girl and the boy. They both look fit to drop but happy, somehow. I'm about to change that.

The boy looks up and sees me. 'What do you want?' he says. He walks towards me holding out a sword. I reckon I could bat him away like a mosquito but she might not like me hurting her pet.

'Hey. Easy now. Just a visit. No hidden weapons, see?'

He reluctantly agrees. There's a tiny whimper from the bundle of cloth on her lap and I'm suddenly curious. 'Can I see it?' I immediately regret my choice of words.

'It's a she,' she says, coldly. This is going well.

She's a beautiful creature. I'm suddenly filled with awe. It's an unfamiliar sensation. I find I'm smiling. The girl is staring at me like I'm nuts.

Then I remember what I have to do.

'Can I speak to you?'

235

There's a bit of negotiation involving the boy. He doesn't want to leave and I don't blame him. Eventually he moves far enough away that he can't hear us but still has us within his sight. That's good, I realise with a sigh. I'm going to have to kill them too, when I'm done with the girl.

Fuck. This is tough.

We have our usual back and forth banter, chit-chat. I'm putting it off, finding anything else to talk about. But it's no use. It's hanging over us like the blade of a guillotine. She's giving me a hard time about being cold, as though I have a choice, as though I can do anything apart from just block it out, shrug it off.

'They're not, that's the point,' I say. Not real. Whatever that means here. 'Anyway, that's not what I came here to say.'

She looks at me like she has low expectations. It's almost a relief to say it.

'I have to kill you.'

She rolls her eyes. 'Again?'

Frustration is building up inside me. 'No. You don't understand. It's different now. And I'm going to do it.'

She laughs. She fucking laughs.

'Listen,' I growl. 'I don't want to do it. I told you that. But she showed me – what comes next.'

Now she's listening. 'What do you mean?'

'I wish you could see what I saw. The place – it becomes – worse. A living death. We'll all die, but slowly. You, me, them.' I gesture to the boy and the baby. 'I'm going to spare you that. That's why I'm here.'

She thinks about this for a moment. Then she looks up.

'Why do you think you get to make that choice?' She stands up. Her eyes are angry. 'I thought for a moment you were a bit like us. But you're not. You're like *them*.' She gestures into the air. 'Trying to control us. Thinking you know what's right for us. It's not your life. It's mine. Now go away.'

I stand up too, anger rising. 'I'm trying to fucking help, you crazy bitch! Do you want to starve to death? Do you want your baby to go through that?'

236

She turns her back on me. The boy stands up and walks over to her, glaring at me.

My fists clench. I hit a tree on my way out of the clearing. It hurts.

Girl

How dare he? How *dare* he?

I groan loudly.

'Ssh! You'll wake her!'

'Why does everyone think they know what's best for us?'

'You're over-reacting.'

'Over-reacting? He wants to kill us.'

'Everybody wants to kill us.'

I stand up and pace. I'm filled with rage. Ali wisely ignores me.

'It's so... presumptuous. We've got this far with hardly any help from anyone. We've walked for miles. I had a baby. We've done so much. It's not fair. It's...'

A thin squawk arises from the bundle. Ali glares at me and picks her up.

And just like that the anger is gone and I'm hit by a tsunami of other feelings. I'm sobbing and gulping, head on knees, swarmed by my emotions. Ali lets me get on with it for a minute or two, then puts a tentative arm around me.

'It's alright.'

I can't speak yet. I'm breathless and overwhelmed. Then it starts to subside and I'm left sobbing quietly.

'It's not fair,' I say, again. I know I sound like a child but I don't care. It's too much. Just for now, it's too much. Everything we've been through and it's still not over. It'll never be over.

Silence returns to the clearing.

'Hey, Girl?' Ali says, after a while.

'Yes?'

'Look.'

He's holding Fish out towards me. Her eyes are wide open. They're a deep, beautiful blue, the same colour as the sky. I take a deep breath and reach out for her.

Boy

I walk and walk without any direction. I just want to be away. Anywhere. Doesn't matter.

I end up on the summit of a hill. I'm forced to stop by the precipice in front of me or I'd probably just keep going until I drop. I flop to the ground, useless and defeated. I lie there for hours, probably. The light fades and I'm left staring at the white line across the sky.

What's up there? Is it like Earth? What do they do? Do they have jobs? Bus drivers? Cleaners?

I pace some more and I think. After a while I sit, my foot still making a soundless tapping movement on the ground. I can see for a long way here; the ground is flat to the horizon, just a few dead trees and shrubs between me and the edge of the world.

My useless attempt at heroism has put me in a shitty mood, which is made even worse by the fact I have nobody but myself to take it out on. I'm doing a lot of pacing. I feel like a caged animal. I have to force myself not to go back, just for the company. Instead I choose a path and just walk.

Later that day I reach the hill where the fight took place. It's empty now. It's as good a place as any to pitch up, so I do.

The next few days pass with painful slowness. Everything is different now. I haven't just lost my soldiers, I've lost my momentum. It was a lot easier to exist in this place before, when I was literally walking towards my goal. Now I have no-one to talk to except myself, and I've never much liked that guy. I'm going slowly crazy. I spend my days walking, hunting, looking out over the emptiness in front of me, not looking up at the emptiness above me. Trying not to think about her, failing.

The evening horror show of memories has become an all-day thing: Mam and Dad, who never stay banished for long. Josef. I see myself cutting his throat again and again and that awful look of relief on his face.

I've probably been here for about two weeks before I finally realise I can't take it anymore. I'm all set to pack up and slink back to her camp when I see them: strangers, heading this way.

They're out in the open; there's nothing to stop me picking them off with arrows if I was minded to do it. But right now I want company. I *need* company.

I haven't seen them before. They're probably from one of the other tribes, the ones who hadn't signed up to help Rosaline.

As they get closer I see that they are a girl and a boy, teenagers. They're approaching me fearlessly. What's going on here?

'Hi,' the girl calls.

'Hi,' I reply, allowing the uncertainty to enter my voice. 'Who are you? Why are you here?'

'Did you see it?' she asks. She's got this enraptured look about her, like a religious convert.

'See what?' I growl.

'The light, from the sky. Did you see it?'

'Oh, that. Yeah.'

'We've been walking for days. We had to come.' She's wide eyed and staring at the line in the sky. 'Is she here?'

'Is who here?'

'The girl. The one who's going to save us.'

What?

'I don't know what you're talking about.'

This only fazes her for a moment. Then she says, in the same voice full of fervour: 'We used to hate each other.' She gestures to her friend. 'I thought he was a monster. He tried to kill me and I tried to kill him.'

'No shit.'

'But then the light came and we saw that we were just the same.' She pauses. 'There are others, too.'

This makes me sit up. 'How many?' I say.

She shrugs. 'A hundred, maybe?'

'Where?'

'All around. They'll be here soon too.' She smiles, broadly. 'Do you want to come with us? We're going to find her.'

I make a quick decision. 'I'll take you to her,' I say.

Her eyes widen again and she looks at her friend. 'See? I told you things would work out.'

I roll my eyes. 'Come on, then.'

At least I'll have company, of a kind.

Girl

I've been counting the days since I had Fish, by marking them off on a tree. She's two weeks old today.

We're all adjusting. We've become a little family unit, Ali, Fish and me. I feed her and he does everything else, except when he's hunting. Which makes it sound like I've got it easy but she feeds All. The. Time. Constantly. Her mouth feels like sandpaper on my boobs, they're so raw. Which makes me grouchy, so Ali takes over when she's done feeding.

She's growing on me, I think. I try not to give myself too much of a hard time over it. I mean, the bond will come eventually. I've had a lot to deal with. It's not surprising I feel a bit numb. And anyway, Ali has more than enough bond for both of us. He won't let her out of his sight, unless she's with me. He doesn't even like Jane holding her.

The quakes stopped for a few days after she was born. And then on day four we felt it again. It wasn't too bad, though. I think perhaps it's this place. We finally made it to the safe haven Jane had prepared for me to have my baby, only a few days late. There's a small hut and a grove surrounded by thick gorse and a protective barrier she's put up. It's shielding us from the worst of the seismic activity.

We'll probably stay here. It's a bubble; I know Afterwards is still there, on the outside, waiting. But for now I can push it aside and if I try really really hard I can sort of believe that I'm living a normal life, with my baby and my best friend. And Conrad too I suppose, although since the fight he's retreated back into himself again. His body has recovered but his mind has gone.

'Rosie.'

And then there's Jane. She doesn't like to let me forget where we are.

I groan and turn away from her.

'Rosie, I need to speak to you. Did you think about what I said?'

No. And I don't plan to.

'You can't avoid it forever, you know.' She sits down, next to me. 'Got a name yet?'

'No.'

'I won't be offended if you call her Jane.'

Is that a joke? I'm not laughing.

'Why would I name her after one of you?' It's more of a snarl that I intended and she looks taken aback. I'm not apologising though.

She sighs, looks defeated. 'Rosie, you know you need to recognise when people are trying to help you,' she says.

'How can I do that when your help always comes at a cost?' I snap.

She's watching me in the way she sometimes does, like she's trying to judge whether to persist. In the end she decides not to and goes to find Ali and Fish.

I sit alone and stare at the blue of the sky and the streak of white light which runs through it. I'm not really looking at it. I'm thinking and my thoughts go like this:

What do we do now?

Can we stay here?

How can I keep them safe?

While another part of my brain is thinking:

Does that look like a building, or is it just a cloud?

The air breathes over me, hot dusty wind. *Get up. Do something. Don't just sit there*. I close my eyes and feel it drape across my shoulders. I'm almost at peace. I could just...

'Rosie!'

I'm jolted awake by Ali, bounding over with Fish tied to his chest in a blanket. I open my eyes reluctantly.

'Were you asleep?'

I give him a look which he ignores. 'Jane's just been telling me about her idea.'

I groan and turn over. 'I'm not doing it, Ali.'

I can't see him but I know he's got that crestfallen expression he has every time I have to deal him disappointment.

'But why? It sounds perfect.'

243

I sigh and sit up. 'Does it?' I ask. 'To me it sounds like a prison.'

She has this plan. A compromise, she said. She's even got the others to agree to it. We're to stay here. We'll be looked after, given what we need to survive. They'll stop trying to kill us. We'll be safe.

'What's wrong?' His face clouds and for a moment I see the teenager he's about to become. 'You're never happy with anything. You always have to find problems. We'll be safe, Rosie. No more running, no fighting.'

He looks older when he's angry, the man peeping out from behind the eyes of the boy.

'Think about it, Ali,' I say. 'If we agree to this, we've lost. Everything we've done has been for nothing. Afterwards will continue as if we were never here and we'll be stuck here in our enclosure, like tigers in a zoo, looking out.'

'We've already lost.' Jane walks back over, her face serious. 'We lost when the world didn't end. That's all we had. I'm just trying to salvage something, for your sake and for that baby.'

'Well, we don't want it.'

Ali looks like he wants to cry or shout but in the end he just says: 'Rosie's right.'

Jane closes her eyes for a moment and when she opens them she starts to speak slowly, as if she's talking to a small child. 'Listen to me. None of us really knows what will happen if you and your baby live out there long term. The world might end. It might not.'

'Then why do you want us to stay here, if there's a chance it might still work?'

'Because it could take years and in the meantime the other side are going to make your lives miserable. And sooner or later they'll find a way to kill you.' She paused. 'They're talking about pulling the plug on the game, starting elsewhere. Do you know what will happen to you if they do that?'

I shrugged. 'They kill us?' *So what?*

'Worse than that. They will abandon you. The world will be

244

closed off so that not even I can help. No more food parcels. A long, slow death from starvation, every day harder than the last. Is that what you want, for him? For her?'

I groan. Another trap in a world full of them. There's no good solution.

'Let me sleep,' I say, lying down again. I need time.

'Well, alright. But don't take too long, or it'll be out of my hands.'

I curl up for a while but sleep doesn't come. After a time I hear Fish's thin wail and that's that. I sit up. Ali brings her to me but he doesn't stay to talk. I wonder if he's still angry.

I'm going to have to take her deal. I have no choice, really. I can't watch Ali die like that. Or Fish. Just like everything else, it's out of my hands. We have to stay here in this earth-blister, being fed and watered and watched. That's all there is for us now.

I'm about to stand up to tell Ali what I've decided when I hear him shout. I hurry over. He's up in a tree, a place he goes to keep a look out, even though nothing can get in or out of the bubble.

'Rosie! People. Coming this way!'

'How many?' I feel a tense knot in my stomach even though I know we're safe.

'Three. No! There's more, behind. Ten, maybe.'

'And they're coming here?'

'It's looks like they are.'

Even Conrad has stirred from his usual comatose position to find out what's happening. He looks rattled.

'They can't get in,' I remind him. He just looks at me with haunted eyes.

He needs help. More than I can give him.

'We just wait,' I say. 'Find out what they want.'

We have a system, not that we've needed it much up till now. I go to the edge, just through the perimeter. I can step back easily enough if I need to and they can't cross the boundary. Ali sits above with an arrow poised, just in case. I have Fish in Ali's blanket-wrap thing. I stand and wait, my heart beating a little faster.

They get nearer and I see him. The boy. He's leading them here, which can only mean one thing. Still, I don't go back inside the bubble. It feels good to make that decision for myself. Whatever he's up to, I'm facing him down.

'Hi!'

The girl he's standing with is smiling this huge smile and I'm thrown completely off guard. The boy sees my face and laughs.

'What's happening here?' I ask, warily.

'They wanted to meet you,' he says. 'They think you're going to save them.'

'*What*?'

The girl reaches towards me. I step back. 'It started when the light came,' she says. 'We'd been fighting. We thought we were fighting demons but when the light changed we could see each other. Everyone could. So we stopped fighting and followed the light.'

She's got this evangelical look which is unnerving me. 'This is nuts.'

'There are more coming too,' says the boy.

'How many?'

'Some from every camp.'

I take a breath, then yell: 'Jane!'

She appears after a few seconds.

'Yes. This changes things, unfortunately.'

'What do you mean? How does it change things?'

'I don't know yet.' She looks worried. 'The game has stopped. The participants are all here, or on the way. This has never happened before. And believe me, they won't be happy.'

'Who won't?'

'The ones who make Rosaline and her associates tremble, never mind the rest of us. The ones *we* have to answer to.' She guides me back behind the line. 'Stay in there. Don't let anyone in, until we know more about what's going on.'

And then she's gone. I glance at the boy before going back into the shelter. He's watching me, as if he's trying to work me out. There's pain in his eyes like Conrad's but he keeps it tucked away. When he sees me looking back he shifts his gaze.

Boy

Things are getting interesting around here. I would love to be a fly on the wall when Rosaline finds out her game's malfunctioning. That the fighters have become devotees, worshipping a human. Ha. I wonder what that's done to their audience numbers? I bet they're tuning in like never before.

'You're correct, in a way.'

Ah. How long has she been there?

'I'm going to make this brief, Niall. Things have turned out differently from how I had hoped, I must admit. But I have cause for optimism.'

Do I reply? Do we have that kind of relationship now? Probably not.

'I have a new task for you,' she says.

'What are you up to?'

Oh. The other one's here too, now. It looks like I'm going to get my fly on the wall moment after all.

'Jane. How tiresome you are.'

'Rosaline. What do you want the boy for now? I thought we had an agreement.'

'Nothing's been agreed yet, as you know. This latest development has changed things.'

'It doesn't have to. If you consent to keep my girl and her family safe I can work with you on fixing your problem.'

'You can't *fix* it. You know that.' Rosaline raised her chin in a sneer. 'Anyway, it barely matters. We don't need special effects to make the humans kill each other. I don't know why we made it so complicated to begin with. They're not civilised beings. They don't need a lot of persuasion to wage war against each other.'

'So that's your plan? Make them fight anyway?'

'Yes. I think the audience will enjoy the new format. More realism.'

'And when they realise that they're gladiators, performing in a show?'

'I doubt they'll care. Given the right incentive.'

They both go quiet for a few moments. Then Jane says: 'And will you let my girl live, if you can get the game running again?'

'That all depends.'

'On what?'

'Whether she stays in her pen.'

When Jane has gone Rosaline explains to me my role in all of this. I'm to start sowing the seeds of disunity among the humans. Start arguments and suchlike. If it works, they'll stop trying to kill her. It's a kind of peace, I suppose.

At least my new job will be a distraction. I've started to feel a bit – disposable. For a while I expected Rosaline to kill me, for betraying her. Then I realised: she can't. Not directly. She has to wait for Afterwards to do it. And while she waits, she might as well make use of me.

And I still don't know where I stand in all of this, in my own head. It's clear Rosie wants nothing to do with me. But I feel this ridiculous urge to protect her, protect them. I know it's stupid. That's what's eating away at me. I can't abide stupidity, especially my own. I'm a contradiction and it's pretty depressing.

So I think I'm going to enjoy stirring up trouble. That's all I'm really good for, anyway. I was only ever going to be the bad guy. Might as well have a bit of fun at the same time.

'Hey. I was thinking. Who's in charge here? Do you think we should elect a leader?'

As good a place to start as any.

Rosie

They've made a camp around the edges of our home. There must be close to a hundred of them out there now.

Ali thinks it's really funny. He keeps scooting up the tree to keep an eye on them and then reporting back that another group has arrived.

It's not funny, though. It's desperate. They need a saviour because Afterwards is horrible and everyone is scared all of the time. I feel the weight of their pain every time I look out.

'There were at least forty people in the new group. They just keep coming!'

Oh and he's prone to exaggeration too.

'Give it a rest, Ali. I don't need constant updates.'

'What are you going to do? Will you speak to them?'

'No. I mean, I don't think so. What would I say?'

'But they've come all this way, for you.'

'Thanks for reminding me.'

The thing is I *do* want to speak to them. But not as some sort of messiah. Just as a girl. I want to tell them – what do I want to tell them? Not to follow me, for a start. That I'm a poor idol. I'm as scared and as lost as everybody else.

And part of me just wants to talk to them because they're people and I'm 17. I miss them.

Later that day I make a decision. I wrap myself up in a blanket, being careful to cover my hair and face like a hood.

'Be careful,' says Ali. He's rocking Fish who's been grizzling all evening.

'I won't be long. I just want to find out what they're saying out there.'

'They'll know it's you.'

'Maybe.'

I sneak out of the protected area by a back exit we've created, by chopping at the gorse. I think I've a better chance of going unnoticed if I can find a way to just merge with the crowd.

It turns out to be easier than I expected. It's chaos out there.

There are people and makeshift tents crammed into every space. It's like the skeleton of a music festival. Everywhere I look there are too-thin people with bones jutting out from beneath their skin and exhaustion and fear in their eyes.

'Move over.' I'm barged out of the way by a tall man with a long scar which runs diagonally across his face, interrupting his right eye which is closed and swollen. He glares at me and I realise I'm standing on his tent. I open my mouth to apologise but then someone else shouts across at me.

'There's no more room here. You need to go further out.'

I start to back up and a shrill cry alerts me to the fact I've just stood on somebody else. I'm getting a bit tired of this.

'Sorry,' I mutter. This is useless. I move outwards, stepping awkwardly over feet and legs and human waste and detritus of every kind.

At the edge of the camp there's a bit more room. I join a group who are sitting by a tree. They're not talking much but they don't look unhappy. When I sit down a girl turns to me.

'You can't sit there,' she says.

I'm starting to get seriously pissed off.

'Why?' I growl.

'Ants,' she says. I leap to my feet and begin feverishly scrubbing them off my legs. They're the brown and yellow ones: long legged and creepy looking but not deadly. Definitely irritating. By the time I'm done I've got a bunch of red spots on my leg.

'Thanks,' I say, although I'm thinking that the warning could have arrived earlier. She looks up and smiles. Actually smiles.

'No problem. Sit over here, instead.'

I step over her and insert myself into a small space between the girl and her neighbour.

'When did you get here?' she asks. I'm guessing this is how small talk goes in this situation.

'Not long ago,' I say. 'What about you?'

'Yesterday. We walked for two weeks.' She points to a man. 'Ben saw her, you know.'

'Saw who?'

'The girl, stupid. Didn't you Ben?'

He has the grace to look uncomfortable. 'Well, I was near the back so I didn't get a good look. But I heard her speak. It was amazing.'

'*Was* it?'

'We're thinking of trying to get further forward tomorrow. See if we can get to the front, see her. Maybe the baby too.'

I'm almost laughing.

'Which tribe were you in?' she asks. 'We were North One. Des and Jilly over there were in North Two. We were fighting for ages without realising who we all were.'

'East Seven,' I say, automatically. The girl's eyes widen.

'That's where she was from. Did you know her?'

I shake my head. 'No. Never saw her.'

'Oh. That's such a shame.'

I take a risk. 'What are you going to do? I mean, what are your plans, after you've met her?'

The girl looks confused, as if she's never considered this. 'She'll guide us,' she says, as if I've said something really stupid. 'That's the whole reason we're here.'

I take a breath. 'But – don't you think it'd be better to come up with a plan ourselves? Rather than waiting for someone else to think for us?'

They've all turned around now. The girl is looking at me oddly. I start to wonder if she's realised who I am, but then she says: 'Hey. If you're from East Seven, how come you're over here? Why aren't you with them?'

I shrug. 'I wanted to meet some new people.'

The man stands up and walks over. 'We've been hearing some stories. About some of the other tribes. Stealing food. Someone was killed, had their throat cut in the night.'

'And you think – what? That I'm that person?'

'We don't know who you are. Maybe you should go back to your people.'

I give up. 'It was nice to meet you,' I say, only half sarcastically. I walk back through the crowd, to where the gorse grows thickly and push my way through, ignoring the thorns.

251

Ali is waiting for me, impatiently. Fish is crying all the more loudly. He passes her to me. 'She won't stop. I think there's something wrong.'

Suddenly every other thought is gone and my mind is focused on one thing. I put my hand to her head. Ali's right. She's ill.

Ali and I look at each other, terror in our eyes.

I unwrap her to try to cool her down but then I'm worried she's cold, so I put the blanket back on loosely. Ali puts some water to her lips. She's crying and crying and the noise is pulling on every nerve in my body. She won't feed, she won't sleep. The ripped up blankets we're using as nappies are coming off her bone dry. I know that can't be good.

We take it in turns to walk with her, trying to soothe her. I shout Jane but she doesn't come. Where is she? She's always here when we don't need her so where is she now? I'm angry and afraid and exhausted and I just want her to stop crying.

And then she does and it's even more frightening. She's clammy and restless, making this snuffling noise. I don't know what to do. I find that I'm praying and then I feel stupid because who am I praying to? But I still do it because I just want her to be alright.

'Jane!' I shout. 'Jane! Where are you?' Nothing.

She goes to sleep eventually and her breathing becomes more regular. We're exhausted as well but too full of adrenaline to sleep. As the first fingers of morning light poke through the trees she wakes again and this time she feeds. And then I can't stop my tears. I'm sitting there in the dawn light, crying and crying, Ali too. We hug each other.

Before we finally go to sleep I tell Ali that I've got a name for her.

Boy

It's been four days since they began to arrive and there must be close to two hundred by now. It's as if they've all seen the same smoke signal. No surprise Rosaline's rattled. They're losing control.

I've been camping with a group of them a few yards from the place where the girl is. I figured it'll be easier to cause trouble from within the group. They're making it really easy for me; they're completely trusting, like toddlers. They want someone to direct them. It seems kind of unfair, if I were someone who dwelt on stuff like that. But, no. I have a job to do and I'm going to do it.

It's different here though. These people aren't arseholes like my previous group were. I mean, they can be annoying. The disciple thing is starting to wear thin now. They talk about her like she's Jesus. I've met her and she isn't. But they're decent people. Sheep with a wolf in their midst, even if that does make me sound like an egocentric prick.

Like this girl. She's called Bee. Cute, right? And funny. She keeps giving me food and asking me questions about myself.

The guy to the right of her is called Green. I don't know why. Names are pretty arbitrary around here. Anyway he found me somewhere to sleep.

Good people.

I'm quietly undermining them.

I spent an hour yesterday dropping tiny suggestions about the other tribes into the conversations and they lapped them up. It's like they were waiting for an opportunity to bad mouth the others. There's not too much to do around here after all. So now these guys are sure that one of the other groups (East something or other) is planning an attack on them, or on the girl. Don't be specific, just plant an idea and let them fill in the rest. That way they don't even notice you're steering them.

It doesn't take long before I start to notice results. A big guy from one of the north tribes has taken a dislike to Green. Most likely because I started a rumour over that side that this group had

253

got an audience with the girl. Jealousy has done its work, as I had hoped. The two men square up to each other and there's a bit of a fracas before Green fells the other, much bigger guy with a decent punch. Good for him.

I'm not enjoying this as much as I thought I would though. It's not that I care about these people. I really don't and ultimately, they're the ones choosing to fight. It feels good to have an enemy, doesn't it?

No, it's not that. What is it then?

I think I'm worryingly close to developing a conscience, which is of no use to me at all. It's her. I can't stop thinking about her. I want her to – what? Like me? Fat chance of that happening. Despise me less, I suppose.

And there's something else, too. An unwanted idea growing inside me like a tapeworm. The kind of idea which is very likely to get me killed. But I can't shut it off. It has an inevitable quality to it; no matter how long I ignore it I think it will win in the end.

I need to go and speak to her again.

Rosie

Dawn.

It's so easy. She feels like a new day.

'It's perfect,' says Ali.

We all get a few hours' sleep and when she wakes up a while later her skin is cooler and she feeds hungrily. We decide to take it in turns to nap. Ali goes first. He doesn't even protest. He can barely keep his eyes open.

Conrad is awake too and looks more lucid than usual. 'Hi,' I say.

'Hi,' he says. He glances at the baby. He's the only one who hasn't held her yet. He seems a bit unnerved by her.

'Want to take a turn?' I ask.

He shakes his head and goes to fetch some food. I lie on the grass with Dawn next to me on a blanket. The sky is forget-me-not blue. It's dazzling. I'm glad she'll get to see some beauty.

'You did that,' I say to her.

I want more than this place for her. I want her to have her prom and to stay out too late giggling with her friends. I want her to wonder if *that boy* likes her too. To have adventures. I want her to feel alive.

All I can give her is Afterwards.

I can't keep her in this bubble for the rest of her life. Even if I wanted to. She'll want to explore, to meet people. And she should want that. I have to give her a chance to live, even if it's here.

Ali's waking up, rubbing his eyes. 'Is she OK?' he asks. I nod and pass her over. He inspects her like a doting grandmother.

'I think Conrad's a bit better,' I say.

Ali glances over at him, then smiles, broadly. 'Breakfast!'

He goes and sits by Conrad, who passes him a bowl.

We're about halfway through the day when I hear a noise from outside. This is unusual. Whatever Jane's done to this place it doesn't allow much sound to get in or out. So whatever's going on out there must be loud. We all turn to it.

'I'll have a look.' Ali climbs up to his perch in the tree.

'They're fighting.' He sits there watching, fascinated. After a moment he says: 'There's someone trying to get in.' Then: 'It's the boy.'

I glance at Conrad, but he's retreated back into his dream state. I stand and walk over to the bushes which mark the perimeter.

'Wait!' calls Ali. 'You're not going to let him in are you?'

I shake my head. 'I'll stay near the line, I promise. I just want to hear what he has to say.'

I step through the tiny gap in the bushes and suddenly there's noise and movement all around me. There's a huge brawl taking place, screaming and shouting and crying. And at the front, the boy, like a circus ringmaster.

'Did you cause this?' I ask.

He shrugs.

I take a breath. 'What do you want?'

'To talk. Can I come in there?'

I shake my head.

'Well, it's a little noisy out here,' he says.

'I don't think I could let you in even if I wanted to,' I say. 'Besides, Ali wouldn't like it.'

He frowns. Then says: 'Let's take a walk. The crowd thins after about a quarter of a mile.'

The fighting around us has stopped and everyone is looking at us. At me.

'I can't.' I make a decision. 'Do you know the spiny tree, on the edge of the valley?' He nods. I lean closer to him and whisper into his ear: 'I'll meet you there in half an hour.'

'Alright.' He turns and stalks off. What am I doing?

Ali is predictably dubious.

'Have you forgotten he's been trying to kill you for months?'

'No. Of course I haven't. But all I have are my instincts and they're telling me to go. Besides, I'll be armed.'

'It won't matter.' He looks stressed. I reach over to hug him but he shrugs me away.

'We need you,' he says. 'It's not fair for you to keep taking risks like this.'

I bite my bottom lip, a nervous habit I didn't realise I still had. 'It's still my life, Ali. I have to make my own decisions.'

'What about me? What about Dawnie?' He's already given her a pet name.

'I'll come back.'

'Will you?'

There's something in the way he says this which makes me pause.

'Ali, what's wrong?'

'Nothing. See you later. Don't die. Again.'

He walks off, grumpily.

Dawn's asleep in the corner. Conrad's sitting by her, staring at nothing. Ali sits on the other side of her. We've made this silent decision that we won't leave her alone with Conrad, but we're trying to be subtle about it.

I put my blanket-cloak on and leave by the back way again. I'm soon in the crowd again but nobody pays me much attention. I push my way through, ignoring the angry voices around me. It didn't take them long to fall out. It sounds like a war is breaking out, demon-masks or not.

The crowd thins out. It takes me ten minutes or so to reach the tree. The boy's pacing. He stops as I approach.

'Hi,' he says.

'Hi. What do you want?'

He looks annoyed. 'Do we have to do this every time? Can't we be civil?'

'Not really. Ali thinks you're going to try and kill me, so let's make this quick.'

'I'm not. I don't...' he pauses. 'I have no interest in killing you, or the kid. Or your baby,' he adds. 'I was – I thought I could, but I can't.'

'You seemed to have no problem killing the people in the resistance group.'

'It's not killing as a general concept I'm having a problem with. It's killing you.'

I stare at him, trying to work out his meaning. 'Because you

257

think I'm real and they're not,' I say, after a while. 'You're wrong about that.'

'No. I mean, yes, partly. But…' He frowns. 'Anyway, I have a proposal to offer you. A kind of truce.'

Is this a joke? A trick? What?

He reads my thoughts. 'It's legitimate, I promise.' He sits, next to the tree, then realises too late it's covered in nasty spikes. 'Son of a…' I try not to laugh.

'How did you survive this long?' I ask.

He looks embarrassed and angry at the same time. 'Surviving is what I do,' he says. He looks morose for a moment, then seems to shake it off. 'Do you know what they are, Rosaline and Jane and the rest of them?'

I shake my head. 'I don't know. But I know what they're not.'

He nods, enthusiastically. 'Yes. That's what I wanted to say. They're not gods. Or at least not in the way they want us to think.'

I glance around. 'How can you be sure they're not listening?'

'They are. I don't give a shite anymore. I want them to know.'

'Know what?'

'That I've had enough.'

'So. You're giving up? You're going to let this place kill you?'

'No. Listen. You know that Rosaline has asked me to cause trouble among the… players? To make them fight.'

'And you did it.'

'Yes. And it was really easy. Depressingly fucking easy.'

'So, what? You were doing what you were told to do. Like the rest of us.'

'Yeah, but the point is, what if we didn't? What would really happen?'

I think about this. 'They'd level the place,' I say. 'Finish it off and start a new one somewhere else.'

'But wouldn't it feel fucking good to say no?'

Boy

I walk back alone to the camp, pretty pleased with myself. She's going to talk to the kid about what I said. She didn't slam the door in my face, so to speak. That's progress.

There's chaos all around me tonight and I'm not in the mood for it. Nor am I in the mood for Rosaline, who appears when I'm just about to eat. She must be aware of what I'm planning, yet she doesn't rush to confront me. I'm way down her list of priorities. So why does she look angry?

'What do you hope to achieve with this defiance, Niall?'

I shrug, taking a bite of meat. 'Pissing you off is a start. Haven't thought it through much further than that.'

She stares at me, her eyes hard. The meat in my mouth changes texture. I'm as cool as can be; I keep chewing despite the fact it now tastes like shite. I shovel more into my mouth. She looks like she wants to grind my face into the ground with her stiletto heel.

'You can't possibly win this. You must understand that.'

That depends on how you define winning.

'Sure,' I say. 'Hey, you got any more of this?'

'You are going to be very sorry you made this decision, Niall.'

A thought enters my head. 'Hey. What does your audience think of me now?'

She smiles, her nasty smile. 'They're watching more than ever, Niall. In that way you've been very useful.'

I laugh, emptily. 'They want to see me die,' I say.

'They're outraged by you. They want to see you get what you deserve.'

'And what about the girl?'

'Some of my people are sympathetic because of the child. But they're vastly outnumbered by those who feel she's a threat.' She pauses. 'You're nothing to them really, Niall. A source of entertainment which can be easily replaced. Don't imagine that you're anything more than that.'

She leaves, but not before she's sent a searing pain through

259

every nerve in my body. 'I own you, Niall. And if you've forgotten that, I will have to remind you.'

I'm sitting by a small fire with a new group. They didn't notice Rosaline at all. I suppose that must be her mojo at work.

When she's gone I vomit up the bad food. Yes, I know she'll know anyway but I'm really past caring. I want the taste of real meat; I want to sit by the fire and watch the flames and think my own thoughts. I'm feeling pretty good.

The next day I get up early and I'm about to go to see her when the ground starts shaking. It's been a while. It sends the camp into total disarray; there are people falling and climbing over each other, trees uprooting and falling on them. I just sit still and wait. I pick up a stick and start carving it, which is pretty hard to do when you're being thrown about and I nearly slice my arm.

It lasts for a minute or two and then everything goes quiet. It's shaken the people out of their little wars; they're helping one another up and dressing each other's injuries. I go to find the girl and am met by Ali instead.

He isn't happy to see me.

'What do you want?' he asks.

'Didn't she tell you?'

He shook his head. 'We haven't spoken since she got back.'

'Well, can you get her? We have things to talk about.'

'It's alright, Ali.' There's a sigh in her voice. Something's going on with them but it's none of my business.

'Are you OK?' I ask. 'Did the quake damage anything?'

She gives me an I'm-not-here-to-chat look.

'Did you think it over? Talk it over?' I ask.

She nods.

'And?'

'And I think you're right.' She takes a deep breath as if she has a speech prepared. 'I've had enough. It's never going to end. They want me to live here, in this fishbowl, forever, being fed and watered until I die. I don't want that. I don't want it for Dawn, either.'

'Dawn?'

She gestures to the baby.

'Oh. Dawn. Nice name,' I say. She gives me a look of mild contempt.

'This doesn't change how I feel about you,' she says.

'Fair enough. You don't have to treat me like a fucking disease though.'

'You killed people I cared about. You were trying to kill me.'

I shrug. 'That's the nature of the game.'

Her eyes harden. 'That's the difference between us. I still can't see it as a game. They were people, with lives and thoughts.'

'Thoughts, maybe. None of us has a life, do we? Even those of us who are still alive.'

'Don't keep saying that.'

'Doesn't make it any less true.'

She stands up. 'I think you should leave now.'

I don't argue. This feels like progress. We had a whole conversation in which neither of us tried to kill the other one.

'I'll come back tomorrow,' I say.

She nods and I go, humming to myself.

Rosie

I can feel the world changing around me. It feels different and I know it's the beginning or end but I don't know which. I'm restless. I have a swarm of bees in my stomach.

I climb up the tree and sit on Ali's look-out perch. It's the closest I can get to being alone without leaving the haven.

What should I do? Am I wrong to trust the boy? What will happen to us?

I think and I question myself for about an hour. At the end of the process I have a headache and the words of a stranger floating in an endless circle in my head. *You can decide your own future.*

I make a decision and climb down. I check on Dawn first and what I find makes me smile. Ali and Dawn are asleep together, curled up in the corner of the hut. That's good; I won't have to explain to Ali what I'm about to do.

'Where are you going?'

Conrad. He looks dreadful; dirty and unkempt, his hair wiry and greasy looking. His eyes are darting about as I speak to him.

'I'm going out,' I say.

'That way?'

I nod. 'Out the front door.'

I expect him to ask what I'm doing but instead he says: 'It's starting.'

I do an inward eye roll but just say: 'I won't be long.'

I take a breath and step outside. The hubbub immediately quietens as faces turn towards me from all around. There are so many people here now I can't even count them. They all look tired and frightened but worse than that, hopeful and that hope is directed at me.

Then the noise starts up again. Hands reaching out, touching me, grabbing me, everybody shouting. I want to run back inside but I won't. I take a deep breath and shout: 'Stop!'

The sound reduces to a murmur. They're waiting for me to speak. Hundreds of eyes on me. The pressure is too much. Then I hear a tiny, reedy cry coming from behind the barrier and I remember why I'm doing what I'm about to do.

I've never made any kind of speech before. I always made sure I was sick on those days at school. But I'm a different person now. And this matters. They've come all this way for me. The least I can do is to set them straight.

'Listen to me,' I shout. 'You've all come here to see me. You think I'm going to save you. Help you get out of this place. I can't do that.' The voices become louder, more agitated. 'None of us are escaping.'

A girl at the front has started to cry. The rest of them don't look any happier.

'I know you want me to tell you what to do but I don't want to. I'm not any kind of saviour. I'm just an ordinary person.' My voice sounds whiney even to myself. I want to cry but I force myself to say the thing that I'm here to say. 'Listen. You need to stop fighting each other. The real enemy isn't the person sitting near you or some person from another tribe. They were brought here just like you. None of us want to be here. But if you fight each other you're letting the real enemy win.'

'And are you going to tell them what will happen if they stop fighting?'

The one called Rosaline is suddenly there, in the middle of the people, who cry out and jump back from her as though she's toxic. She seems taller than before, glaring down at us like we're cattle trying to escape from the pen.

There's total silence.

'It doesn't matter!' I shout. 'We've already had the worst that they have to give. They've made us kill each other. They've sent monsters and famine and disease at us. They have nothing left. We need to start resisting!'

They're all paying attention now.

'Oh, we have plenty left,' says Rosaline. 'But we won't need any of it. All we need to do is leave. Perhaps you've never noticed how much help we give you. I don't just mean the packs. Or the food we give you when you fulfil your side of the bargain. No, we maintain this environment. It isn't a natural habitat, even if it feels like it. What do you think will happen if my technicians stop working?'

I haven't an answer to give. *Technicians?* The crowd is silent, listening to her every word.

'The lights will go out,' she says.

'So what?' I shout. 'We'll survive. And even if we don't, isn't that better than being a slave?'

'Perhaps the easiest way is to give you a demonstration.' She clicks her fingers and suddenly everything goes dark, apart from the crack of white light which glows eerily above. And it's cold. Really teeth chatteringly cold. Screams begin to sound all around us. 'Let's see how you feel after a couple of days of this. Oh, and Rosie?'

'What?'

'Jane won't be coming to help you anymore.' The way she says this makes my skin feel as if it's crawling with ants.

'Why? Where is she?'

She takes my hand in hers. Hers is cold, as if she is dead. She leads my hand to something. I can't see at all, but I can feel. I can feel Jane's hair, soft and wavy.

'Jane?' I say, quietly, even though I know.

There's a flash of white light and in that instant I see Jane's head, detached from her body. I step back, fighting the urge to vomit.

'You have two days, Rosie. At the end of that time you can decide whether to play the game our way or to continue to survive alone, in an empty world.'

Then she's gone and I haven't got the luxury of crying or shouting because that's happening all around me and I need to do something to help them. I try to make myself heard over the clamour of voices but it's like singing into a storm. Then a loud whistle cuts through the noise, followed by another voice.

'Hey. Listen up. Quiet. Listen.'

The boy.

'We need to start co-operating if we want to survive, OK?

264

Fighting isn't an option anymore. Now, we need to make a fire. We'll make one and then the rest of you can use it to start your own. Anyone got any flint in their pack?'

There's a rustling sound as people feel about in the black. Then another cry starts up.

'They've taken our packs. They're not here!'

The place is in uproar again as people realise everything they owned in this shitty place is gone. No blankets to protect us from the cold. We're left with whatever we happen to be wearing.

'Shut the fuck up!' shouts Niall. 'There's no point in braying like fucking donkeys. We can still make a fire. Everything's dry. We just need some friction. You! Yeah, whatever it is, I don't care. Go and find some rocks or sticks or something and start rubbing them together. You know how this goes. Get on with it. You, and you, do the same. The rest of you, start trying to find food. Use your senses. It's not fucking difficult.'

He's done it. They've calmed down and are doing what he says.

'Thank you,' I say.

'You don't need to thank me,' he says. 'I just want them to shut the fuck up. We're all screwed. We can't survive on a dead world. But if they're busy trying to prolong their pointless lives they're not here, giving me a frigging migraine.'

I frown at him, a useless gesture in the dark. 'Well thank you anyway.'

I go back into the haven which, I realise on the way back in, is no longer protected in any way. This realisation panics me enough to make me hurry back to Dawn. It's easy to find her, at least: she's wailing like a banshee.

'She's hungry,' says Ali. He passes her over and then starts to walk off.

'Hey,' I say. 'What is it? You've been weird for days.'

'I'm fine.'

'No you're not. Tell me, Ali. There's no point in keeping secrets here is there?'

'I'm fine.'

He's gone and I realise I haven't told him about Jane. I bite

265

back tears and turn my attention to Dawn who attaches herself to me like a ravenous zombie. I allow myself to drift into a hormone induced calm as she feeds herself to sleep.

It won't be long before they realise they can get in here. I decide to make the most of the quiet space while I have it, and settle back with my eyes closed. It's really cold. I pull Dawn closer to me.

My thoughts clamber about in my head, fighting for attention. Can we survive this? Am I insane, picking a fight with them? I'm hungry and I'm cold and frightened but I can't afford to be any of those things because I have to be something else, this leader who knows what she's doing and definitely isn't just making it all up as she goes along.

And underneath all of that I have another feeling which is sitting there unacknowledged because I don't want to think about it. I'm lonely. I haven't felt like this since I met Ali, all of those months ago. But now he's avoiding me and I need him. I can't be alone in this place.

'Rosie.'

It's as if he's heard my thoughts, echoing about in the dark.

'What's wrong, Ali? Why won't you talk to me?'

'I know, Rosie. I know that you didn't want to come back.'

Silence falls between us, as tangible as a wall.

'How did you find out? Did *they* tell you?'

'Does it matter?' He sounds so sad and small that I want to hug him but I don't want him to push me away. I don't think I could take that at the moment. 'You were going to leave me in this place, alone.'

I take a breath to try to steady myself. 'You don't know what it was like, Ali. I wanted to come back but... it was like I'd woken up from a bad dream.'

'You knew it wasn't a dream.'

'Yes, sort of. But I wanted to believe it was.' I take his hand. He doesn't move away. 'I would have come back to you in the end. I would.'

'Would you?' His voice has a wobble. 'I never thought you'd leave me. I didn't believe them, but they showed me.' He looks down. 'I thought we were each other's family.'

'We are.' My heart is shattering. 'I love you, Ali.'

He pulls his hand away. 'But you love yourself more.'

'No. It wasn't like that!'

He goes quiet for a moment. Then he says: 'I want it to be OK. But it's not. I can't stop thinking about how you didn't want to come back. How you just left me here.'

'Ali, they're trying to divide us. You know that. You can't let them win.'

'They always win. There's no point in fighting it.' I hear his footsteps moving away.

I pick Dawn up even though she's asleep. I just want to feel less alone.

The darkness is beginning to feel oppressive. I feel like it's pressing down on me. I can't breathe but I don't know if it's the dark or the cold or my rising panic. I haven't felt this helpless since *that* night. Funny, really. All this time I was living in Hell and it didn't break me. Now I realise it was Ali keeping me going. I need him. We need each other. I hope we need each other.

I can't do this without him.

I must have stumbled into sleep because some time later I'm waking, alone. Where is Dawn? She was in my arms. Has Ali been back? Has he taken her?

'Ali?' I call. The only sounds are coming from outside. 'Conrad?'

Panic is starting to press down on me. I try to push it aside. Not useful. *But where are they? Where is Dawn?*

'Ali? Conrad?'

Nothing. I shiver and reach for a blanket. This way. He went this way. I think.

I squash down the cold and the fear and head in the direction think I heard Ali leave. It's overgrown; I have to push my way blind through stinging weeds and brambles.

All the while I have a series of worst case scenarios running through my head, all of which end in me finding them dead. I can feel panic rising in my chest, making me choke. Breathe. Just breathe. In out in out.

'Ali!' My voice sounds crazed and shrill. 'Conrad! Are you there?'

I'm crashing through the overgrowth clumsily, forcing myself on, when suddenly I'm forced to stop. I've reached a ravine, of sorts. Except that from the bottom, instead of darkness, light is pouring out. *What is this?*

And then the next terrifying thought: what if they fell in?

I shout again.

Wait – what was that?

I shout again and there it is, for certain. I can't make out what he's saying but it's Ali. Thank god. Thank god.

'Where are you?'

Nothing. I look down into the wide crack in the earth. It slopes down more steeply than I'd like. Then after a hundred yards or so, bright white light. Could I even get out of there if I went in?

'Rosie!' His voice is weak but at least he's conscious. And he isn't in the ravine. 'I can't move my foot.'

It's hard to see his foot and I have to hold on with everything I have to avoid falling. I manoeuvre myself around him and reach for him. I feel my grip slipping but I manage to catch myself on a root before I go completely.

His foot is wedged between two strong roots. I try to pull the ones around Ali's foot apart but I can't. I take my knife and start sawing away. It's slow going but eventually I can snap it away.

'Can you get out?' I ask.

He moves, slowly and awkwardly, grimacing with pain. It's agonisingly precarious: one careful step at a time, the ground shifting beneath us. We cling to one another and stumble away from the chasm, to a darker, safer place where we both collapse in a mess of snot, tears and exhaustion.

'I'm sorry,' breathes Ali, after a minute. 'I'm really sorry.'

'I'm sorry too,' I say. 'I would have come back, Ali. I would. It just wasn't easy.'

'I know.'

I find my breath and try to focus. Clarity returns. 'I need to find Dawn.'

'Where is she?' I can hear the panic in his voice.

'I don't know. I think Conrad has her. I don't know where they are.'

We make our difficult way back through the brambles, Ali leaning on me the whole time. Then we trip out into the enclosure.

'Conrad? Are you there?'

There's still no reply. Where has he taken her?

'I need to find them.'

I'm about to leave when there's a tremendous ripping sound and suddenly the sky is filled with light again. I'm frightened and I don't want to look up but I have to. The sky is torn in half and light is streaming through. No longer a crack; now a fissure. And in the fissure is a city, beyond the sky.

Boy

Well, would you look at that? It's happening at last. The place is collapsing. I'd like a deckchair and some popcorn to watch it all go down – how often do you get to see a world disintegrate around you? But I'll have to make do with what I have, which is nothing. Once the ground stops shaking I hike up to the highest point I can find and just sit.

It's crazy. The sky has been torn in half and there's light pouring out of the gap, flowing into the sky and painting it purple, red, orange, white. It's pretty fucking special, let me tell you.

And when you look past it all into the gap there's a city out there. Lots of weird shaped buildings, like a futuristic London maybe, or how I imagine Tokyo to look. That's where they live, these gods-who-are-not-gods, the lords and ladies who are in charge of our destinies. That's where they wake up and do whatever it is they do when they're not watching humans kill one another for sport.

She's done it. She's destroyed the world. And I'm not sorry to have come out on the losing side.

I'm just going to sit here awhile and think.

Are they watching me, watching them? I have the really strong impression that I'm being focused on. 'Are you watching, you bastards?'

I stick a half-hearted middle finger into the air, then I feel kind of stupid because to them the gesture probably means something different.

So I pull down my trousers and take a shit, and even though I've done this a million times while I've been here this time it feels different because I know, I just know they're watching.

That'll be a ratings killer.

It's the small things.

When I'm done with my business I go back down to see how the troops are getting along. I've somehow become their leader, despite having no aptitude in that area. I'm only really interested in my own skin, hers at a push. Now I'm supposed to start thinking collectively. But, they're kind of helpless without a leader, so here I am, playing the role of the good guy.

They've managed to get a couple of decent fires going, which is pretty good work given the earthquake and all. I think they've figured out that time is running out, so we may as well be comfortable. I can even smell meat cooking.

I'm almost beginning to relax when the girl comes running towards me.

And I know instantly that something is wrong.

Girl

I can't think about what it means yet. I have to find her first.

The light from the fissure is enough to see where I'm putting my feet at least. I leave by the front door. I'm no longer worried about being seen. They've had long enough to work out that I'm a second rate hero.

'Have you seen the baby? And a man? Did they pass this way?'

I'm asking the same questions over and over and getting no answers. They just look at me with weary faces and go back to what they're doing.

I scream with frustration which makes a few heads turn. But still nobody tries to help. Apart from Niall.

He's sitting alone with that intense look he has. When he sees me it softens.

Why did it have to be him? *Anyone* else. But there is nobody, so I approach him.

'I need help. Conrad's vanished. I think he has Dawn.'

He's on his feet immediately. 'Did you see which way?'

I shake my head. 'No. She was in my arms when I fell asleep. When I woke up they were both gone.'

He nods, thinking. Then he whistles, loudly. Everyone stops.

'Over here. All of you. Now.'

They drift over to us lazily, no urgency, like an army of zombies. Niall divides them into groups and sends them away to search, with instructions to return immediately if they find anything.

We're heading towards the canyon where I gave birth to Dawn. I'm not sure why we're still walking together. It makes more sense to split up. I open my mouth to say this when he interrupts me.

'Can we be friends, do you think? Ever?'

The confusion I'm thrown into by the strangeness of what he's asking is enough to silence me for a few seconds. Then I recover.

'No! Of course not. How could we ever – I don't know why you think I could…' I'm literally lost for words.

He looks unsurprised. 'I know that's fair. It's just – I'm not such a bad guy, really. I'm a fuck-up, obviously. I've had a shit life and I just got used to fighting my way out of trouble. It's been pretty useful here, except— He goes quiet, frowns.

'What?' I sigh. 'Why do you even want to be friends with us? There are loads of other people here now.'

He looks at me as if I'm stupid. 'Why do you think?'

'Are you still trying to get back at them? Rosaline and all the others?'

'No! Well, yes, partly, I suppose. But...' he pauses, before taking a breath. 'It's you. It's always been about you.'

He stops walking. 'I know you hate my fucking guts. I don't blame you. But – I can't help it. I feel like we're – the same. I...'

I stare at him, horrified. 'No! Don't. Don't say it.'

'Why not?' He looks like he's in physical pain. 'I don't expect anything from you. But you may as well know. I never even believed in love, till now. But it's like you're the missing part of me. The good part.'

I don't know what I can possibly say to this. 'I can't deal with this at the moment,' I say, refusing to look at him. 'I just want to get Dawn back.'

'Yes. Let's do that.'

We carry on walking in an extremely awkward silence. I'm embarrassed and I'm angry that he's distracted me from what I actually care about. Suddenly I'm back to being a girl and I can't do that now, I have too many other things that are more important.

There's a shout and we turn around to see someone running towards us, waving his arms frantically. We hurry back towards him. I'm staring at his face, trying to judge what he's going to tell me. I feel sick.

'They've found her blanket. And...' He looks at me, eyes wide, staring into the headlights.

'Just say it!' I snap.

'There's blood on it,' he says.

I go cold everywhere. 'Where?'

'In the woods.' He gestures for us to follow. I glance at the boy. He looks worried.

'Come on,' I say.

We walk on, each of us dreading what we might find.

Boy

I did it. And yeah, I feel like a bit of a twat. But, none of us are leaving here alive, right? So there's really no point in prevaricating.

Actually I feel pretty good, despite the fact that we're all cold and hungry and the woman I love hates the bones of me. Doesn't matter.

I have to pull myself back down to – well, here, to focus on what I'm doing. Finding the baby.

I *knew* that Conrad guy was tweaked. He always had that look about him, even back then, before—

No. I can't hide from it. I made him that way. I created this particular monster. Just like my father made me the man I am.

Just like that, my good mood is gone, replaced by images of my old man in various stages of inebriation and anger and me, following in his footsteps like a good little bastard.

I'm silent until we get back to the camp. She probably thinks I'm gutted at her less than overwhelming reaction to what I told her. I don't mind letting her think that. It saves me the complication of having to explain what I'm actually thinking about.

There's a search party waiting for us and they show us where they found the blanket. It's covered in dark blood stains. The girl says nothing. Doesn't cry, doesn't shout. Nothing. It's like she's shut down. Then the kid comes over and puts an arm around her. He's limping. Another casualty. She holds him tightly and I feel a stab of jealousy. I push it aside.

'They went that way,' I say, pointing. I'm no tracker but it's obvious; there's a blood trail.

She starts to walk. The boy comes with her but she shoos him away. Good call. He'll be a liability in that condition. I catch up to her. We've acquired a party of hangers on, eager to help. A procession of ghosts in search of a tiny drop of living humanity. It's like a reversed day of the dead parade, but the costumes are grey rags and everyone smells bad.

He hasn't made much of an effort to cover his tracks. The plants are trampled down and spotted with blood. We follow the trail as far as we can and then without warning the ground disappears in front of us. A sheer cliff face, 200 feet down. Rosie's swaying slightly. I grab her arm to stop her falling over.

She looks at me without really seeing me. 'Are they down there?' she asks.

I take a breath and then look down.

'No. I can't see them.' I glance around. The trail picks up to the right. 'They've gone this way,' I say. She starts walking again without a word.

We've walked for a while when the trail begins to lead sharply upwards. It's hard, hot work; we climb upwards for what seems like hours, our feet slipping on loose pebbles and getting caught in foliage.

It finally brings us out at the top of a hill. We can see miles of the surrounding land from here: our camp, the lake, the start of the desert. A network of cracks criss-crosses the land.

'What's that?' I say, more to myself than her.

She looks over to where I'm pointing. 'I... I don't know.'

I know what it looks like. It looks like nothing. Like the ground has broken away and there's fuck all underneath, just a big hole.

'I guess the world really is ending,' I say.

She ignores this and she's about to start up walking again when a shrill cry stops us both. It's coming from below us, where the side of the hill is steep and sheer. We follow the sound and then we see them. Conrad has the baby on a tiny ledge, a little way down the hill. A step either way and they'll both be dead.

Girl

She's alive. That's my first thought, before my brain has the chance to catch up with the situation. And then I can't act. It's like I'm frozen, watching it all happen in front of me.

The boy is calling out to Conrad. 'Just stay really still, OK? I'm going to help.'

'No.'

Conrad's wearing this look of frightened determination. 'We're staying here. She isn't safe up there.'

The boy looks at him and then at me. He puts his hand to his head. 'You – you think you're helping her? Jesus, Mary and – you're all fucking crazy!' He lies down on his belly and starts inching down, slowly, slowly. Conrad pulls Dawn towards him protectively.

Something wakes up inside me. 'Conrad! It's me. I'm her mother. You can give her back to me.'

'She isn't safe,' he says again, holding her closely.

Dawn's crying starts up again. 'She needs to feed!' I shout.

'They're going to kill her. I need to keep her safe.'

The boy has almost reached them. His foot slips and he's tumbling down towards them. It looks like he's going to fall on them but he manages to grab onto something and steadies himself in time. Conrad is leaning back terrifyingly close to the edge.

The boy climbs up and says something to him. Conrad leans away again, a wild look in his eyes. Then Niall says something else, his arms stretched out. He nods to Conrad who seems to be thinking.

He passes the baby over. Then he walks off the ledge.

A scream starts in my throat and gets choked away. It doesn't matter. Conrad doesn't matter. Get her back.

Niall is scrambling up the sheer hillside with one hand, holding the baby in the other. As soon as they're close enough I stretch down and pull him up. When they reach the top he hands over the baby, wearily.

'Thank you,' I say, burying my face in her. He flops down to the ground.

The world stops, briefly. All of my attention is on Dawn. Her smell, the feel of her skin, her soft black hair.

The sound of soft crying pulls me out of the dream state I'm in. 'It's OK,' I say. 'It's OK.'

We make our slow way back.

Once we're there, I take a look at Ali's leg. I'm pretty sure it's broken. I'm trying to recall anything about treating a broken bone. I have the vague idea that it needs to be put back in the right position and then he has to rest it. I'm just not sure of any of it. Mum would know.

'I broke my leg once,' says Niall. 'Or, it was broken for me. You've got to try to push it back in, then let it heal itself.'

'Can you do that?' I ask.

'Me?' He pulls his face. 'No thanks.'

'Please?'

'No! Not him,' Ali says.

'I can help.'

Rosaline.

'No thanks,' say Ali and I at the same time.

'I won't hurt him. What would be the point?' She stands over Ali.

'No,' he says.

She shrugs. 'Sorry,' she says, before wrenching at the broken bone. He screams. She looks at me. 'Bandage it up with a splint.'

I step between her and Ali. 'Leave him alone,' I say.

'Oh, hush. I helped him.' She nods at me and Niall. 'You two. I need to speak to you. You can bring her, that's fine.'

She leads us out of the hut, into a quiet part of the woods. She gestures for us to sit, but we don't.

'What is it?' I say.

'I'm here to warn you. I'm not a monster, not really.' She takes a breath. 'We're going to clear the domain. It isn't working. We're resetting Afterwards.'

We're startled into silence. Then we both start speaking at once. She smiles, her nasty smile.

'Oh, I know it's a shock. But what did you expect to happen?' She pauses and then continues as though she's in a boardroom meeting. 'The next move from our part is likely to be some kind of mass clearance.'

She lets us take these words in.

'By 'mass clearance' you mean – extinction?'

She nods. 'Yes. We've invested too much in Afterwards to simply abandon it. The most viable plan is to get rid of the problem and start again.'

I look at her calm face and I'm suddenly filled with rage. 'Why are you telling us this? What are we supposed to do about it?'

Rosaline continues, in a vaguely bored tone. 'Some of my associates thought it fair to give you the chance to fix this. It can be fixed, you know.'

'You want us to get them to fight again,' says Niall.

She nods. 'Yes. What we have here now is serving nobody. Nobody's fighting. They're all here, quietly existing. People up there are getting bored. There's no point to it.' She stares at me. 'This is your last chance to do the right thing. I can still keep you safe, if you help.'

I can't believe what I'm hearing. 'Then – everything we did was for nothing.'

'You were always on the losing side. There's no choice, Rosie. You've reached the end.'

'Go away,' I say, turning to leave.

'I could squash you now if I wanted to. You're an insect.' She smiles. 'Popular opinion has turned against you, you know. Nobody will mind very much if we clear the arena of its pest problem.'

'Then why don't you?'

'She needs permission,' says Niall. 'Isn't that right? You're not in charge up there.'

She looks down her nose at him. 'When I have it, you'll be the first to know.'

And she's gone.

We go back to the hut. Ali's eating, which always cheers him up. I flop down next to him. He pauses long enough to give me a hug.

'They found food, then?' I say.

He nods. 'There are a couple of good hunters in the group. Not up to my standards, course. Get some of the meat before it's all gone.'

I take a handful off his plate.

'Hey! Not mine. It's over there.'

I laugh and eat it anyway. 'Sorry.'

'What did *she* want?'

I told him what she had said.

'So she wants them to agree to fight?'

'Yep.'

'Are you going to tell them?'

I frown. 'I don't know. Do you think I should?'

He thinks about it and finally shakes his head. 'No.'

I bite my bottom lip. 'But – if I don't…'

'She'll wipe us out and start again.'

'Yes.'

'Well, so what?'

'Aren't you afraid?'

'Yeah, but I'm always scared. All the time. What difference does it make?'

I look into his eyes. 'I can't believe how brave you've become.'

He snorts and turns his attention back to his food. Then after a minute he looks up again. 'Rosie?'

'Yep?'

'I don't mind that I'm here, you know. I wouldn't have met you otherwise.'

I feel tears start to prick my eyes. 'I know, Ali. But I wish you were still alive. I don't want this for you.'

He shrugs. 'We're here and that's that. Now let's eat.' I reach out for his food again but he's ready this time. 'Not mine!'

I think it's evening but I can't tell really because there's no change to the light anymore – we live in a permanent half-light caused by the torn sky. I'm restless. Once I've fed Dawn I pass her over to Ali.

'I'm taking a walk.'

He glances at Niall, who's sitting nearby, staring into the fire.

'Do you want me to stay?' I ask. Ali shakes his head.

'It's OK.'

Niall looks up. 'Don't worry, I'll go.'

Neither of us protest.

'I won't be long,' I say.

I retrace yesterday's path, through the woods and up the hill to where we found Conrad. It feels big here and I can breathe. I sit on a rock and just look. Grass and hills and desert and a gap where the world has broken. And the ever present wound of light in the sky.

This is where I've landed. A year after my death. What would you think of me, Mum?

It isn't going to be long now, before we end or the world does. The clock is ticking for us, one way or another. I find I don't mind too much.

'Hey.'

Niall.

'Hi.' I mask my irritation as well as I can.

'I can go back, if you want,' he says.

I shake my head. 'You don't have to.'

We lapse into a silence that I don't care to break. I'm enjoying the quiet up here.

'Hey! Look at that!' he says, pointing. Fireflies. I've never seen them before. They're pretty.

'Why did you kill yourself?' he asks. This is what counts as small talk around here.

I think about it for a few moments. 'I was lost,' I say. 'I couldn't see a way out.'

He looks at me appraisingly. 'I don't see it,' he says.

I scoff. 'You don't believe me?' *How dare he?* 'You don't know me.'

'I didn't say that. You just seem so – together.'

Hah. 'Shows what you know.' I ask the question that I feel he's waiting for. 'What happened to you?'

'The usual. Parents were a waste of space. Couldn't wait to get out.'

'Oh.'

He's pulling at a plant, thoughtfully, then looks down at his hand. 'Shit!' His fingers are swelling up rapidly. I glance about and spot what I'm looking for. I pull up a broad leaved plant and hand him the root. 'Rub that on it.'

He does and the swelling stops. 'How do you know all this shit?'

I shrug. 'I've been here for a while. People tell you things when they're not scared of you.'

He accepts this, then says: 'How come you weren't? Scared, I mean?'

I look at him. 'For one thing, you remind me of someone.'

'Who?'

'Someone I knew before. He was a dick, too.'

'Thanks.' But he's smiling. 'You're like nobody I've ever met.'

I turn to him. 'Why do you keep saying things like that?'

He looks astonished. 'What are you on about?'

'Compliments. Saying that you...' I falter.

'That I love you?' He stands up, his face red. 'Well maybe, just maybe, it's because I do.'

'No, you don't.'

He starts to pace. 'Look. I don't expect you to say it back. I don't expect anything from you. Except...' He pauses. 'Don't tell me that I don't feel what I feel. We're the same, you and I. We're made of the same stuff. I don't mean because we're the only living souls in this... shithole. It's more than that.'

'No. You're wrong.'

He makes a frustrated sound and walks off.

I lie back and try to find the tranquillity I had when I arrived. But it's gone. My head is full of angry thoughts.

Niall

I'm not going to be morose about the fact I don't get the girl. Guys like me don't, that's the reality of it. Athletic guys like Conrad do, unless they've lost their mind. Not scrawny little shits with adult acne. All I have to offer is my wit. God help me.

I think I'm losing it too. I feel weirdly euphoric. Perhaps they've dialled down the O2 and I'm hypoxic. Or perhaps it's my brain catching up with what my body knows; I'm dying. My days are numbered. I don't know why. I just know it's true.

'It's a side-effect.' Oh. I'm surrounded suddenly by a group of *them*. I don't recognise them, so I guess they belong to the other side.

I raise my eyebrows. 'What side effect?'

'We could never be sure how a mortal would react to living here. We tried a few before you and Rosie, you know.' The speaker is a pale woman, with long blonde plaited hair.

'What happened to them?'

'Oh, most of them died pretty quickly in the usual ways. And the ones that didn't-'

'-got sick,' I finished. 'So how long do I have?'

'Once they started to realise what was happening it wasn't long. A month, maybe.'

'So… Rosie?' It's worse, I realise, to think that she's dying too.

'Well actually, she's fine at the moment. Her body seems to have adapted. We're not sure how.' She narrows her eyes. 'Don't you mind that you're going to die?'

I shrug. 'Not like I have much choice. Besides, I knew.' Having it confirmed still sucks, but I don't tell her that. 'Anyway, I already died.'

'That isn't technically true.'

'It's true enough to me. It's true enough to mean I never got to have kids or see the northern fucking lights or any of that shit.'

She gives me a look of sympathy.

'Don't do that,' I snap. 'Don't pretend like you care.'

'We do care. Why else would we be doing this?'

Something dawns on me. 'You're here for a reason. What is it?'

'You're perceptive. We want to talk to you about something.'

I don't like the sound of that. But at this point, what's the worst that could happen?

'Go on then. Spit it out.'

'I have a suggestion for you.'

She outlines their plan. It's pretty solid, I have to admit.

'Can I trust you?' I ask.

'You don't have to. You know we can't lie.'

'Mmm. Well, your compatriots have a way of getting around that.'

'Regardless. It is true. Knowing what you know of me, you must see that it would make sense, from my perspective.'

'Yep. But I've got to be careful.'

'I agree, you should. Answer this: what does she stand to gain from my plan?'

She has a point.

'Will you do it?'

I shrug. 'Why not?'

She looks relieved. 'I really think this could work. We need to get the timing right though.'

She runs through the plan with me one more time.

'You know which way to go?'

'Yeah. I mean, it's right there for me to see. Just head towards the big hole in the fabric of the world.'

'That's right. I need to check on a few things. I'll send you a sign when it's time to go.'

'What sign?'

'You'll know it when you see it.'

She's gone, leaving me with my thoughts.

I'm not feeling like being alone right now so I head back. Rosie's probably still pissed off but that doesn't matter too much now.

But when she sees me she doesn't look angry. She looks – embarrassed, if anything. I think that's worse.

'Are you alright?' she asks. I'm astonished. That sounds like actual concern for my wellbeing. It throws me off balance.

'I'm fine,' I growl, avoiding her eyes. 'Why?'

'Something – is happening. Or is going to happen.'

I force a laugh. 'Since when are you mystic fucking Meg?'

She doesn't look amused. 'I just know.'

The kid is looking at me like I just flushed his hamster. 'Why is he still here?' he asks.

'Don't worry, I'll be going soon,' I say.

'Where?' asks the girl.

'Why does that matter?' I reply.

'It doesn't,' says the kid. I shrug.

I have a tightness in my chest. It takes me a minute to work out that I'm panicking. I haven't felt like this for a long time.

Everything seems to be in focus all of a sudden. My senses are going crazy. I can smell the woody damp smell from the forest and the smoke from the fire and roast meat and I'm ravenous.

'Is there any food left?' I ask.

She nods and passes a plate over. I demolish it in seconds.

'That was good,' I say. 'Would love a Murphy's to wash it down, but can't have everything.'

I stand up, trying to ignore the words *last meal*, which are bouncing around my skull. I forget about the plate which clatters to the ground. I stare at it stupidly, then look at Rosie.

'I wish things had been different,' I say.

She looks perplexed, but she just says: 'Me too.'

There's a commotion outside. One of the girls from the camp pokes her head around the doorway.

'Come and look! It's amazing.'

We go outside. It *is* amazing.

'What is that?' asks Rosie.

I laugh. 'It's the northern fucking lights!'

The sky is streaked green, pink and gold. It's breath-taking.

It's also, unmistakably, a sign.

'Got to go,' I say.

286

Rosie

The sky is, I have to admit, one of the most beautiful things I've ever seen, even when I was alive. I help Ali walk out. He can't miss this. We sit there outside the hut, staring up at the colours chasing one another and merging and morphing, the fireflies skittering about below, oblivious to the beauty. Electricity crackles across, making transient bridges over the sky city, where they're undoubtedly watching this too.

It's only after we've been looking upwards for a while that I begin to wonder why this is here, now. I mean, this is an artificial environment. Which means somebody created this. For what?

Then I recall Niall's reaction to it. He was acting oddly to start with: restless, nervy. Perhaps that's what he's always like. I don't know. But when he saw the sky he fell about laughing and then left in a hurry.

Something's going on with him.

'You're right.'

'Jane?' For a second I hope; that I was wrong about her, that it was another trick. But I've never seen this woman before. 'Who are you?'

'Not Jane. She's gone. But I'm on the same side. Your side.'

She reaches over for Dawn but I move her away. 'I'm sorry,' I say.

'No. That's alright. I understand.' She sits on the ground. 'Sit beside me, will you? I need to explain something to you.'

I sit, keeping Dawn close.

'What is it? Is it about Niall?' I grow suddenly suspicious. 'What's he going to do?'

'You don't need to worry. I asked him to do it. I'm hoping it will be enough.'

'What do you mean?'

She glances about. 'We haven't long.'

'Go on.'

'You must have noticed that there are some places where the environment is beginning to malfunction.'

287

'The patches of light. We saw them from up on the hill.'

'That's right. Those areas are gaps in the infrastructure.' She pauses. 'When this place was built, some of my people were a bit concerned about it. Not for the right reasons, of course. They were worried about your people breaking through and reaching our world.'

My mouth fell open. 'But – that's – is that possible?'

She nods. 'Yes. Quite possible. We have portals to take us from here to there. So there was a serious concern that one or more of you might find a way out of this world and into ours. And then—'

'Take our revenge.' My brain is working quickly. 'Is that where he's gone? Niall?'

Jane shakes her head. 'No. Let me finish. They were so worried that they built in some fail-safes. If a human were to get backstage, so to speak, the system temporarily shuts down and all humans become suspended until it's started up again.'

My brain is trying to shape this into something which makes sense. 'So – is that what he's going to do?'

She nods. 'In about three minutes, he will jump into the largest of the holes. This will cause Afterwards to close down and admin power will automatically go to the guardian of the highest rank inside the system.'

'Which will be you, right?'

'That's right. I've created a little distraction for Rosaline and her friends. It won't last long, but we don't need long. I know exactly what I'm going to do.'

'What?'

'I'm going to change the system so that none of us has access. It will continue to run for centuries on its current power supply and it was built to be a self-sustaining environment. You don't need us and I'm going to make damn sure we can't get back in.'

I go quiet as I take her words in. Then: 'What about Niall?'

She sighs. 'He and I have both assumed that he isn't going to survive this.'

My thoughts are racing. I don't know what I feel about any of this. I fall back on anger because it's easier than trying to sort it all out in my head.

'How can you be OK with that? Just asking him to give up his life, like it's nothing?'

'It was his choice. Always his choice.'

'But it's not! It never is. You manipulated him. You're no better than Rosaline or the others.'

'You may be right about that.' She looks sad.

I look away from her, tears building behind my eyes. The sky is still streaked in colour. 'Why did you do that?' I ask. 'What was the point?'

'He wanted to see it. I figured I owed him that much.' She took a breath. 'This may be hard for you to hear, Rosie, but he wanted to go. There's no place for him here.'

'There could have been. You have no right to decide that!'

She doesn't reply.

Then it happens. It's as if the world has short-circuited. She's gone without a backward glance, so she won't have realised that she was wrong about one thing at least: I'm not frozen.

The grass which was under my feet a moment ago is gone. The beautiful, immense sky is gone. The hills, the forests, the deserts. I'm in a gigantic white room. The only thing that's the same is the enormous rip above me and that's clearer now. I can see buildings, lights, clouds.

And all around me are the other players, frozen in the act of whatever they were doing. Laughing, eating, walking. Ali caught mid-scratch. This is Afterwards, undressed.

289

Niall

I'm concentrating on putting one foot in front of another. That's the only way I can make myself do this. See, I'm a coward, when it comes down to it. The first time I died, sort of, was unexpected. Now I'm being asked to literally step into the abyss.

One foot at a time. That's all we ever do, anyway.

The hole in the world is on me before I know it. It's massively uninviting; a big, empty mouth. Oblivion awaits.

I throw up a bit. Not exactly heroic, am I?

I know I have to make myself do it and I know I don't want to. I imagine my old man standing beside me, calling me all of the chicken shit bastards under the sun. Doesn't work.

Then I imagine myself going back to Rosie, skulking back and trying to slip back into her life. Even if she doesn't know about this plan, which she undoubtedly does by now, I have no place there. I have no place anywhere here. So this is where I am.

In the end it's the exhaustion that gets me to do it. I've had enough. So I stop deliberating, close my eyes and walk forwards.

I have a terrifying second or two when my feet don't connect. Then I land, or rather I stumble, face down. My eyes flick open to see that the world has gone. Factory settings have been restored. And it seems that I am not dead.

I climb to my feet, staring around me with my mouth open like a guppy. I'm standing inside a gigantic nothing. I know there's a floor because I feel it but my eyes are giving me nothing that isn't attached to me.

And then pop. Pop. Pop.

Rosaline. Comb-over. Princess. And finally, pop. Other Jane.

'Do you think we're stupid?' hisses Rosaline. Actually hisses, like a snake.

'I'm going to do this, Rosaline. You're not going to stop me.'

'Did you think we'd just let you take the habitat we've invested so much in? Just hand it over?'

'It's the right thing to do.'

'For whom? Not for us or our stakeholders.'

'For them.' She points to me.

Rosaline makes a pfft sound. 'They're happy enough. We give them food, water. They can't expect to do nothing in return.'

New Jane frowns. 'You don't understand how similar they are to us. If you took the time to actually watch the show you're so proud of, you might…'

'Oh, hush. I'm tired of pointless philosophical debate. Do you know how much this interruption in transmission is costing us?' She smiles, her nasty smile. 'Still, at least I can be sure this will remove one thorn in my side.'

'Yes, I know I'll lose my job. That doesn't matter anymore.'

'You'll be lucky if it stops at your job. My people are calling for your neck.'

'Well, in that case I had better make sure it's worth it.'

New Jane turns and opens up a panel in the floor, a grey metallic patch in the endless white. Rosaline and Comb-over start towards her but they're stopped by – what? A barrier of some kind. Rosaline makes an irritated sound.

'Emergency override. Command code Pegasus 8.' She listens. I hear nothing, but she says: 'What? Why?' Then vanishes. She returns seconds later with a man with white hair.

'Emergency override. Command code Aries 1.'

'Supplemental code Pegasus 8.'

They wait for a moment, then rush at New Jane. The man pushes her out of the way and starts trying to undo what she's done.

'What did you do?' snarls Rosaline.

'You know what I did.'

'What can you hope to achieve? We'll get back control eventually.'

'That won't matter.'

Rosaline looks from New Jane, her face incredulous. Then realisation dawns. 'You intend to shut us down.'

'All I need is time.'

The man looks up from the panel. 'I can't access it.'

Rosaline emits a deep guttural growl and throws herself on New Jane, who's too startled to react at first. Rosaline tears at her like an animal. New Jane recovers herself but she hasn't a chance against Rosaline. I can see how this is going to go. I need a plan, because once she's finished with her rival it'll be my turn.

I begin walking away in a random direction. It doesn't seem to matter which way; I have nowhere to hide, nowhere to go. Endless nothing to walk through.

And then it doesn't matter. The system reboots with me on the right side of it, them on the other. I'm in a clearing, god knows where, but for now I'm safe. I collapse onto the ground and just lie there.

Rosie

Things are different now.

Afterwards is our world. It's not perfect; we still have to contend with monsters and poisons and all of the other little traps they built for us. And of course, each other. Sometimes that's worse. There are no new arrivals anymore and *they* can't interfere. There's just this, until the end.

Dawn is getting bigger daily. She can sit now, her chubby little arms and legs sticking out like a doll. I wish I could offer her more than this but sometimes, when I see her smiling at Ali and him beaming back at her, things don't seem too bad. Death is what you make of it.

I wonder if they still watch us, now that we don't fight for their pleasure. Do they scrutinise our interactions, our little love affairs, our arguments? Or have they moved on? Perhaps they've built another one, somewhere else.

We can still see their city in the hole in the sky. The quakes have stopped and the tear hasn't got any bigger. It's just there, a huge permanent reminder of what we were. Or, if you're of a positive mind-set, what we've achieved. We stared the gods down. We did that.

I live with Ali and Dawn in a hut that Ali built. Niall lives nearby, with a girl from the camp. Every now and again I see him looking over and I wave, but that's about it.

This is what I want, for now. As for the future, who knows? I'm still unused to the idea of a future. Our only function is to stay alive and to find tiny bits of joy wherever we can.

We will never be anything. We will never go anywhere. This is our reality. This is all we have.

But actually, I think that's enough.

~~~~~~~~~

About the Author

Karen Kendrick is a writer and creative writing teacher from the North West of England. She writes poetry and fiction which straddle the boundary between reality and fantasy. She lives in Astley, Greater Manchester with her husband, two sons, a dog and a snake, and many plants. *Afterwards* is her first novel.

Like to Read More Work Like This?

Then sign up to our mailing list and download our free collection of short stories, *Magnetism*. Sign up now to receive this free e-book and also to find out about all of our new publications and offers.

Sign up here:
   http://eepurl.com/gbpdVz

Please Leave a Review

Reviews are so important to writers. Please take the time to review this book. A couple of lines is fine.

Reviews help the book to become more visible to buyers. Retailers will promote books with multiple reviews.

This in turn helps us to sell more books... And then we can afford to publish more books like this one.

Leaving a review is very easy.
Go to https://amzn.to/3WlXGH8, scroll down the left-hand side of the Amazon page and click on the 'Write a customer review' button.

Read More of K M Kendrick's Work in These Books

The Salford Manifesto in
Salford Stories
Published by Bridge House (2016)

Order from Amazon:

Paperback: ISBN 978-1-907335-44-0
eBook: ISBN 978-1-907335-45-7

The Road to Nowhere in
Citizens of Nowhere
Published by Bridge House (2017)

Order from Amazon:

Paperback: ISBN 978-1-907335-53-2
eBook: ISBN 978-1-907335-54-9

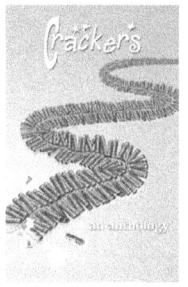

Snap in
Crackers
Published by Bridge House (2018)

Order from Amazon:

Paperback: ISBN 978-1-907335-59-4
eBook: ISBN 978-1-907335-60-0

Other publications by Bridgehouse Imprints

Face to Face with the Führer
by Gill James

Käthe wants to be a scientist. She sees herself as more than a housewife and a mother. And she is in her own eyes definitely not Jewish.

Life in Nazi Germany sees it another way however. She has to give up a promising career and her national identity. She has to leave the home she has built up for her husband and daughter. But she is not afraid of challenges. She enlists the help of a respected professor to help her fulfil her ambition, she learns how to use a gun and how to drive a car. But what will she do when she finds herself fact to face with the Führer or, indeed, with the challenges of modern life?

Face to Face with the Führer is the fourth novel in Gill James' Schellberg cycle.

Order from Amazon:

ISBN: 978-1-910542-99-6 (paperback)
978-1-910542-00-9 (ebook)

Chapeltown Books

Dry River
by Alicia J Rouverol

Sara Greystone's career as a public defender is spiralling after a
disastrous court case, and now her husband's IT career is also in
jeopardy. A move to California is supposed to get them both back on
their feet, but the state is in the midst of a crippling economic
downturn-and then Sara's mother falls seriously ill. In the face of
migration, illness, unemployment, and the tantalising possibility of
infidelity, Sara has to work out who she is and what she really wants.

Spanning 1997 to 2012, *Dry River* echoes Wallace Stegner's classic
Angle of Repose, moving across place and time to chart the slow
collapse of a marriage alongside a declining US economy.

"Beautifully written story of life's crossroads," (Amazon)

Order from Amazon:

ISBN: 978-1-914199-44-8 (paperback)
978-1-914199-45-5 (ebook)

Invisible on Thursdays

by Peppy Barlow

Peppy Barlow is a playwright and screen writer who lives her life looking for meaning and material in all her experiences. In this book she and her friend Persephone/Lucia explore childhood memories - both good and bad - and travel with their children to Crete where ancient myths emerge to haunt them.

A very personal account of a friendship which takes Peppy back to England and ends with Persephone returning to the Underworld. Authentic, brave, honest, funny and touching - the author's voice shines out from these pages.

Author Peppy Barlow guides us through her turbulent and rich life adventures. Truly a life well-lived.

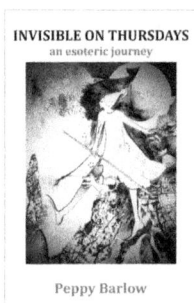

INVISIBLE ON THURSDAYS
an esoteric journey

Peppy Barlow

"I loved it… what a roller coaster ride. Living life as it occurred. For me there were laughter and tears in equal measure." (Amazon)

Order from Amazon:

ISBN: 978-1-914199-17-2 (paperback)
978-1-914199-18-9 (ebook)